COUNSELOR UNDONE

COUNSELOR UNDONE

LISA RAYNE

FIRE SIGN
PRESS

Kansas City | Los Angeles

COUNSELOR UNDONE

Fire Sign Press,
a division of Fire Sign Media Group
PO Box 9150, Kansas City, MO 64168
www.firesignpress.com

This is a work of fiction. Names, characters, places, and incidents are
either the product of the author's imagination or are used
fictitiously. Any resemblance to actual persons (living or dead),
business establishments, events or locales is entirely coincidental
and in no way reflects the nature, character, business practices or
opinions of any person or entity for which a resemblance may exist.

Any trademarks or trade names mentioned are the express property
of their respective owners.

First Edition (August 2015)

ISBN-13: 978-0-692-50813-8 (Trade Paperback)
ISBN-10: 0-692-50813-9

Front cover design by The Cover Collection.

Two . . . One . . . Happy New Year!

Despite the two flutes of champagne he held in his other hand, the gladiator turned her deftly into his embrace. The shawl she'd wrapped around her shoulders fell to the ground as plastic horn toots erupted inside amidst cheers. He slid his occupied fist behind her back, gripped the base of her neck with his free hand, and kissed her thoroughly. She pushed hard against his chest. When she opened her mouth to tell him he'd made a mistake, he took the liberty of sliding his tongue inside to play wickedly with hers. She moaned softly, which caused him to chuckle.

She didn't know who this man was or why he thought he had an open invitation to make love to her mouth, but her ability to think straight slowly evaporated. She'd never been kissed like this—like the last beautiful woman on earth. Her libido sparked, making her excited and appalled at the same time. She'd been unattached for fourteen long months, and this hunk's skill with his tongue sent hot flashes to an area of her body she'd almost forgotten existed.

This book is dedicated to

KAROL JARVIS and **BONITA THORNTON**

for always believing in the dream.
Every person should have cheerleaders like you in their
corner: people who never doubt, never discourage,
and always lift up. This book would never have been
completed and published without your unfailing support.

ACKNOWLEDGMENTS

Few authors are lucky enough to start their career with a book club behind them before the first manuscript is even finished. I happen to be so lucky. To the ladies of STCC Book Club (www.stccbookclub.com), many thanks for your support, beta reading time, and invaluable feedback on the storyline and characters of this book (particularly Donna Scoggins, Beverly Jackson, and Laverne Rodgers Smith).

To the ladies at the fragrance counter at Macy's Metro North Mall in Kansas City, Missouri (Nancy, Mary, Cathy, Alicia, Paula, and Pam), you *rock*. The writing and fine-tuning of this book would not have been half as much fun without your constant support and feedback.

To Dr. Kerrie Herren, although you will probably never read this book, know that I appreciate your diligent and "gentle" pushes to hold me accountable to finish.

To the awesome Cherry Adair, thank you so much for your invaluable time and guidance during and after your pre-convention plotting courses at the Kansas City and New Orleans RT Booklovers Conventions. Figuring out turning points and black moments and how to raise the stakes in fiction shouldn't have been such a blast.

And finally, to my new readers and future fans, I'm happy you took a chance on this book. I'm planning a few additional books in this series so please let me know what you think. You can find me online at www.lisarayne.com.

Happy reading!

Lisa Rayne

COUNSELOR UNDONE

Chapter 1

*M*ichael Remington had never had to work so hard for a one-night stand in his life.

It went against his grain and his ego.

He'd long ago become jaded about love and all things Cupid, but he generally had no problem finding a casual bedmate when he wanted. As a named partner in a prestigious law firm with political connections and ties to the social elite of Kansas City, women practically threw themselves at him. Yet, here he stood at the local bar association's annual New Year's Eve masked ball—at five minutes till midnight—looking for a woman who had made herself scarce. If he hadn't been the one to walk away from his elusive prey earlier, he'd think he'd lost his touch.

"What are you doing standing here all alone?" Chase Hager, his best friend and law partner, snuck up behind him and slapped him on the shoulder. "The whole point of my convincing you to come was so you could meet someone new."

Michael grunted. "I must have been out of my mind. And I can't believe I let you talk me into this ridiculous costume. I feel like a piece of meat on display."

Chase laughed. His eyes scanned the costume that made Michael look like an ancient gladiator *sans* breastplate. "How do you expect to attract quality prospects if you don't show off the merchandise?"

He rolled his eyes, finding the comment ironic coming from a guy whose costume kept all his significant body parts covered. "You know I'm not in the market for quality prospects. I'm not in the market for *any* prospects."

"Oh really?" Chase eyed the two champagne glasses in Michael's hand. "It looks like you're in the market for something. Didn't mean to interrupt. Carry on." Chase walked away, loud chuckles accompanying his self-satisfied grin.

Tuning out the annoying sound of his friend's retreating mirth, Michael resumed the search for his evening entertainment. She wore a Juliet costume. Other than that, he didn't know much about her. He hadn't bothered to ask her any questions or even get her real name. It hadn't mattered. The moment she'd spotted him, she'd turned on a flirt that promised more than good conversation.

Not one, usually, to go for the vampy come-on, he'd humored her. He may be jaded, but he wasn't rude. She'd made a pouty complaint about her Romeo having gone off "roaming" and suggested Michael play her knight in shining armor. He'd laughed and responded, "Wrong costume."

When she'd looked at him with a blank stare, he'd realized she couldn't make the distinction between a Roman gladiator and a knight of the realm. He'd wondered if her Elizabethan-styled wig covered a natural blond. Then he'd chastised himself for the insensitive stereotyping. A woman certainly didn't have to be blond to be intellectually challenged. He'd met enough female cerebral lightweights to know.

Categorizing Juliet as good for an easy lay, but never one to rise above an occasional late night tryst, he'd politely excused himself. He hadn't originally felt like playing the game tonight. He'd recognized her type and the hunger in her eyes immediately. He avoided—or fought off—women like her all the time, women set on attaching themselves permanently to a rich professional with a strong reputation in the community. He didn't make himself available for that kind of liaison.

At thirty-eight, he'd seen enough of his buddies take the marital plunge only to end up doing the sap two-step when romantic bliss turned into an episode of reality TV divorce court. He'd almost made that mistake once, with a firm colleague no less, and his engagement had ended in disaster. He'd learned his lesson. He didn't believe in forever-after, and he didn't think this masked ball would net him a Cinderella. He had one use for women currently—a physical use, which is exactly where his one-night stand came in, if he could find her.

He glanced at the two flutes of champagne in his hand, tempted to down them both. He abstained. He'd probably had one too many drinks already. After he'd escaped

Juliet, he'd had a few to take the edge off his boredom. That had been a mistake. He'd only managed to slide his boredom into frustration.

His gladiator costume had brought out the predator in otherwise reserved ladies. After being groped and propositioned relentlessly by women he knew—despite their masks and costumes—and a few he didn't, he'd decided to go with it. Maybe getting laid for the first time in four months would improve his disposition. Unfortunately, now that he'd decided to give in to dimwitted Juliet's offer of a sure thing, she'd disappeared.

He should have stayed home and watched the ball drop over Times Square. Better yet, he should have gone to the office to figure out how a box of discovery documents had gone missing in his multimillion-dollar patent infringement case. He planned to build the firm founded by his late father and his grandfather into a national powerhouse. He wouldn't succeed if he dropped the ball on the intellectual property case of the year, a case journalists predicted would change the legal landscape for pharmaceutical patents. He sighed. He'd deal with his case issues tomorrow.

Banishing work from his mind, he stepped onto the balcony of the penthouse condo. A smile spread across his lips. A lovely vision stood staring out over the railing. He'd found her.

&? &? | ?? ??

Mask still in place, a costumed Juliet stood on the balcony wondering why she hadn't left this party. The couple she'd planned to meet, her first cousin plus one, hadn't shown and she didn't know anyone else here. She planned to give her mysteriously absent cousin a scathing piece of her mind for pressuring her to attend this party then leaving her high and dry.

She hated New Year's Eve parties. She didn't need to wax nostalgic about the past year. Betrayal and heartbreak had haunted most of the last three hundred and sixty-five days. She'd left the unpleasant memories behind in Los Angeles six months ago, and she never wanted to revisit them. As for New Year's resolutions, the only resolution that mattered mandated letting nothing—and no one—distract her from making partner by the end of the year at the KC law firm to which she'd recently transferred.

She'd only come to this midnight-fest foray—against her better judgment—to appease her cousin. Then she'd compounded the mistake by letting her cousin arrange for her costume. She'd wanted Cleopatra, but a mix-up at the costume shop had led to the delivery of this Juliet getup instead. By the time she'd realized the mistake, the shop had closed and she couldn't make an exchange.

The sound of the balcony door sliding open drew her attention. She turned towards a walking piece of art wearing a gladiator costume.

Four . . . Three . . .

"Juliet! There you are!" the masked gladiator cooed, his baritone voice slightly singsong from one too many glasses of wine . . . or something. "I wondered where you'd gone." He placed a strong hand around her arm.

Two . . . One . . . Happy New Year!

Despite the two flutes of champagne he held in his other hand, the gladiator turned her deftly into his embrace. The shawl she'd wrapped around her shoulders fell to the ground as plastic horn toots erupted inside amidst cheers. He slid his occupied fist behind her back, gripped the base of her neck with his free hand, and kissed her thoroughly.

She pushed hard against his chest. When she opened her mouth to tell him he'd made a mistake, he took the liberty of sliding his tongue inside to play wickedly with hers. She moaned softly, which caused him to chuckle.

She didn't know who this man was or why he thought he had an open invitation to make love to her mouth, but her ability to think straight slowly evaporated. She'd never been kissed like this—like the last beautiful woman on earth. Her libido sparked, making her excited and appalled at the same time. She'd been unattached for fourteen long months, and this hunk's skill with his tongue sent hot flashes to an area of her body she'd almost forgotten existed.

Without removing his lips from hers, the gladiator backed her into a corner alcove west of the sliding glass door, not stopping until her back nearly touched the stone wall. With a bit of apprehension, she noticed darkness covered the alcove he'd selected, the few existing patio sconces not aggressive enough to throw their light around the turn in the wall. Her mind began to whirl. She shouldn't be here—not at this party and definitely not in this man's arms.

The thought made her push harder against his chest. *"Please."*

"Honey, there's no need to beg. Whatever you want, I plan to give it to you *all night long.*" Pulling back slightly, he handed her a glass of champagne.

She accepted the glass on reflex. "You don't understand—"

"Here's to the New Year," he interrupted and lifted his glass dramatically. He paused, as if searching for a more mindful toast, but simply added with a wicked grin, "It's suddenly looking very promising." He downed his champagne in one gulp then tossed the flute onto a cushion-covered wrought iron chair not far away.

"Drink up, Juliet." He wrapped his fingers around hers on the stem of the glass she held and assisted it to her lips. "Don't you know it's bad luck not to drink to a toast made on New Year's Eve?"

She took a sip while pressing persistently against his chest with her other hand. He budged a smidge. Her breathing came easier with the space she'd created between them until she realized his stingy costume left most of his chest bare. Her hand rested against the wall of his smooth pectorals, and what a wall it was. He sported the physique of a Calvin Klein underwear model, all planes and bulges and six-pack. Those reawakened body parts began to liquefy.

"Y-You've made a mistake," she murmured, flustered by her unexpected female response to him.

Though she could count the number of lovers she'd had on half of one hand, she didn't lack sexual experience. Still, none of her lovers, even the man to whom she'd once been engaged, had stirred in her with a simple kiss a fraction of the heat currently rising inside her. "I think you're looking for someone else." *And that's a shame*, she thought, surprising herself.

The gladiator smiled down at her. She stood approximately five feet ten in the flat leather sandals she wore, but he still stretched several inches above her. He had to be well over six feet tall.

She'd gotten a brief look at his face before he embraced her and noted odd colored eyes in a rugged face. He wore his hair a little long. The back brushed the top of his epaulettes, and a wavy wisp fell across his forehead, touching the top of a dark brow. Given the paucity of the starlight, she couldn't quite discern the color of the tresses—black or maybe a deep brown. He qualified as objectively handsome by any woman's standards, but she didn't understand this intense attraction. Even with his olive-toned skin, he didn't fit her usual type.

Removing her champagne glass with one hand, he pressed his other over the hand she rested on his chest. "No, milady, there's no mistaking you. How about we get better acquainted, like you suggested earlier?" He tucked his face into the curve of her neck. "Mmm, you smell good. All flowers, and sweetness, and woman."

His lips trailed kisses along her neckline while he showered her with words of seduction. The sound of his voice, two parts sexy and one part awe, stirred her. She became enraptured by the risqué words he whispered. When he got to the part about what he wanted to do with his tongue, she shivered.

He took her mouth in another rousing kiss. His tongue sliding warm across her lips, then along the length of her own, evoked sheer bliss. Wrapped in the feel of him, she didn't notice the hand he slid to the split at the side of her costume until that hand invaded the fabric and moved up her thigh.

Through a haze, she became conscious of his fingers caressing the side of her bare bottom, the stringy thong she wore giving him full access. His fingers massaged the firm muscles of her buttock. He still held her half-full champagne flute in his other hand, but the burden didn't slow him down. He pressed at her back until she leaned flush against him from hip to shoulder. The long hardness of his arousal met her abdomen, and her hips swayed in a manner that made him groan aloud.

When that old R. Kelly song about a little bump and grind began to play in her head, she decided she'd lost her mind. What was she doing in a darkened corner—outside no less—with a stranger, making out like a horny teenager?

Something in her consciousness chided she needed to stop him, but she couldn't muster the will to resist. She felt as if he'd put a spell on her. Maybe he should have come dressed like a warlock. He'd been looking for another Juliet, but he'd magically homed in on the one so deprived of a man's touch she'd let him have his way with her outside on an open balcony.

Everything happens for a reason, her grandmother always said. Taking grandmamma at her word, she wondered if there was a reason she'd ended up dressed like Juliet on this particular balcony at midnight so Mr. Gladiator could kiss her until she turned into a shameless hussy. At the moment, a reason escaped her, but perhaps she needed to accept the serendipity of the evening to truly appreciate the divine order.

What would happen if she completely surrendered to the moment? Why not enjoy her first real New Year's Eve kiss—not counting the kisses from her godchildren last year—in three years? She was long overdue for a serious, grownup New Year's Eve kiss so surrender to the moment she did, with gusto.

The act marked a defining moment in her life. Her nature didn't include spontaneous or frivolous. She was the intellectual in her group of friends, the deep thinker, the analytical one. Known as a FranklinCovey planner junkie, she couldn't get through her day without a prioritized daily task list. She didn't take uncalculated risks, and she didn't even kiss on the first date. Despite those deep-set character traits, she slowly raised her hand, pushed her fingers into his long, silky hair, and kissed him back as if he were the love of her life.

ॐ ॐ | ॐ ॐ

Michael yielded to her unrestrained response and fireworks ignited inside him. Heat pulsed through his veins, and a thousand pinpricks of light exploded behind his eyelids. The colors flashed brilliant, more magnificent than poppy fields on the way to Oz and just as dangerous. The onslaught to his senses stunned him. Unfamiliar feelings shook the buzz off his intoxicated haze, warning him he needed to be more aware of the moment—more aware of *her*.

The sound of her soft moan lured him further into her magic, but the need to breathe forced him to release her lips. "Damn," he gasped, leaning his forehead against hers. "Lady, you pack quite a kiss."

She chuckled softly. "You're not so bad yourself,

Spartacus."

He smiled. "So, you figured it out."

"Figured what out?" Her brow creased.

The puzzled expression she wore perplexed him. The disconnect between his encounter with her earlier and her current demeanor deepened. In the parlor, she'd all but bluntly stated her obvious attraction to him. Now, she acted as if she'd never met him. Was she playing hard to get? He sensed a playful intelligence about her, but no coyness. This couldn't be the same woman he'd met earlier. No way would he have let this woman walk away from him.

He stepped back and glanced down at her costume to determine what new diva he'd encountered. His perusal confirmed the same Juliet dress he remembered. He shook his head, annoyed with himself. He really should have laid off the cocktails an hour ago.

"Never mind." He reached for the mask covering the top half of her face.

"No." She stayed his hand, knocking her wig slightly askew.

"I need to see your face."

"*No.*" She pressed more firmly against the hand he had at her mask. She had no intention of letting him see her face.

He watched her breasts rise and fall. Like him, she hadn't yet recovered from their soul-shattering kiss. He studied her eyes, which looked soft brown in the dim light. He could have sworn he noted greenish eyes before. Dismissing the discrepancy as a trick of the shadows, he captured her hand and pressed his full lips against her palm in an open-mouthed kiss. Although she didn't make a sound, he felt a deep inhalation shudder through her.

His thumb rubbed across the soft skin of her upraised palm before he turned her hand over. Her long, graceful fingers ended with well-manicured, medium-length nails she'd painted with nothing more than a clearcoat. His thumb and index finger rubbed one of her fingertips, and he discovered they were her natural nails.

"You have beautiful hands," he whispered, admiring the golden undertone to her complexion he hadn't noticed when her tanned hand had touched him inside earlier.

To think, he'd been about to give up his search when he'd spotted her standing on the balcony. He'd gotten a full view of her soft, curvy hips and round, full bottom in the sexy, modernized costume. The snug plum velvet, with its mid-thigh split and wispy, diaphanous overlay had accentuated her womanly figure and billowed seductively about her ankles. How had he missed all those luscious curves before?

He placed her hand back on his chest. His heartbeat raced beneath her palm. Her fingers curled against his bare skin, and the butterfly caress made him hum with appreciation. Releasing her hand to its own temptation, he moved back against her. "Do you have any idea what your touch is doing to me?"

"Wha—?" Her words disappeared inside the startled gasped that rushed from her lungs when his hand brushed the front of her dress. Her nipples beaded at his touch.

"Yeah, my problem exactly," he murmured. "Everything about you makes me hard and swollen, too."

Her eyes darted to his. Despite the dim light, he could

read the desire burning in their depths. His fingers played along a nipple before he palmed her and relished her heavy roundness. Her breast filled his grasp. She had to be at least a C cup, an all-natural C cup. The thought brought a smile to his lips. He pressed those happy lips against her neck and massaged her budded peak with deep, deliberate pressure. His hips moved.

She groaned when he began to lower his head. "Wait." She placed her hands on either side of his face to still its descent.

His voice pitched low, husky. "Wait for what, sweetheart?"

"I—I . . ."

Her inability to form words amused him until he noted the look in her eyes. Sincerity and definiteness of purpose filled her gaze, with some confusion and uncertainty mixed in. Whatever the vibes she'd sent his way in the parlor, she appeared to have had a change of heart. The thought disturbed him. He couldn't pinpoint what had happened between his gathering of two champagne glasses to track down a one-night stand and this moment of genuine human attraction. He needed more time with this woman to figure it out. Something about her beckoned him to get to know her and not only in the biblical sense.

The melodic sound of her voice replayed in his head: *You've made a mistake. I think you're looking for someone else.*

An uncomfortable uncertainty tickled his nerves, invoking the feeling again that the woman before him differed distinctly from the woman he'd conversed with earlier. The moment of unease caused the lingering alcoholic fog around his brain to lift completely.

Spurred by the possibility she might pull away, he wrapped his arms around her. "Be mine tonight, Juliet. Let me give you your first pleasure of the New Year."

ॐ ॐ | ॐ ॐ

Juliet managed only a whimper in response to the gladiator's entreaty. Her voice completely abandoned her. His nibbling lips returned to her neck. His warm hand fondling her breast, coupled with his well-endowed shaft riding above the throbbing apex of her thighs, built an erotic pressure deep inside her center and hinted ecstasy lingered only a small pelvic alignment away.

A battle raged inside her. The level-headed intellectual in her kept telling her to nix this behavior before this stranger bashed her in the head, did horrific things to her, and dumped her body in some toxic ditch, making her a tragedy worthy of an episode of *Criminal Minds*. The passionate woman in her, the one she'd buried beneath a deluge of disillusionment and cured with a heavy dose of compulsive career focus, started fighting her way free of the self-imposed fourteen-month cell of abstinence.

She pushed his hip, trying to put space between their thighs. "Please," she tossed the impassioned plea at him, not really sure what she was asking.

Was she asking him to stop? *Yes.*

Was she asking him not to stop? *Yes.*

She'd never understood the notion of mixed signals. She'd always thought it a simple matter of you did or you didn't—you wanted to or you didn't want to. How self-righteously ignorant she'd been. Heaven help her. Everything about this man turned her on, and she didn't even know his name.

His hand dropped from her breast and reached under the folds of her costume. "Tell me, Juliet, are you as wet for me as I am hard for you?"

She squirmed. A deep flush spread over her body. She *was* wet. She blocked his hand with her leg, trying to shield the evidence of her arousal and stave off the orgasm that surely would occur if he touched her.

He squeezed his hand between her legs and cupped her intimately. He lifted triumphant eyes to hers. "Why would you want to hide this from me?" he murmured gruffly.

"I can't . . . ," she started, but didn't finish. Her train of thought vanished with the glide of his fingers over the damp satin triangle of her thong. A sound squeezed from her throat she didn't recognize, having never before vocalized this particular note of tortured bliss.

"Don't deny me, Juliet. You're the best part of this whole miserable New Year's Eve for me."

Despite herself, the urge to rock her pelvis against his fingers grew strong. She bordered on emotional overload. She couldn't reconcile the pleasure she felt from his touch with the horror rising inside her for her uncharacteristically loose behavior. That this man's kiss, his words, his illicitly placed fingers, could give her the most stimulating sexual encounter of her life both puzzled and overwhelmed her.

Her feminine walls started to pulse and tremble, but she couldn't allow him to continue. She slid her hand between them, inadvertently brushing the back of her hand against his erection. His sharp intake of breath rattled her already shredded composure.

She wrapped her hand firmly around his broad wrist and closed her eyes to steady herself. When she thought she'd conquered her emotions, she opened her eyes and peered into his watchful gaze. "We have to stop." She squeezed his wrist. "*I* have to stop. Please, let go."

A few seconds passed before he moved, letting his hand drop. A question built behind his eyes, and he whispered, "Who are you?"

She hesitated a moment, contemplating her response. She could tell by his expression he'd finally accepted she wasn't the woman he'd come looking for. Did it bother him? He seemed simply curious not angry. Nevertheless, innate self-preservation made her glance around for an escape route.

The gladiator placed a hand firmly on her waist to hold her in place. "Tell me your name. Your *real* name. I have to see you again."

Her mind raced. Nothing good could come of a midnight tryst with an intoxicated stranger whom you almost let get inside your panties without even trading your real names. She needed to get away.

"No." She moved aside abruptly. "Let me go."

"Wait!"

Their voices overlapped. Her movement caught him off guard, and he dropped the forgotten champagne flute he'd been holding. The bubbly liquid spilled down her back before the sound of shattering glass rent the air. She jerked and the corded shoulder gathers of her dress snagged on the curlicue design of his epaulettes. The cords unraveled and the bodice of her dress drooped, completely exposing her to the waist. Her mouth dropped open. Mortification overtook her when the gladiator's eyes widened at the display of her naked breasts.

Footsteps sounded near the sliding glass door of the balcony and a giggling voice carried across the night. "Are you sure no one else is out here?"

"Don't worry, baby," came a masculine reply. "You're safe with me."

The gladiator recovered quickly and clasped her to his chest, shielding her from view with his larger body.

The giggling increased when the amorous couple passed them. "See, I told you someone else would have thought of this," the female voice admonished.

"Baby," the deep male voice replied humorously, "they're so into each other they won't even know we're here. C'mon. Let's find our own private corner."

Their footsteps faded, and Juliet became aware of her bare nipples squished against the gladiator's chest. Instead of alarming her, the warmth of him felt oddly comforting. Instinctively, she understood he'd grabbed her to cover her wardrobe malfunction, which impressed her as oddly gallant under the circumstances.

"Thanks," she murmured, disengaging to attend her bodice.

When she couldn't get the shoulder piece back together, he intercepted her frustrated fumbles. "Here. Allow me."

The chore stumped him as well until he discovered a small clasp hidden beneath the gold cording. The clasp was bent, having snagged on his shoulder piece. He pressed it back into shape with a firm squeeze between his thumb and forefinger then latched it closed over her shoulder.

Adjusting her dress, she stepped towards the door, careful to avoid the broken glass at her feet. "I have to go." She spoke without looking at him.

"I really want to see you again."

"No, you don't." She shook her head and almost laughed at his shocked expression. "What you want is an easy lay. And I'm not that woman."

"That's not—"

She placed three fingers against his lips to silence him. "Look, this isn't who I am. I don't know what came over me tonight. I've never done anything like this before in my life. Ever. So, you can forget about your all-nighter. You won't be getting lucky with me." She took a deep breath before she continued. "Unfortunately for you—" She sighed. "—well, for both of us really. I'm the kind of girl who needs a commitment, not the kind of girl you keep in your little black book for late-night hookups."

He removed her hand. "Whatever you say. All I'm asking is for you to give me a chance to find out who you are for myself."

"I don't think so." She laughed and shook her head again. "Something tells me that after tonight, we'd be hard pressed to rewind to getting-to-know-you drinks or dinner and a movie. How about we simply leave it at our midnight rendezvous, and I'll revisit the memory of tonight whenever I need to remind myself even someone as provincial as me can have a bit of a naughty girl inside."

Still holding her hand, he insisted, "At least tell me your first name."

She smiled fully for the first time. "What? And ruin the

mystique? I don't think so." She began to walk away. She made it halfway to the balcony door before she hesitated. She turned to see his pensive profile staring off into the night. "Hey, Spartacus," she called.

He turned his head towards the sound of her voice.

"You're one hell of a kisser. Whoever your true Juliet is, she's one lucky lady." She returned to the party, but not before she heard him murmur under his breath.

"*You* are my true Juliet," he whispered, not knowing she could hear him.

CHAPTER 2

M ore bothered than he cared to admit about Juliet's refusal to tell him her real name, Michael stood at the balcony railing staring into the night. *New Year's Day*, he mused. *A day for new beginnings.*

He surveyed the sparkling Christmas lights on the retail and office buildings of the Country Club Plaza. Over two hundred eighty-seven thousand multi-colored Christmas lights covered approximately one hundred thirty-nine square miles of Spanish-inspired architecture. The Kansas City novelty thrilled locals and holiday tourists alike. The beautiful sight would stay lit for another two and a half weeks before being doused until the next annual lighting ceremony to be held, as per tradition, on Thanksgiving night.

From his position atop the upscale Wornall Hills condo building, Michael could see the entire fifteen-block display. The postcard-perfect visual made a fitting back-drop for what had turned into the most romantic encounter of his adult life. Two things were certain: One, he would never view a simple kiss the same way again; two, the woman he'd kissed tonight was definitely *not* the same woman who had accosted him earlier in the parlor.

The feel of his Juliet lingered across his fingers and across his senses. A strange sensation flowed through his consciousness. *Amore a prima vista.* He hadn't thought about the concept in a long time. He didn't believe in it—the notion that when a man met the woman right for him, he would recognize her instantly.

As he stood alone with his thoughts, he remembered his father telling him often about the day he'd first seen his mother. His father always claimed it had been "love at first sight." When he was young, Michael had loved listening to the story of how his parents had met. After all, his mother was beautiful. How could a man not fall in love with her instantly? Once he reached his teens, he became more skeptical, and his skepticism had grown over the years.

His personal experiences with women suggested no such magic exists. In his opinion, what his father had felt for his mother amounted to lust at first sight, and his father had simply gotten lucky. His mother had turned out to be as beautiful on the inside as she was on the outside. More often than not, the women Michael encountered showed themselves to be calculating, manipulative, and creatures of false passion or coyness.

He found it interesting that the most genuinely passion-ate encounter of his life had occurred with a complete stranger. The woman had been not only beautiful, but also spontaneous and sexy and the most naturally responsive woman he'd ever touched. And what had he done? He'd let her walk away.

He tensed. *Idiot!*

Turning abruptly, Michael rushed into the party. His eyes skimmed the crowd. Packed from wall to wall, the normally cavernous room shrank to a tiny blockade. Couples huddled together, discreetly making time or swaying together on the makeshift dance floor. Groupings of friends and acquaintances chatted and laughed. The crush made his search dense work, but his height allowed him to see over ninety percent of the party guests. When he didn't see Juliet immediately, an unfamiliar wave of anxiety rushed over him.

Anticipation slipped towards dread. His eyes scanned the room again and finally located her on the platform leading to the front door. She stood talking on a mobile phone. Her demeanor turned animated. He couldn't hear her side of the conversation, but he recognized signs of distress in her expressions. After a few moments, she closed her eyes, lowered the phone, and blew out a breath. That she might have trouble concerned him. He moved towards her, his desire to learn her identity now coupled with a strong need to make sure she was all right.

He'd only taken a few steps when she looked up and saw him advancing towards her. A look of astonishment crossed her face. Turning quickly, she opened the door, exited, and closed the door behind her.

Michael quickened his pace, muttering apologies as he pushed past people left and right. When he finally made it to the door, he swore. His unsuccessful tugging revealed she'd locked it. Disengaging the lock, he simultaneously admired and cursed her ability to keep her wits about her while making a hasty getaway. He'd lost precious seconds in his pursuit.

The door finally swung open, and relief washed over him. She stood in front of the lone elevator located at the end of the hall.

"Wait!" he called.

A resonant ding announced the arrival of the elevator a half second later. She raised her hand, palm out, before stepping inside. He couldn't tell if she'd meant to wave goodbye or simply tell him not to follow her. Either way, he had no intention of letting her get away.

He dashed into the stairwell. The overly bright white lights shocked his pupils after the soft yellow lighting of the hallway, but he didn't slow down. He descended each flight of stairs in a rush, leaping three and four steps at a time. The tinny reverberation of his footsteps on the metal stairs bounced around the whitewashed walls. The sound mocked him with the possibility of failure.

He made it to the lobby level in time to glimpse the hem of Juliet's flowing gown flutter on a gush of air and disappear inside the revolving panes of the glass exit. He pressed forward. Darting into the slowing turnstile, he pushed hard, but the natural lethargy of the revolving door fought against his urgency.

Trapped inside the circular, mechanical obstruction, he watched a taxi pull to a stop in front of Juliet.

She reached for the door handle.

"Porca Madonna!" His exasperation defaulted, without

conscious thought, to his mother's native Italian tongue and sweat beaded his brow. *No. No. No.* Getting this close and failing became untenable. With one last burst of muscle, he plowed his way free. "Please wait!"

She stopped and eyed him over the taxi door she'd pulled open.

Gulps of air expanded his lungs in a staccato rhythm. Trying not to spook her any more than he already had, he stood immobile at the building entrance. "I just want to talk to you for a minute."

She waited, but didn't speak.

"I have to know your name."

"Just call me Juliet."

He swallowed his disappointment. "Okay, I get it. You don't want to tell me your real name. I'll have to live with that. For now." He ran a hand through his hair, shoving wayward locks off his forehead. "Let me buy you dinner tonight."

A shake of her head silently rejected the offer.

"Tomorrow then or any day you choose. Give me a chance, Juliet. I realize I didn't behave . . . um . . . like a gentleman upstairs. And I apologize if I offended you. But, I promise I'm not an axe murderer or a stalker or generally a molester of women—"

She laughed, a light airy sound. "I don't know why, but for some reason, I believe you."

"Then have dinner with me."

"I can't. I don't think it's a good idea."

He opened his mouth to protest and took a step forward.

Her hand went up to stop him. "No. Try to look at this

from my perspective." She paused briefly to duck her head inside the cab and murmur something to the driver. When she looked back at him, her lips held a reluctant smile. "If we had met under different circumstances, I'm sure I'd find your dinner invitation flattering. Tonight, well . . ."

The hand she'd rested on top of the cab door tightened. Although he stood some distance from her, Michael noticed the gesture. It didn't bode well.

She averted her gaze. The taxi had stopped outside the parameter of the security floodlights so shadows danced across her masked face. "My friends are always telling me I need to be more spontaneous." She looked back at him with a simper. "I doubt our meeting upstairs is exactly what they had in mind, but I'd like to be able to look back on tonight and remember it as my adventurous rendez-vous with a sexy stranger. That will be a lot easier for me to do if I don't have to face you tonight or the next day or the day after that. Please try to understand. I need you to let me go."

For several seconds, neither of them spoke. They stood quietly regarding each other.

Finally, he nodded and gave a half bow. "As you wish, milady."

Her lips curved up at his gesture before she slid into the back of the yellow cab.

The taxi door made only a faint click when she closed it, but the snick reverberated in his ears as if the door had been slammed. The psychologically deafening sound echoed the finality of an unexpected opportunity slipping forever out of his reach.

❦ ❦ | ❧ ❧

Six days later, Michael sat at the large mahogany desk in his corner office staring blankly out a wall of windows while a tablet stylus did somersaults between the fingers of his left hand. He was supposed to be choosing a new second chair for his patent infringement case not browsing the downtown skyline from his twenty-fifth floor Remington Towers office suite near Crown Center. Chase currently served as his second chair, but Chase needed to take the lead in another case because the wife of one of their equity partners had recently been diagnosed with cancer, and the partner needed time with his family.

A file folder of forgotten resumes sat open on Michael's desk. He'd read through them several times and had narrowed his selection to one of two candidates. They both looked good on paper, but the non-quantifiable qualities that didn't show up on paper meant a lot as well.

This case represented a significant opportunity for his firm, both in dollars and legal notoriety. He considered it the linchpin in his strategic plan to launch the firm as a national player in the world of business litigation. A successful outcome meant instant nationwide publicity for the lawyers involved. He'd already been interviewed for write-ups in prominent legal and business journals. He needed to make the right choice. Yet, he couldn't force his mind to focus on the task at hand.

On days like these, he'd usually take a motorcycle ride to clear his head. Nothing like speed on an open road to get the blood flowing to all extremities including his brain. Unfortunately, it was too cold for a ride. Although this winter's weather had stayed unusually mild, it would be several months before the temperature warmed enough to take the bike for a spin. Which reminded him he needed to make an appointment with his mechanic to get his bike checked and prepped for the spring riding season.

Michael looked at the electronic tablet on his desk. He made himself a reminder to get a service appointment then glanced at his court docket. Maybe he should work on reconciling his calendar. He'd promised his baby sister he'd attend the annual family Independence Day gathering. He'd committed to staying for the entire picnic this year and not simply putting in an appearance then rushing back to the office to bill more hours. He hated to disappoint Raina, but given the current status of his case, that might be a tall order.

He tossed his stylus onto the desk in frustration. The opponent's motion for summary judgment had arrived this morning. The motion requested the court decide the case in the opponent's favor because, according to opponent's counsel, the factual information exchanged by the parties during discovery mandated a judgment be entered in its favor by law — no need for a trial.

If the motion prevailed, it was game over for Metra Pharmaceuticals. His client would be held liable for patent infringement, ordered to cease the manufacture and sale of their extremely successful immunotherapeutic drug Davrosil, and forced to disgorge to the opponent all profits made from selling the drug.

While this would normally be enough to concern him, today a whole other distraction worried his brain. A week had passed since he'd touched her for the first time.

Fleeting thoughts of her hounded him from time to time, but for some reason, today the memory of her wouldn't leave him alone. *Juliet*.

Where was she? What was she doing? Whom was she doing it with?

The last question in particular bothered him.

He slid his hand into his right pant pocket and fingered the sterling silver chain he'd been carrying around for six days. He tended to finger it absently when his mind wandered to Juliet. He needed to get to work. If Chase caught him daydreaming about her, Michael would never live it down. His buddy already ragged him heartlessly, and without remorse, about being hung up on what Chase had dubbed his "mystery woman."

Michael knew better. Curious? Definitely. Hung up? Hardly. He had no intention of letting any woman put the shackles on him. Of course, you couldn't tell Chase anything. Chase and his wife had been happily married for four years before he lost her. Marriage wasn't for Michael, but he'd more than love another chance to experience the sumptuous creature he'd kissed by accident on New Year's Eve.

He'd searched for her. He'd tried to let it go, let her go, but by the end of the next day, he'd felt a driving need to find her. The search had required Chase's help since Chase had served on the party planning committee. Chase had contacted every guest and inquired about each of their companions. Strangely, no one could identify the mystery woman *or* the original Juliet as legitimate invitees. He and Chase had concluded, on top of everything else, his Juliet might have crashed the party. It figured.

The guest chair to his right squeaked, and Michael pulled his hand from his pocket. What was that old expression? Think of the devil and the devil shall appear. Okay, so maybe it was "speak" of the devil, but for the moment, it was all the same.

"Chase." Michael acknowledged his partner with a bland look.

"Welcome back." Chase took a seat opposite Michael's desk.

Michael's perplexed expression made Chase grin. "I stood in your doorway for several minutes. What were you thinking about?"

"Nothing."

"Or should I ask *whom* were you thinking about?" Chase made absolutely no effort to hide the amusement in his sky blue eyes.

Annoyed, Michael turned squarely to his desk, picked up his stylus, and let it resume its somersaults between his fingers. "Did you need something?"

At Michael's curt avoidance of his question, Chase sighed. "Man, tell me you are not still hung up on your beautiful party crasher."

"Don't start with me, Chase. I'm not hung up. Let it go."

"I don't understand what it is about this woman. You couldn't have spent more than thirty minutes with her tops."

"Forty-five minutes." He'd looked at his watch when she'd ridden off in the cab. She'd pulled off at twelve forty-five a.m. exactly.

"I stand corrected," Chase deadpanned then leaned back in his chair. "I'm starting to worry about you, man.

It's not like you to become so preoccupied with a woman."

Michael shook his head. "I don't know what to tell you, Chase. I really can't explain it. Something about her won't let me go."

Chase studied him. For the first time, Michael saw his friend's dawning acceptance that his interest in Juliet wasn't some passing fancy.

"I can't believe the untraceable, unnamable duplicate Juliet bewitched you so completely." Chase ran a hand through his ash blond hair. "Michael, I did what I could to determine who she may have come to the party with. You're going to have to accept you might never find her."

"Intellectually, I know that, but my head isn't winning on this. Something tells me she's closer than I think. Something I noticed about her that night or something she said holds the clue to finding her. If only I could figure out what I've been overlooking."

Chase leaned forward in his chair. "Don't go all dog-with-bone on me. I know how you get when on the trail of a missing link—that one piece of evidence an adversary doesn't want found or the discrepancy in an argument that would shatter an opposing counsel's whole legal premise. You do it better than just about any lawyer in the country—which is why we have several Fortune 100 clients on the firm's roster—but this isn't high-stakes litigation.

"I don't know what more we can do to find the mysterious Juliet. I'll admit, I'm more than a little intrigued by the lady. She's the first woman in whom you've displayed more than a passing interest in over a year. It's the main reason I made such a pest of myself with the association's party guests in an attempt to locate her. But, no luck.

Maybe it's time you let this go."

Chase laced his fingers together and lapsed into silence.

Michael saw the wheels begin to spin behind his eyes. Sensing trouble, he warned, "Don't even think about it, Chase."

"What?" Chase's look of faux innocence almost made Michael laugh.

"I know what you're thinking, and I'll have none of it. I'm not interested in dating another one of Grace's friends." Grace was Chase's late wife. She'd been relentless in trying to pair Michael off with one of her friends. Since her passing two years ago, Chase had made it his mission to pick up where she'd left off.

"What's wrong with Grace's friends?"

"There's absolutely nothing wrong with Grace's friends. I'd simply rather not be privy to any more of your matchmaking by proxy. It was bad enough when I had to deal with Grace. Do me a favor? If you think these women are so great, you go out with them."

Chase got a faraway look in his eyes. "You know there's not a woman on the planet who can take the place of my Grace."

"I'm not talking about replacing Grace, Chase." Michael's voice dropped to a hushed tone. "It's been two years. It's time to move on."

"Says the dyed-in-the-wool bachelor who, after being betrayed by his fiancée, staunchly proclaims he's never getting married."

The forgotten stylus stilled in Michael's hand. He couldn't argue with that.

"You know, Michael, I'm beginning to wonder if your

mother's right."

"Right about what?"

"She believes despite not knowing her real name, you fell instantly and completely for the mysterious Juliet, which is why *you* can't seem to move on."

Michael waved his hand in dismissal. "My mother is a hopeless romantic."

"That she is, but maybe she knows what she's talking about. It seemed to work for her and your father—that whole get engaged after knowing each other only two weeks fairy tale. Have you seriously considered that maybe you're—"

"*No.* I haven't." His voice took on an edge. "Enough about the missing Juliet. What brings you here?"

"Well . . ." Chase's smile immediately made Michael more nervous than the direction their conversation had started to take. "I'm wondering if you plan to grace us with your presence at this week's briefing session. The new laterals and associates have been here for months, and you've yet to meet them."

Michael sighed. He really didn't want to participate in the weekly war room session they used to supervise and train new lateral hires and associates. "Can't you continue to handle these on your own? I'm not in the mood to manage the egos of another bunch of young professionals with a penchant for high-school-level drama."

Chase chuckled. "I know you eschew these administrative duties, which is why you've resisted for another year taking over the Managing Partner position your grandfather vacated when he retired three years ago. But you agreed to co-chair our group's Associate Development

Committee with me this year, and you've been extremely lax in your duties. Not to mention you know I need to take over the Werner case from Jackson soon. So, you need to make a decision on my replacement for the Metra Pharmaceuticals case. At some point, looking at resumes isn't going to be enough."

Snagging the folder of pedigrees Michael had ignored all morning, Chase flipped through the dossiers of the senior associates on their team. "Eventually, you need to meet these guys in person to determine which one will suit your purpose best." He tossed the folder back on the desk.

Chase made a good point. No matter how many times Michael went over the resumes, it always came back to the same two possible candidates—on paper. Time he evaluated the next level. He flipped open the folder and placed the photo-included resumes of his top two candidates side-by-side on top.

Unfolding from the chair, Chase stood. His tall frame towered over Michael's desk. "Avoidance time is done. You're coming to the meeting today. I expect to see you in the South Conference Room in fifteen minutes. If you're not there on time, I'm going to personally pick one of the new female hires to come escort you down."

Michael's head jerked up. As he suspected, a mischievous smirk graced Chase's lips. His friend had a wicked sense of humor, and Michael knew he meant it. The only thing Michael hated more than the administrative duties associated with partnership was fending off the female groupies who considered him the firm's most eligible catch. Every year, a new bunch arrived.

Sometimes, he felt like a mouse in a house with a dozen

cats. He had to be careful when he came out of his hole. The Mediterranean complexion he'd inherited from his mother gave him a perpetual-tan look the opposite sex found attractive. Still, he'd learned what most interested females were the size of his bank account and the power associated with having the same surname as the firm's founding partners. He didn't do office relationships. He'd been there, done that, and had the battle scars to prove it.

"I'll be there," he finally replied. The last thing he needed was for Chase to sic some overzealous female associate on him. Chase had a knack for picking the ones with a biological clock ticking so loud it could be heard throughout the tri-state area. The last time it happened, Michael spent weeks trying to dissuade the young lady from her pursuit. In his opinion, there wasn't a species on the planet more tenacious than a female lawyer. He doubted even a mother lioness could hold her own.

"Good." Chase turned and exited the corner office.

Michael's chest rose and fell with a deep breath as he rubbed his left hand through his hair. His Monday morning hadn't stacked up so well. He'd let Chase catch him daydreaming about his mystery lady. He'd let thoughts of *her* distract him from the case he should have been working on.

Opposing counsel had made it clear during their last telephone conference that the plaintiff, Dexter Drug, wouldn't talk settlement unless the deal included a full assignment of Metra Pharmaceuticals' patent rights in its competing drug. Of course, Metra Pharmaceuticals wouldn't agree so he needed to survive the summary judgment phase. If he did, this case might actually go to trial.

Looking at his calendar again, he noted that would put him in court right around the Fourth of July picnic. Raina was going to skin him alive. On top of that, he now had to go play mentor.

He rose from his deep, black leather chair, grabbed his suit jacket, and headed for the South Conference Room. He didn't know why, but he had a sudden premonition his day was about to get even more complicated.

CHAPTER 3

*J*ordis Morgan stood to the side of the half-full conference room, gripping a cup of chai spice black tea. Subconsciously, she categorized the different personality types in the room. She excelled at reading people, a skill that had proved useful during her career as a litigator.

In some ways, she was an anomaly. She had a reputation as a fierce litigator. She rarely lost and could pick apart an adversary's case with the efficiency of a swarm of locust stripping a field of crops. Yet, her easy smile and youthful demeanor lured opposing counsel into a relaxed mood that often resulted in their underestimating her. By the time they realized under her easygoing exterior laid the heart of a predator, she'd shredded their legal theories and left their clients defeated.

While her colleagues didn't qualify as adversaries per se, competition inevitably reared its head among the ambitious group. She lumped the women on her team into distinct categories, from hot-to-trot to damsel-in-distress to no-nonsense career woman. She turned her attention to the men, but got distracted when Michael Remington walked into the conference room. The head of every female swiveled his way and lingered longer than necessary to simply acknowledge his arrival. Jordis, too, took a few extra minutes to admire the tall, muscular dark-haired lawyer in his tailored navy Armani suit. His confident loose-limbed walk said athletic. This man didn't simply chisel out a physique in the gym to impress the ladies; he used his body for activities more engaging than static barbell repetitions.

Michael made his way around the room, shaking hands and introducing himself. He lingered with a couple of guys whose faces became particularly animated after introductions. Jordis couldn't hear the entire conversation, but apparently one of them had attended Michael's law school alma mater.

The younger of the associates, Jonathan, like her was a lateral hire and new to the firm this year. The other associate, Eric Covington, was a firm veteran and the group's egomaniac. Covington had wasted no time rubbing Jordis the wrong way. Her hand tightened around her cup as she watched him try to ingratiate himself with Remington.

When Michael Remington finally excused himself and walked her way, he hesitated a second before extending his hand. A less observant person wouldn't have noticed the infinitesimal pause, but Jordis noticed.

"Michael Remington." His hand hovered in front of her.

She shifted her cup into her left hand and shook his with her right. "Jordis Morgan."

Up close, Jordis took note of his alluring gray eyes. She'd never met a man with gray eyes. She'd read about them in works of fiction, and now seeing the real thing, she understood why hordes of women would fantasize about having a man look lustfully at them through gray lenses.

Those exquisite eyes narrowed slightly as he examined her face more closely. "Have we met before?"

"No." Jordis shook her head. "At least, not officially."

"Not officially?" Michael, who had continued to hold her hand, glanced down when she slid her hand casually from his grasp. "How so?"

"I've worked at the firm for four months." She flashed an easy smile. "Maybe you've seen me lurking in the halls."

Out of the corner of her eye, Jordis caught Alyson McGovern watching her with a none-to-happy look on her face.

His hands slid into the pockets of his slacks, and he considered her response. "Maybe, but I don't think that's it."

Rumored to be the hottest guy at the firm, the future managing partner had a reputation as a chick magnet. A die-hard workaholic, associates rarely saw him outside his office. She'd joined the firm shortly before Labor Day, and until today, she hadn't met the man in person.

She didn't put much stock in rumors or innuendo, but she had to admit, the talk didn't do him justice. He didn't have a classically handsome face in a pretty-boy way. His features leaned towards the rugged. Square-jawed with angled cheekbones and full brows below a balanced forehead, he had a straight nose that gave nice symmetry to his face. His brown-black hair had been shaved short around the sides and back of his head, but left full in the top. With his athletic build and those compelling features beneath a smooth olive complexion, he exuded an animal magnetism hard to ignore.

Before he could make another comment, Chase called the meeting to order.

"After you." Michael stepped aside and motioned her towards the conference table.

A voice interrupted their parting. "Excuse me, Mr. Remington."

Michael looked down to see Alyson smiling at him.

A petite woman, Alyson stood about a head shorter than Jordis, making her look delicate next to Michael. "I'm going to top off my cup of coffee." Her sweetly reticent smile suggested a shyness contradicted by the offer in her eyes. "How about I get you a cup?"

"No thanks, Alyson. I appreciate the offer, but I'm good." Michael motioned Alyson to the coffee service. "Why don't you hurry and freshen your cup so we can get started."

From her spot at the conference table, Jordis watched Alyson's smile turn into a frown once Michael could no longer see her face. After topping off her coffee cup, Alyson moved to the conference table and placed her cup in front of her seat before adjusting the wide leather waist belt on her red designer shirtdress. Alyson glanced at Jordis and gave a fake smile. Jordis returned the smile in turn, internally pleased at the disappointment masked on

Alyson's face.

Jordis didn't have time to examine why the interchange between Michael Remington and Alyson pleased her so much because Michael surprised her—and Alyson—by walking over to the coffee service and pouring his own cup of coffee. Jordis discreetly caught the expression on Alyson's face as the woman took notice of the gesture and the silent message it sent: she wouldn't turn Michael Remington's head easily.

Ms. Hot-To-Trot would have to up her game if she intended to make a serious play for the sexy partner. Why this pleased Jordis, she'd have to examine more closely later.

ớ ớ | ở ở

"Okay, the last order of business," Chase stated, "is to select this year's litigation pro bono case." He flipped open a file folder in front of him. "Each of you has a copy of the synopses for the five potential cases selected by the Pro Bono Review Board. The matter is now open for discussion. Recommendations?"

Michael looked casually around the table. He covertly evaluated this latest crop of lawyers, trying to determine who'd likely have a long-term stint at the firm and who'd likely be gone by the end of the fiscal year. Good grades and high test scores were important, but they encompassed only a small part of what it took to be a great lawyer. He believed in recruiting from the top ranks of prestigious law schools, but intangibles such as drive, discipline, empathy, and integrity meant as much as academic success. Talent alone was never enough. When they got lucky and found associates with the triple combination of academic talent, emotional intelligence, and those amorphous intangibles, then he knew they'd hit pay dirt.

He lifted his cup of now cold coffee and tried to focus on the discussion. He was having an unusually hard time paying attention to the various topics. He sat at the opposite end of the table from Chase, and the long-legged associate with the unique name sat two chairs down on his left. He couldn't take his eyes off her, though he made sure to be discreet. Where had he seen her before?

Maybe he *had* passed her in the hall, but the thought didn't ring true. He'd noticed her immediately upon walking into the conference room. Something about her posture and body language as she'd stood alone surveying the room had tugged at the recesses of his memory.

When he'd introduced himself, her striking eyes had taken him off guard. The swirls of browns, golds, and greens mixed together to make an alluring tapestry of color more intense than any hazel eyes he'd ever seen before. She wore minimal makeup, but her eyes appeared large and seductive. Combined with her light caramel skin tone, the exotic eyes gave her a stunning appeal that would make any man look twice.

High cheekbones graced an oval face enhanced by perfectly arched eyebrows. She'd pulled her straight hair back and secured it at the base of her neck with a flat barrette. Its chestnut brown fullness fell between her shoulder blades against a gold-colored blouse she'd paired with a black pencil skirt. The skirt stopped decorously right above her knees, but the cheetah print pumps she wore accentuated her shapely length of long legs.

To his chagrin, when she'd walked away to take her seat, his eyes had dropped to the sway of her hips. He'd looked up to find Chase watching him with a questioning look. Michael had taken a quick glance around to see if anyone else had noticed where his eyes had strayed. No one had seemed the wiser.

He angled his conference chair to the left and leaned back in the comfortable black leather swivel rocker. With his right foot propped over his left knee, he kept Jordis Morgan directly in his line of vision. Every once in a while, she flicked her left hand and rubbed her left wrist. She wore no watch. He wondered if she'd forgotten to put one on this morning and subconsciously missed it.

She had nice hands with long fingers and soft skin. A French manicure in beige instead of white tipped her nails. Her hands kept busy, either casually fingering the rim of her cup or fiddling with her pen. The constant movement fascinated him. He could imagine those hands trailing languidly across his naked body. The place on his anatomy he'd most welcome her touch twitched at the thought. When she opened her mouth to lobby for the landlord-tenant matter of a single mom in a depressed neighborhood, he squashed his wayward thoughts and shifted his awareness of the discussion from the back of his multitasking brain to the forefront.

"Look, sweetheart, I feel for the little inner-city single mom as much as the next person," Eric Covington said to Jordis with barely disguised superiority.

Michael's right hand, which had heretofore absently

twirled his pen atop a yellow legal pad on the table in front of him, stopped abruptly. *Did he just call her "sweetheart" in the middle of a business meeting?*

Michael looked at Chase who slowly raised an eyebrow, confirming for Michael he hadn't imagined the inappropriate appellation.

"However, we have the opportunity to be the legal face of a major patent dispute that could lead to some historical legal precedent. Here—" Eric tapped the folder of his preferred case. "—we have an everyday guy whose brilliant innovation was ripped off by a major corporate conglomerate." He leaned forward in his chair, getting into his pitch. "It'll be great PR. We'll be touted for fighting for the underdog. We shouldn't pass that up for a case that could easily be handled by Legal Aid."

Jordis leaned back in her chair and simply stared at Eric. Michael watched a slow smile creep across her face. He'd swear he'd seen the same look on the face of his uncle's favorite tomcat right before he took out a family of rats. He thought to intervene, but something about Jordis's relaxed poise made him bide his time.

"Excuse me, *studly*, but I thought the point of the firm's Pro Bono Program was to make a difference in the community, not to select cases with the intent of improving the firm's PR profile."

Eric glowered at Jonathan, to his right, who came down with a sudden coughing fit at Jordis's use of the word *studly*.

"Legal Aid is a charitable organization with a finite annual budget," Jordis continued. "There's no guarantee they'll be able to take on this woman's case, at least not immediately. If the patent case has such promise, I'm sure some other firm will be more than happy to take it on a contingency fee basis. Besides, we already have a high-profile intellectual property case on the firm's docket. Using the Pro Bono Program to add another smacks of personal hubris not community service."

"Jordis, I can understand wanting to fight for the social underdog." Eric's voice held a slight edge of condescension. "But let's look at this logically."

She lifted an unopened water bottle from the table, twisted the cap off, and took a sip. Setting the bottle back on the table, she slowly swiveled her chair to the right, crossed her long legs and responded with a quiet air of nonchalance. "Logically?"

Eric grinned his pretty-boy grin, expecting his charm to carry the day. "Exactly."

Jordis smiled back, not with joviality, but with the look of someone who recognized an insult and intended to pick up the gauntlet thrown down before her.

The foot Jordis dangled in the air bobbed twice. Michael tried to keep his eyes on her ankles, but they were drawn up her shapely calves and beyond to where her pencil skirt had ridden up her thighs. His thoughts wandered to what she might be wearing under that skirt. A vision of Jordis uncrossing her legs to plant her cheetah-pump shod feet wide enough apart to give him a peek flashed through his brain. The image hit him hard and shocked him with the instant hardening impact on the muscle between his thighs.

Looking up from Jordis's thighs, his eyes met those multi-colored orbs he found almost as entrancing as her legs. Her eyes shifted color. Her facial expression remained neutral, but she'd noticed where his attention had been focused. He dropped his foot to the floor and turned his seat squarely under the table, needing to be discreet about his lap's abrupt change in appearance.

Dammit. He couldn't believe he'd been caught, not once but twice, during a rare flare of female gawking. He didn't usually ogle woman, particularly not at the office. He had a strict personal policy against fraternizing with associates or any firm staff. He'd learned the hard way while a junior associate working with his father and grandfather that having the Remington name on the building and on his driver's license made him a target for schemers and gold diggers. If they couldn't coax him into marriage or trap him into fatherhood, they weren't beyond claiming a consensual encounter constituted sexual harassment.

"So," Jordis replied to Eric Covington, shifting her attention back to the discussion at hand, "are you saying I didn't use logic when evaluating the case the first time or you simply think I'm incapable of making a logical, coherent analysis without your assistance?"

Eric's smile faltered at the edges. "I didn't say anything like that. All I'm saying is we need to look beyond personal biases and analyze each possible pro bono matter objectively."

Michael leaned forward in his chair. He didn't like the direction the discussion had taken. He was about to put a stop to it when Chase warned him not to interrupt with a subtle shake of his head. Michael accepted the warning and held his tongue. It didn't sit well with him, but Chase had shepherded the group alone for the last few months so he would defer to Chase's judgment for the time being.

Jordis's direct gaze never wavered from Eric's face. "Ah. So you feel I'm biased and unable to be objective in this matter."

Eric held up his hands in a gesture of truce. "Jordis, there's no need to get defensive. Let's not make this personal."

The corner of Jordis's mouth lifted in a half smile. "Oh, *let's*," she replied with a lilt on the last word. "Eric, why don't you explain to us exactly what personal biases I might have towards this potential client?" When Eric didn't reply immediately, she pressed him. "Is it the fact she's a single mom or that she lives in the inner city? Or, is there some other connection you believe we have?"

A vacuum of sound permeated the conference room. Everyone stared at Eric, awaiting his response. His jaw tensed, and he ground his rear molars together. Anger stewed beneath the guy's cool, macho surface.

Jordis had put him on the spot. He either had to retract his statement or come up with a creative answer. If he failed to answer, everyone would assume he'd based his comment on personal biases in the vein of those he'd claimed should not be a part of the debate.

Michael looked at Jordis. She sat relaxed, a neutral but pleasant expression on her face. Her right hand found its way back to her mug, and her fingers once again traced the rim of the cup. She had the demeanor of one simply waiting for her opponent to make his next move on a chessboard. He wondered if she stayed this cool in court. The lady was no shrinking violet. She handled tough situations head on and took the direct approach to handling personal affronts. He liked that about her.

Intrigued to see how Covington would handle the situation, Michael sat back in his chair. As he did so, he glanced back at Chase who gave him a slight tilt of the head as if to say, *I told you so.*

৵ ৵ | ৶ ৶

Eric Covington was not a happy camper. He stood watching Jordis Morgan leave the conference room chatting conversationally with a redhead. By the time the pro bono case discussion concluded, Jordis had won the day, and the single mom had new legal counsel.

"Hey, dude, don't feel bad," Jonathan said to Eric as he swatted Eric on the shoulder. Jonathan's eyes followed Eric's down the hall to the retreating back of Jordis Morgan. "You know if you're going to take on Ms. Morgan, you'd better have done your homework. That lady has the sharpest mind in the department. Actually, probably in the whole damn firm. Don't let the pretty face fool you. Underneath her ladylike exterior lies the heart of a pit bull."

"*I* have the sharpest mind in the department," Eric replied.

"Well, it sure didn't come off that way today, *studly*. Keep telling yourself that." Jonathan laughed as he gave Eric's shoulder another pat then headed for his office.

Eric frowned, internally acknowledging Jonathan was right. Jordis had made him look like an idiot and in front of Remington, the future managing partner of the firm. By the time they'd finished debating the intricacies of their respective preferred pro bono cases, he'd come across as a pretentious snob. She'd made it look like he'd assumed because of her race she'd have some special affinity for an inner-city dweller and the plight of a single mother.

He'd looked even more foolish when Jordis had pointed out the prospective plaintiff was a young white woman named Cynthia Gardner who'd gotten pregnant at the end of her senior year of high school. Rather than stand by her, her high school sweetheart chose to accept a college basketball scholarship and abandoned the teen to her own devices. After her judgmental, self-righteous parents put her out, the single mom had found it hard to support her child without state assistance and subsidized housing.

Granted, he probably did have some preconceived notions about how Jordis had gotten her lateral position in the firm. Diversity initiatives were all the rage in major law firms across the country. No matter the firm propaganda about being more aware of subconscious biases that had excluded qualified candidates in the past, he figured women and minorities simply got special consideration. No way that leggy, supermodel type had credentials or a professional record to match his. He intended to be the star senior associate of this division, and he wasn't going to let some woman upstage him.

His father always said a woman had two places: behind a man or beneath him. Jordis Morgan needed to learn her place—behind him like the rest of the women in the group. Then again, he thought as he watched her feminine curves disappear down the hall, maybe she'd be better off beneath him. Getting her in his bed would certainly give them a better outlet for the sparks that flew whenever they were in the same room together.

Eric slid his hands into his pockets and creased his brow. He looked over to find Michael Remington watching him. Chase put his hand on Remington's shoulder and guided the partner out of the conference room.

With a nod at the two partners, Eric headed for his own office to consider his next move.

Chapter 4

*J*ordis entered her office with Vivian O'Connor on her heels.

Vivian perched on the arm of one of Jordis's guest chairs. Natural blond strands laced her long red hair. The fiery color almost didn't look real. She had green eyes and flawless fair skin sprinkled with freckles across her upper cheeks and the bridge of her nose.

With her classic Irish beauty, Vivian had the looks to play the sexuality card to get what she wanted if she so chose, but she preferred to let her brains and her work product speak for themselves. Her lips twisted with barely contained mirth. "So, what did you think of Mr. Managing Partner finally gracing us with his presence?"

Jordis sat down behind her desk. "Future managing partner."

"O-*kaay*." The eye roll Vivian gave her would have done

any sixteen-year-old diva proud. "What did you think of Mr. *Future* Managing Partner?"

"What's to think?"

"What's to think? Are you kidding me? Every woman in that room looked like she wanted to dribble chocolate all over him and lick it off."

Jordis chuckled. "If you say so."

"If I say so?" Vivian leaned forward. "Are you telling me you found the elusive Mr. Remington to be something short of delicious?"

"Look, he and Chase are our supervising attorneys. I'm not even going to go there. Besides, he's not really my type."

Vivian gave an unladylike snort. "If that man isn't your type, then either you don't do white guys or you're gay."

With an indulgent smile, Jordis silently shook her head.

When Jordis failed to respond, Vivian pushed, "Well, which is it?"

"What difference does it make?" Jordis flipped open a file folder and picked up her pen.

Vivian ignored the dismissive action.

"You need to get out of my office and go bill some hours."

"Oh, come on, Jordis. Give me something here." Vivian slipped into the chair. "Are you going to make this a three-way competition for Mr. Remington's affections?"

"Three-way competition?"

"Yep. Everyone knows Alyson has the partner in her sights. And all Lizzie talks about is how gorgeous Michael Remington is. You'd think the child had never seen an attractive man before."

Only one year out of law school, the blond Lizzie was the youngest of the bunch and still had a college-sorority-girl vibe going on. Jordis half expected her to drop her books the next time she came across Michael Remington in the hall with the hope he'd stop to pick them up for her. At thirty-two, Jordis found the peppy, boy-crazy antics of the younger woman annoying.

"Well, Lizzie is still young. I doubt the guys at her law school had quite the machismo of Mr. Remington. I suspect those twenty-something hormones of hers are pinging all over the place." Jordis dropped her pen back on her desk. Vivian clearly wasn't going anywhere until she'd gotten the chance to talk this thing through. "What about you? Wouldn't it be a four-way competition?"

Vivian laughed, leaned back and crossed her legs. "Honey, I definitely don't do white guys!"

That made Jordis laugh, too. "Vivian, you're a mess!"

The redhead simply smiled at her, a genuine smile. She'd started at the firm a few weeks before Jordis. A down-home kind of girl, Vivian lived a what-you-see-is-what-you-get lifestyle. She spoke her mind and didn't pull punches, which was one of the many reasons Jordis liked her, but Vivian did have one major flaw. She was a die-hard gossip. If office gossip existed, Vivian would ferret it out and happily divulge what she'd learned. Jordis had no intention of sharing any personal opinions with her about their gorgeous senior partner.

"Look, Vivian, there is no way I'm dishing with you about Michael Remington. You aren't going to stand around the coffee station gossiping about me. Alyson and Lizzie are welcome to him. I've got one thing in my sights—partnership at the end of this fiscal year."

Vivian gave Jordis a look that suggested she doubted whether to believe her. "If you say so." She rose to leave. "As for gossiping about you around the coffee machine, I'd never do that to you. Anything you said to me would be strictly between us." Vivian made her way to the door before she added, almost as an afterthought, "Oh, and fair warning, beauty queen. Alyson's a vulture. If you decide Mr. Tall-Dark-And-Wanted floats your boat after all, watch your back. She's not above putting a knife in it."

Jordis grimaced. Not because of what Vivian said about Alyson. Jordis had already figured that out. What grated her was the "beauty queen" moniker. Others called her that behind her back, and she hated it. Vivian was the only one with the guts—and the integrity—to say it to her face, and Vivian mostly did it to get a rise out of her.

Vivian noticed Jordis's grimace and chuckled on her way out the door.

෨ ෨ | ෫ ෫

In Michael's office, Chase leaned against the closed office door with his arms crossed over his chest.

Michael lounged on the office sofa. "Okay, start talking." He placed his feet on the mahogany sofa table and crossed them at the ankles. "Are associate meetings always like that?"

"See what you've been missing?" Chase grinned.

Michael shook his head. "What's the deal with this Covington character?"

"He's a real piece of work isn't he?"

"He's an arrogant, sexist prick is what he is."

Chase laughed. "Yeah, that too." Pushing off the door, he moved to the armchair perpendicular to the sofa.

"So, remind me how we ended up with Mr. Personality?"

"He's the nephew of Stormy Willis over in Business and Finance. He's been at the firm since he was a first year associate but only switched to IP litigation about three years ago. Apparently, he went to a top-tier law school, finished in the top third of his class, and has an impressive courtroom record. And, of course, no one is more impressed with his credentials than Covington himself."

"Clearly. Do he and Morgan go at it like that every week?"

"No. You just got lucky today."

Michael snorted.

"Seriously," Chase continued. "Eric is a smartass to pretty much everyone in the group. As you witnessed, he tends to act more patronizing with the women. He's tested Jordis for weeks. Until today, he hadn't pushed her too hard so she's responded with enough fire to check him but hadn't engaged any heavy artillery. For some reason, Covington decided to grandstand today to make a point. Perhaps he was trying to impress you."

Michael snorted again. "Yeah, right. He certainly failed at that."

Chase nodded. "Well, I've been waiting for the day Jordis decided to take off the kid gloves. I always suspected in head-to-head combat, I should bet on the lady."

Michael gave an appreciative whistle. "Man, she's one cool customer. Is she always that smooth?"

"I've never seen her lose her temper, but rumor has it she's not a lady you want to cross. From what I could find out about her, when she goes after an opponent she does it with a smile and the finesse you witnessed earlier. Apparently, they don't realize they've been sliced and diced until they're lying bleeding on the floor."

Chase rose and wandered to Michael's desk. He looked down at the two photos clipped to the resumes Michael had abandoned earlier. He grabbed them and turned back to Michael. "I guess you have a better understanding now of your possible replacements for me." He tossed the dossiers onto the coffee table, one of Eric Covington and one of Jordis Morgan.

"Yeah." Michael placed his feet on the floor. "I certainly like Jordis's fire. Not to mention she clearly does her homework. She spouted the relevant facts of the Gardner file without once looking at any notes. That's impressive."

"The entire group is really bright, but yeah, Jordis stands out when it comes to the details. She's helped me a couple of times with some motions and a few deposition preps. She has a real knack for reviewing large quantities of information and finding patterns and connections others miss."

Michael aligned the photographs side-by-side. "And if I were grading them on their arguments today, Covington wouldn't make the cut."

"Well, then, I guess you have your answer." Chase sat back down. "Jordis would certainly be my choice for my replacement."

Michael wasn't so sure. He had no doubt the lady lawyer would perform beautifully as his second chair, but the sexual effect she'd had on him today gave him pause. He couldn't remember the last time he'd gotten a hard-on in a business setting. In fact, he didn't think he ever had. If she had that effect on him in a full conference room when they weren't interacting directly, what would happen if they worked closely together for an extended period of time?

Chase probed into his silence. "Michael?"

"Yeah. Maybe."

"Maybe? What maybe? A mind like a steel trap, exceptional debating skills, and extensive courtroom experience. What's your maybe?"

"I don't know." Michael blew out a breath. "Nothing. You're right. Jordis is the clear choice." It wouldn't be fair to select Covington over her because Michael couldn't keep his libido under control. He'd simply make sure to keep his focus on the case and off those long shapely legs. His mind drifted at the thought.

"Not to mention, all that comes in a package perfectly designed to make a man want to come home to her every night."

It took a few seconds for the comment to register with Michael. He looked up with a frown to find Chase watching him with a knowing half smile. "Hey, what happened to all that 'no woman can replace my Grace' business?"

"I'm widowed, not dead. My eyes work just fine. As do yours apparently." Chase gave a look that dared Michael to challenge him.

Michael's expression veiled. "I have no idea what you're talking about."

"Oh, puh-leez." Chase pushed to his feet. "You forget

to whom you're speaking. You can drop the poker face. I know you too well. I saw you checking her out . . . more than once."

Michael looked at Chase without responding.

"Yeah, that's what I thought." Chase headed for the door. Before he opened it, he turned back towards Michael. "You know, it looks like Ms. Morgan is going to shake things up around here in more ways than one." Smiling, he added, "Perhaps the cure for your infatuation with the New Year's Eve mystery woman is in the office around the corner and down the hall."

Michael flipped him the bird. Chase laughed and exited the office. Michael could still hear him laughing after the heavy mahogany door clicked shut.

To his frustration, Michael spent the rest of the afternoon trying to dissect the weaknesses in the Dexter Drug motion for summary judgment without success. Caramel skin, hazel eyes, and gams the stuff of erotic fantasies kept traipsing across his concentration. He wanted to talk to her again. That niggling feeling he'd met her before still bothered him. He felt uptight and on edge, and Jordis Morgan was the cause. She drew him on a biological level even though his intellect kept sending his impulses the exact opposite message.

He pushed up abruptly from his desk and grabbed his duffle bag. Maybe a good, hard workout would take his mind off the distracting Ms. Morgan. He needed to talk to her about stepping into the Metra Pharmaceuticals case, but he wasn't ready to do that yet. He would put it off for a few days. He needed time to get his head on straight, maybe even get laid. He suspected his drought in the area of sexual relations fueled a lot of his lusty enthusiasm for Ms. Morgan.

He hit the weights hard then took a two-mile run around the track. By the time he finished, he was loose, sweaty and relaxed. A quick shower made him feel like a new man. Under the heat of the blow dryer, he ran his fingers through the cropped hair at the top of his head. He'd only recently gotten his hair cut this way. He'd worn it long through the first part of winter, like he had in college. Back then, it got him more play with the ladies. Now, the longer hair didn't gel with his professional, killer litigator persona. He tended to keep his style short and neat when he had to appear in court, like he had this week.

After he returned to work, the rest of the workday progressed with productive efficiency. The following day, however, he found himself drifting into the same unfocused predicament. He also found himself in the weight room and on the track the following day and each of the two days after that. The sight of Jordis in the hall or during the briefest interaction aggravated his restlessness. Now that he'd met her, he felt as if he ran into her constantly. It was like buying a new car. Once you decided on a particular model, the number of similar cars on the road seemed to multiply by a thousand.

Pondering his new daily two-hour workouts and the woman who drove him to them, Michael strode towards the elevator Thursday night. The faint sound of music interrupted his thoughts. He lifted his wrist and noted eleven fifteen on the face of his TAG Heuer watch. When he rounded the corner, he saw light streaming from Jordis's office. Why he'd passed this way tonight instead of taking his usual route to the elevator—which took him in the opposite direction—he didn't really want to analyze at the moment nor the rush of exhilaration at the sight of her.

She sat at her desk listening to a tune with a relaxed groove while she reviewed the documentation in an open file folder. Her bare feet rested on the edge of her desk, bopping in time with the music. She held the file propped on her knees. With her other hand, she cradled a refillable twenty-ounce travel mug she sipped from absently every few minutes.

He sat his briefcase at his feet and leaned against her doorjamb. Those long legs enthralled him as much as the first time he'd seen them. He noticed her toes were painted in a French pedicure to match her fingers and even her bare feet looked sexy. Every once in a while, she sang along under her breath with the female vocalist about working what you've got. She hadn't noticed him. He wondered how long it would take. Until she did, he contented himself with watching her.

இ இ | ஒ ஒ

Jordis stilled. Sensing a presence at the door, she slowly glanced up. Michael Remington stood with his jacket pulled back, hands thrust in the pockets of his pants. The stance accentuated how the tailored cut of his slacks caressed his muscular thighs. Today, he'd paired a charcoal gray suit, possibly Gucci, with a soft lilac shirt and a shiny silk tie in a deeper almost royal purple. Above his square jaw and strong chin, his full lips pressed together as if he deeply pondered something. He had the look of one of those brooding, sporty types displayed in Armani or Dolce & Gabbana cologne ads.

Her breath caught in her throat. She hoped Michael thought it was because he'd startled her—which he had—but, in truth, her breathlessness was due more to an unexpected kick of hormones than a frisson of fear.

"How long have you been standing there?" She grabbed a small remote off her desk and pointed it towards her music player to quiet Mary J. Blige.

"Long enough." He slid his fingers through his hair, giving it a tousled look.

Jordis's eyes followed the movement. She'd seen him do the same during the team meeting. Now, like then, she wondered what it would feel like to run her fingers through that thick, coffee-brown mass.

Something about Michael Remington exuded sexual energy. She was uncomfortably aware of him as a man and that wasn't good. When she'd spied him at her door, a soft *mmm mmm* had reverberated through her head. She'd had a similar reaction when he'd walked into the briefing meeting three days ago. He had swagger she didn't usually associate with men of his background. When he'd approached her in the conference room, all her girly parts had started to vibrate.

She'd convinced herself her reaction stemmed only from objective appreciation for a beautiful male specimen. Like admiring a male model in a magazine ad, you could look all you wanted, but you knew you'd never actually touch. Then she'd caught him staring at her legs during her tête-à-tête with Eric Covington. It had taken every ounce of her self-control to stay on point with Eric and keep her voice from reflecting the tremors in her belly set off by Michael Remington's perusal.

She no longer believed what she experienced when seeing the partner qualified as simple aesthetic appreciation. Those girly parts were vibrating again, and she needed to cut it out. He was one of her supervising attorneys for Pete's sake.

Michael walked to her desk and picked up the file folder she'd set aside. "You know, I'm usually the last one out of the office at night. It's after eleven o'clock . . ." His last sentence trailed off in a distracted manner.

A rough clearing of his throat caught her attention. His eyes focused on her lap while he rubbed a hand over the back of his neck. A quick look down by Jordis revealed her unladylike position hiked her brown pencil skirt past mid-thigh. Heat of embarrassment climbed up her neck. Heat of another kind crept down her belly and radiated through her lower abdomen. Jordis quickly put her feet on the floor and adjusted her skirt.

Michael averted his gaze while she slid her feet into a pair of brown, three-inch leather platform pumps with ankle straps. "What are you still doing here?" he finally asked.

"Chase made me lead counsel on the Gardner pro bono case." She leaned from her chair to buckle one of her shoes. "Since I've got a deposition tomorrow on my trademark infringement case, I wanted to get up to speed today because I'm meeting with Miss Gardner the day after that."

His eyes moved from the contents of the file to her face. "That's Saturday."

She smiled. "Yes, sir. I'm well aware of the weekly calendar."

An odd intensity darkened his eyes. "That's good to know . . . *ma'am*."

He said it with a straight face, but Jordis sensed his facetiousness. She never would have suspected he had a sense of humor. He seemed so straight-laced and buttoned up.

"The client works weekdays and has to collect her child from daycare by a certain time every night. I didn't want her to have to miss time at work to meet with me or have to pay someone to watch her child. She has enough challenges without it costing her money to meet with lawyers who are supposed to be helping her for free. Saturday afternoon worked best for her schedule, and this way, she can bring the child with her."

She rose to pack up. She took the pro bono file from his grasp and placed it in her designer Michael Kors *MK* signature tote. When she reached for the chocolate brown suit jacket that coordinated with her skirt, Michael stepped around the desk to help her. The gesture caught her off guard. She hesitated before allowing him to assist her.

He slid the jacket onto her shoulders, and his knuckles brushed her silky white blouse. As his hands fell away, he fingered a length of her hair. Jordis started. A warm tingle sizzled from his fingertips up through her scalp. Her gaze snapped over her shoulder. His eyes met hers and held while time suspended itself.

An eternity of awareness passed between them in the mere second it took Michael to take a quick step back. He frowned. From the look on his face, he'd surprised himself as much as her.

Looking away, he shoved his hands in his pocket. "I'll walk you to your car."

Jordis turned. An odd sensation tugged at her, stemming from the coincidence of him caressing her hair when moments earlier she'd daydreamed about what it would feel like to run her fingers through his. She tamped down the emotion. "That's not necessary."

The clipped tone of his offer made it less than appealing. She didn't think he really wanted to walk her to her car.

"Yes, it is. The parking garage will be abandoned this time of night."

"Security will—"

"I'm your security for tonight." His jaws tightened into a don't-argue-with-me position.

She stared at him. From the moment he'd touched her hair, his demeanor had gone short and gruff. What was his problem?

He headed for the door and picked up his briefcase. "If you're ever here this late by yourself again, make sure someone walks you to your car. The security desk is too far from the garage for them to be of much help if someone decides to make mischief."

He waited for her to respond.

Annoyed by his demeanor and his tone, she made her way to the door. "You know, I'm a big girl and—"

"Yes . . . you *are*." He gave her a long, slow perusal, making it clear he appreciated all the grown parts of her. When his eyes made it back to hers, he stepped to her, placed his hand at the base of her throat, and rubbed his thumb along her jawline. In her three-inch heels, she could nearly look him directly in the eyes. His voice dropped to a bedroom whisper. "But you do realize big girls get accosted all the time?"

His cologne—something woodsy and seductive—seemed familiar as it permeated Jordis's senses and stirred her underworked sex drive. Those magnetic gray eyes held her, and her heart began to pound. Self-preservation mandated she step away from him, but she couldn't get her legs to move. She had an inkling of what a Cobra's prey must feel like, held paralyzed by eyes that hypnotize even knowing a fatal strike was imminent.

"I expect you to be careful. No case is worth your safety. Okay?"

She wanted to tell him to stop treating her like an idiot; that, of course, she paid attention to her safety when she left the building. That's what she would normally have done. She didn't like being told what to do by anyone, let alone by bossy macho types. Right now, however, she struggled to keep her concentration on something other than his lips. Their shape fascinated her. When he spoke, they were almost sensuous in movement.

As she became conscious of her thoughts, warning bells clanged loudly in her head. Having a pissing contest with her boss about safety precautions late at night seemed foolish when a whole other dynamic appeared to be at play. She needed to end this confrontation before she did something stupid, like lean up and press her lips against his.

"Okay," she agreed in a voice softer than she intended.

His gray eyes darkened to the color of cumulous clouds. Her voice had come out breathy and flirty. The thought made her cringe internally. She didn't do breathy and flirty. What was this guy doing to her?

Michael held her gaze for a long moment, his thumb rubbing seductively against her skin. When his eyes dropped to her lips and then to the pulse beating rapidly at the base of her throat, she broke contact and reached down for her tote.

His expression shuttered. He mumbled, "I'll take that." He lifted the bag from her and merged it into his left hand with his own briefcase. "Let's go." He placed his free hand at the small of her back.

After the moment they'd just shared, they were both acutely aware of the location of his hand. Jordis looked over at him after a few steps. She wondered why he continued to guide her along, but she didn't shake off his touch. The depth of color in his darkened eyes gave him a smoldering look that sent waves of adrenaline pulsing through her veins. She felt like the protagonist in one of those thrillers she liked to watch on television. She had the sense ominous music should be playing in the background, the kind that presaged getting into tight quarters—like an elevator—alone with him might be a colossal mistake.

CHAPTER 5

When they reached the elevator bay, Michael removed his hand from Jordis's back to push the *Down* button. Although he no longer touched her, the ghost of his hand lingered along her back. He didn't speak. He stood quietly at her side staring straight ahead. Jordis didn't speak either, too busy trying to make sense of the odd current that had passed between them back at her office.

She thought about the look in his eyes when he'd caressed her face. He hadn't tried to kiss her, but she'd gotten the impression he'd wanted to. But that was ridiculous, right? Michael Remington didn't do office romances. The talk around the office made that clear.

The elevator arrived, and they stepped in together. Michael continued his silence. Jordis continued her silent musings about him. They'd known each other for only a few days. How had he managed to get under her skin with no more than a few touches and a challenging look from those hypnotic gray eyes?

Okay, that wasn't exactly true. This pull stemmed from more than his physical appearance or a few touches. The guy intrigued her. He had from the moment he'd walked into the conference room three days ago. Since then, she'd run into him in the hall a few times and finished a research memorandum for one of his cases on appeal. Reviewing the file for that case had added to the admiration she'd already developed for his courtroom style. The man wrote one hell of a brief. His written legal work stood in equal measure with his courtroom flair.

Uh-oh. Personal curiosity, physical attraction, and professional admiration. This could not be happening. She was not developing a thing for a guy at work . . . and a white guy at that. Was she out of her mind?

Jordis glanced at Michael. She'd learned to thrive in the predominantly white school and work environment she'd been immersed in since her days at the all-girl college prep high school her mother insisted she attend, but she'd never dated outside her race. If she were going to start, now was not the time to develop an appreciation for tall, vanilla swagger. Well, given his luscious olive skin tone, maybe he was more like butter toffee swagger. Either way, a fling with a senior partner, even one—especially one—as sexy as Michael Remington was definitely not in the cards.

Nothing undermined a female lawyer's credibility in the office quicker than talk she slept around with fellow associates. Carrying on with a senior partner? That constituted premeditated reputation suicide, a quick way to get herself labeled an opportunist set on sleeping her way to the top.

As if sensing her pensive mood, Michael slowly turned to face her. "Something wrong?" His deep baritone voice reverberated within the steel box of the elevator. Warmth poured from his gaze.

Her senses prickled with apprehension. "No."

"Then why are you looking at me like that?"

"Like what?" Her pitchy tone belied her calm outward appearance.

His eyes cruised heatedly down the length of her body, and she hoped that wasn't the answer to her question.

"Like you're considering . . . the possibilities?"

He took a step in her direction, as if propelled by a force outside himself. His movement caused a waft of his cologne to drift over her, and she was once again struck by the thought the fragrance was familiar. That prickly feeling intensified.

She took a measured step backwards.

Michael continued to advance, and she continued her slow backstep until the wall of the elevator interrupted her retreat. Michael's eyes focused on her mouth. He reached for her and slid his thumb across her bottom lip. Jordis closed her eyes against the influx of arousal coursing through her.

"Michael," she whispered before she opened her eyes, "this isn't a good idea."

"I know," he replied right before he touched his mouth to hers.

Jordis stilled herself, bracing for a forceful, passionate kiss, but Michael took her mouth nice and slow. His gentle lips tested, searched. The unexpected tenderness short-circuited her defenses. Unprepared for the sweetness of his mouth or the seductive current flowing from the fingertips he brushed along her neck and jaw, she melted.

When he slid his tongue along the seam of her lips, it felt like the most natural thing in the world for her to open to him. He murmured softly in response. A distance thud signaled he'd dropped their briefcases. She wrapped her arms around his neck without forethought. He accepted her embrace as an invitation to take the kiss deeper and his exploration further.

The hand at her jawline slid down her neck and kept southbound until his palm slid inside her jacket to rub a beaded nipple through her blouse. Michael's other hand slid around her waist to rest at the small of her back. He pulled her hips tight against him. Heat pooled between Jordis's thighs and simmered under her skin. She had the sudden urge to remove her jacket . . . and her blouse . . . and everything else to release the blaze engulfing her. More importantly, she had an urge to remove the jacket, shirt and—oh, yeah—just about everything else off Mr. Future Managing Partner to see if he looked half as good without his clothes as he did in them.

Michael must have been thinking along similar lines because a sudden burst of cool air blew across her chest. He'd undone the top two buttons of her blouse without her noticing. Where his hand played along the curve of breast displayed above her demi bra, her skin flared hot. Everywhere else, she had goose bumps.

She moaned. His manhood went from semi-erect to rock hard instantly. He broke their kiss, emitting a sound between a growl and a groan, and transferred his touch from her breast to the wall above her head. The hand at her back slid to rest on the side of her waist. The relaxed hold removed her core from direct contact with his arousal, but she knew his physical state. She'd felt the evidence of his virility the instant it rose.

Michael looked into her eyes, fighting some battle with himself. She stared back at him, knowing she could halt the ardor happening between them with one word. Yet, that word wouldn't come to her lips. She came to the uncomfortable realization a part of her didn't want the encounter to stop.

∝ ∝ | ∝ ∝

Jordis's eye color shifted to a deep forest green and her pupils dilated. Michael's gaze dropped slowly to her lips. When they parted, seemingly in slow motion, the thoughts he'd been warring with fled his mind.

He pressed himself against her, bending his knees slightly so his shaft fit in that perfect spot at the juncture of her thighs. He rested there, relishing the feel of her against him. He wanted her desperately. The sexual current between them sparked intense, volatile, but he wanted more from her than just sex. He wished he could absorb her through his skin until he knew her completely inside and out.

He'd watched her all week. Sharp and always on point when analyzing a legal issue, her intelligence made the outer package that much more attractive. She always appeared to be in a good mood, her behavior surprisingly courteous and polite to everyone including the support and janitorial staff, but she accepted no foolishness or disrespect.

The interesting dichotomy of the woman fascinated him. Add to that her sensitivity in putting the needs of a down-on-her-luck single mom ahead of her drive to bill hours or whatever weekend plans she could have made, and he was in a whole mess of trouble. He'd been drawn to her looks and legal acumen on a conscious level, but a connection this strong had to come from someplace deeper. How could he fight an attraction that was turning out to be so much more than physical, especially if he allowed his physical needs to dominate his interactions with her?

The voice of his mystery woman resounded in his head: *Something tells me that after tonight, we'd be hard pressed to rewind to getting-to-know-you drinks or dinner and a movie.* Perhaps she'd imparted a lesson he needed to heed. Wasn't he about to make the same mistake?

Michael fought his urge to devour Jordis. Indecision haunted her eyes. They needed to downshift.

She wrapped a finger through the belt loops on either side of his pants to steady herself. Her grasp shifted him slightly, causing his erection to rub against the *V* shielding the pleasure point beneath her pubic bones. A look of intimate bliss filled her face. Her eyes closed, and her head fell back against the wall. An odd sound squeezed from her throat. The sound whipped him mentally back onto a night-shrouded balcony where another woman had made a similar sound.

Juliet?

Jordis's eyes flitted open.

Had he said that name out loud? Michael was searching her face for some clue she'd heard and recognized the name when the elevator bounced to a stop with an annoying ping.

He quickly stepped back.

Saved by the bell, he thought. But who had been saved — her or him?

Jordis redid the buttons on her blouse with fast, adept fingers. The elevator door slid open with a hydraulic hiss, quelling the mood inside the elevator. Michael picked up their briefcases and placed his hand against the retracted door, waiting for Jordis to exit. His eyes strayed to a round black recessed globe in the upper right corner of the elevator. He did a double take. *Shit.*

Without making eye contact, Jordis moved past him and headed for the glass doors leading from the elevator bay.

The parking garage had that eerie glow that came from low wattage florescent light bouncing off grayish concrete walls, pillars and floors. Very little traffic cruised this part of the city late at night so quiet hovered around them despite the garage's open access to the adjacent two-way street.

Stepping into the lowest level of the five-story structure, Michael scanned the parking garage and noticed a Dodge Charger SRT SuperBee in vibrant orange parked to his right. He allowed his eyes to glide over the racy sports car in appreciation before moving on to the silver Lexus SUV parked two spots closer. Michael headed for the Lexus, the only other vehicle visible inside the garage besides his black Lincoln Navigator.

The sound of Jordis's heels striking the concrete floor echoed through the garage, punctuating the noticeable lack of conversation between them. When they reached the driver's side door of the Lexus, Michael turned towards her and extended his hand. She looked blankly at him.

"Keys?"

Without taking her eyes from his, Jordis reached into her jacket pocket and pulled out her key fob. She leaned forward, bypassing his outstretched hand, as if to unlock the door. At the last second, she turned the fob towards the Charger and hit the automatic unlock button.

When the Charger's lights blinked in concert with a pitched mechanical beep, Michael's eyes widened. "She's yours?"

"She?"

Michael shrugged. "With a body like that, every man on the planet would consider that Bee to be a woman."

He'd driven the Navigator today instead of his Jag because the forecast had included a chance of snow. Even though he drove a foreign sports car, he loved a good ole American muscle car. In fact, he had a classic '69 Camaro, which had belonged to his father, at home in his four-car garage.

Jordis's SuperBee was a thing of beauty, and it suited her right down to the sassy color. It had sleek lines, strong curves, and lots of power under a pretty hood.

Jordis walked to the Charger and opened the door. Michael recognized the move as a blatant display of independence.

He followed her into the triangle of the open car door.

His eyes searched hers, trying to decipher her hidden thoughts. The unreadable look on her face made him sigh.

"Look, Jordis, about what just happened . . ." He stood in a quandary. That he'd kissed her raised a myriad of job-related issues they needed to address, but, selfishly, he held another topic uppermost in his mind. *How did you ask a colleague if she'd made out with you anonymously on New Year's Eve?*

"Don't." She placed her hand against his chest.

A jolt shot through him from the spot where she rested her palm. She snatched her hand away and quickstepped back.

He looked down; she scrubbed the offending hand absently against the side of her skirt. He'd bet she'd felt it, too. "We need to talk about it."

"No, we don't. We made a mistake. We both know it shouldn't have happened." She moved to get in her car, but he blocked her way. She heaved a sigh. "You're my supervising attorney, Michael. It can't happen again. I think we both can agree on that. So, let's just forget about it and move on."

He stared at her for a minute. He wanted to explore why kissing her had triggered a memory of New Year's Eve. More than a simple kiss had transpired between them. Pretending it hadn't happened didn't seem the way to go, but the parking garage late at night probably wasn't the best place for the discussion. So, despite his burning question, he stepped aside.

Jordis lowered herself into the driver's seat, and his eyes followed her skirt's rise up her thighs. The exposure of more of those long golden legs exacerbated the lingering discomfort in his pants. He rubbed a hand across the back of his neck, fighting the urge to pull her from the car and pursue the matter.

He handed her the tote he still held. "Do you have far to go?"

"No, I don't live far. I should be inside my apartment in about twenty minutes."

"Okay."

She reached for the door handle, but he didn't move. "Michael, I really have to go."

"You don't need to stop for gas or anything, do you?"

"*No.*" She tugged at the door, but his hand stayed its movement. Shaking her head, she released the door and gripped the top of the steering wheel with both hands. "I'm good. Trust me. I know better than to make pit stops alone this late at night."

He nodded and closed the door. Instead of stepping away from the car, he motioned for her to roll down the window. "If you need anything, call me."

"What could I possibly need between here and home?" Her voice dripped with exasperation.

Her rising anxiousness to be on her way lightened his demeanor and tempted him to delay her a bit longer. "You could run out of gas," he said for the simple sake of argument.

"I told you I had plenty of gas."

"No. You told me you didn't need to *stop* for gas. For all I know, you're one of those people who like to ride around on *E.*"

She looked at him with an expression that said *as if.*

Michael fought a smile. "You could get a flat tire."

"I have roadside assistance."

"Yeah, some strange guy in a tow truck meeting you stranded by the side of the road in the middle of the night. That really reassures me. Take my mobile number."

"Michael, really. I appreciate the escort to my car, but I'll be fine from here."

Michael's shoulders lifted as he heaved an exaggerated sigh. He pulled his smartphone from his inside jacket pocket. Punching buttons, he asked, "Do you have a cell phone?" He took her eye roll as a yes. "What's the number?"

She rattled off ten numbers. He punched them into the keypad. A few seconds later, her phone rang inside her bag. Jordis's mouth turned down in a perplexed frown at the late night call before she glanced at the phone in his hand and saw it had an active outgoing connection.

He pushed the *End* button and slid the phone back into his pocket. "Now you have my number. Call me if you should need anything on the way home. If not, great. But, do call me when you get home so I know you arrived safely."

She opened her mouth to protest, but he cut her off. She gave a short laugh. "Okay, okay. I'll call you to let you know I made it home. Can I go now?"

He backed up.

Not giving him a chance to say anything else, she shoved the car into *Reverse* and zipped out of the parking space. She hit the breaks to shift into *Drive*, and her eyes met his one more time. "Goodnight, Michael," she said quietly.

His responding farewell came out in an unintentionally

husky voice. "Goodnight, Jordis."

Her fingers clenched the steering wheel. She looked away quickly and maneuvered out of the garage. When she cleared the gate, he dropped his head back and closed his eyes.

What was he doing? All he had to do was walk her to her car and say goodnight. Instead, he'd made out with her in an elevator and harped about her safety as if he were dropping off a date.

Turning toward his SUV, he pulled out his key ring and hit the remote unlock button. The SUV's lights blinked at him as the keyless entry system chirped. Michael walked over slowly, pondering that he'd given Jordis his mobile number.

He took great care to make sure few people had his mobile number. It avoided problems, especially those of the female variety. Only his assistant, Chase, and a few key senior partners had his personal cell number. If anyone else needed to reach him, they could leave him a voicemail message at the office—he picked those up religiously—or contact his assistant who always knew how to get in touch with him.

How ironic that women usually tried so hard to get his personal number and the one time he offered it willingly to a female associate, she didn't want it. He was almost insulted, but he suspected with Jordis it came down to a show of independence. His display of old world manners had thrown her. He'd caught her look of surprise when he'd helped her don her jacket. That bit with her car keys—not letting him open the door for her—had also been revealing.

Michael slid into his ride. He put the key in the ignition, but didn't start the car. He glanced over at the elevator bay, pulled out his phone, and made a call.

When he finished, the scene in Jordis's office flashed through his mind. He'd almost kissed her then. When he'd touched her in the doorway, he'd wanted only to challenge her bravado a bit, but the smell of her perfume—a hint of sweet and floral with a crisp aquatic note—had drawn his mind from her late night lawyering habits to her womanly curves. Once his hand contacted her warm skin, all he could think about was how soft she felt, how beautiful her eyes were, and how much he wanted to explore those luscious lips.

He'd watched her eyes shift colors like they had in the conference room when she'd caught him staring at her legs. The vein in her neck had pulsed at Mach speed, and he'd wondered if anxiety or attraction fueled the response. She didn't seem the anxious type. Given her response to him in the elevator, he'd like to think it had been attraction. Yet, when he and Chase had walked past her office after Monday's meeting, he'd heard Vivian ask her about her sexual preferences. Her nondescript response left questions to which he'd like to know the answers. It would be his luck that she was indeed gay.

A gush of disappointment skittered across his gut, making him grab the steering wheel and squeeze tightly. Shaking off the implications of his reaction, he chastised himself. *Get a grip, Remington. There's no way she would have responded to you that way if she were gay.*

Kissing her had felt right, like coming home. His gut churned and an odd tremor rolled through him at the thought of her uniquely familiar moan when she'd pulled him against her. She'd taken him to a place he'd been before. Why? What was there about this woman that stirred him so?

He rubbed both hands down his face. His still semi-firm erection throbbed with a need for release he suspected could only be found between those long, long legs of hers. When he'd admired those legs as she'd lowered herself into her car, he'd appreciated the golden hue of her light caramel skin.

His head snapped up.

New Year's night, he'd admired the second Juliet's tan, her *golden* tan. He hadn't considered that her color might be natural instead of sun-induced.

"Ah, hell." The words burst from him as he flopped back against the seat. "It *is* her."

He let the knowledge wash over him, unsure what to do with his certainty. All this time, he'd been looking for Juliet, and she'd been right under his nose. Chase had called it. Jordis Morgan shook him up in ways a colleague—or any woman for that matter—hadn't in a long time.

Until his midnight run-in with the mystery woman a couple of weeks ago, he couldn't remember experiencing an instant emotional draw to a woman. Instant sexual attraction? Sure. He'd been there and done that. He handled instant hormonal urges easily. He did what came naturally and forgot about it, and the woman, once he'd slaked his need.

Unfortunately, what he felt now went beyond mere biological appetency and therein lay the problem. The instant emotional attraction he'd experienced on New Year's Eve hadn't been a fluke. Jordis was his mystery woman, and her emotional pull on him tugged stronger than ever. Why on earth did these stirrings have to arise for a woman who worked at the firm? Life had taught him the dangers of that. He could be setting himself up for a shakedown.

What would she want? Would she vie for key case assignments or guaranteed partnership? Or, would she maneuver covertly for a more permanent setup, perhaps one that came with eighteen-plus years of child support payments?

She came across as a straight shooter. She didn't seem the type to play games, but he had to wonder with which head he'd formed that opinion.

Of course, the question of whether she "did white guys" had yet to be answered. He hadn't been able to hear if Vivian had gotten any additional information on that query. Wondering if she had a racial preference didn't disturb him as much. This second hurdle, if it existed, didn't seem insurmountable. He wouldn't mind being Ms. Morgan's first. She certainly hadn't responded to his kiss as if she'd been concerned about anything other than the feel of his tongue inside her mouth.

A wicked smile on his lips, he leaned forward and started his car. The dashboard lit up and displayed that over twenty minutes had passed since they'd said goodbye and, of course, Jordis hadn't called.

He wondered which would explode first, their battle of wills or the sexual time bomb they'd ignited with that kiss in the elevator. Whatever happened between them, he doubted either one of them would be able to "just forget" what had transpired tonight.

Now, he had to figure out what to do about it.

CHAPTER 6

*J*ordis pushed into her Northland loft apartment and tossed her keys onto the entry table. Her heart pounded in her chest. Without turning on the lights, she let her tote slide to the floor and pressed her forehead against the closed door.

What had she done?

She'd let Michael Remington kiss her. Worse, she'd kissed him back.

It was that damn cologne he wore. The scent had taunted her from the moment he'd approached her three days ago and had continued to draw her under his spell with their every encounter. For days, she'd been fighting an attraction she didn't want to feel. After tonight, the situation had escalated to a whole new level.

Never in her life had she lost herself like that with a first kiss — except once. Spartacus. And tonight it had happened again. When Michael backed her against the elevator wall and pressed his lips to hers, she'd known. The kiss had been sweet and seductive, not overwhelming and passionate, but she'd known.

Michael Remington smelled like New Year's Eve.

His scent reminded her of the midnight kiss she'd shared with a stranger under the stars. The familiar scent had wrapped around her and kissing Michael had felt almost predestined. When his lips had touched hers, the same vortex of attraction and passion and overwhelming lust she'd experienced on that dimly lit balcony had coursed through every cell in her body.

She'd felt almost as if she were reliving that night. In fact, she'd momentarily become disoriented. When she'd grabbed Michael's pants to steady herself, she'd thought she heard him whisper "Juliet" right before the elevator dinged.

She was losing her mind. No way, he'd called her Juliet. Had he?

What were the chances of that? What were the odds Michael Remington, of all the men in the greater Kansas City area, would turn out to be her gladiator? A million to one? Two million to one?

Her mind had to be playing tricks on her. Her gladiator had that long, sexy hair that gave him a bad-boy, devil-may-care vibe. Everything about Michael Remington, from his short-cropped hair to his expensive tailored suits, shouted proper, straight-laced, and . . . *lawyerly.*

Surely, she could blame her behavior tonight and her temporary mental deficiency on the olfactory déjà vu effect. One minute, she'd been reminding herself of all the reasons she shouldn't be attracted to Mr. Remington. The next minute, she'd been wondering what he looked like without any clothes.

She sucked in a breath. The visual that came with the thought was almost too naughty for words.

No. She rapped her forehead against the door thrice. *Stop it. Stop it. Stop it.*

She'd only recently escaped the viper pit of law firm scandal. She couldn't handle scandalous hookups part two. Yet, ever since Michael Remington had walked into the conference room on Monday, an inappropriate curiosity had haunted her.

Was he dating anyone outside the office? Rumor had it he didn't do serious, but did he have a current go-to girl?

The last question in particular had warned her she was headed into dangerous territory. She'd weathered the personal aspersions cast her way at her prior firm when she'd been accused of fraternizing with a senior partner in exchange for special treatment. How ironic would it be for her to walk into the same scenario at RHM?

Actually, it wouldn't be ironic. It would be *mega stupid*. She'd already experienced several setbacks in her career. RHM was her last stop on the law firm partnership track. She needed to make partner here or rethink her career path. She'd previously considered the logistics of starting her own practice. She had the drive, the people skills, and the knowledge to make it work. But, starting a business from scratch when she had a perfectly good set up at a great firm with a built-in support network didn't sound appealing.

With that in mind, it would be the worst form of self-sabotage if she walked consciously into the fire this time by actually sleeping with her boss. But how on earth was she supposed to resist this attraction to him if every time she was near him, his cologne made her think of her encounter with Spartacus? It was the sexiest night she'd ever spent with a man, and they hadn't even taken off any clothes.

Shaking her head, she walked to the open vertical blinds covering the floor-to-ceiling sliding glass door that led to her deck at the back of the building. She had a great view overlooking a large swimming pool and a meandering walking trail. Floodlights usually lit the pool area, throwing brightness into the apartment. Tonight, only the dim glow of security lamps poured in because the pool was closed for the winter.

She stared into the night, the elevator kiss still foremost in her mind. Having made the connection between Michael's cologne and Spartacus, she understood, in part, this odd pull she felt towards her boss. *But was it just his cologne?*

Had she simply been trying to relive New Year's Eve tonight or was there more to it?

Before she could seriously consider the issue, her cell phone rang. She snatched the vertical blinds closed, flicked on a light, and darted to where her bag laid abandoned by the entryway. She fished out her phone. Looking at the number on the screen, she smiled. "Hey, you. To what do I owe this late night call?"

"Hey, sis," her brother replied. "Just checking on my favorite girl."

"Yeah, right. You must be in between hoochies at the

moment or you would definitely be otherwise occupied this time of night."

Her brother laughed. "Well, for someone complaining about the lateness of the hour, you sound awfully bright-eyed and bushy-tailed."

"Well, I'm just getting in from the office."

"What! Jo, what have I told you? I don't like you alone in that office building so late after business hours."

She rolled her eyes and plopped down on her plush oversized sofa. Here we go again, she thought. "Look, dude, you're not the boss of me," she joked, reverting to their childhood banter. "A girl has to make a living."

"That's crap and you know it. A girl can bring her work home with her and do it from the safety of her own apartment. Isn't your laptop working?"

Jordis thought about the laptop her brother had recently overhauled for her. It had been top of the line when she'd bought it four months ago. Now, she wouldn't be surprised if the US military considered it a classified secret weapon with all the RAM and microchips and whatzits he'd added.

An electrical engineer by training, her brother spent most of his time tinkering with anything electronic or mechanical, trying to see what he could do to "make it purr." He'd been a Bond fan as a kid. Jordis had always thought if MI6 ever needed a hip quartermaster, her brother would be the perfect candidate. If he weren't such a looker, he'd be considered the quintessential nerd.

"My laptop is fine. Although, I'm afraid to turn it on now. Last time I went to use it, it tried to take over a small country in the Middle East."

"Ha, ha. Very funny," her brother replied dryly. "I'm serious, sis. What's the point of having remote access to your office network if you're going to stay at the office no matter what? Hell, what you need is a man. Then you'd have something to do besides play Perry Mason and perfect oral arguments."

"Perry Mason was a criminal lawyer."

"You know what I mean."

Jordis sighed. "Yeah, and I need another man like I need a hole in the head. The last one I had didn't know the meaning of the word supportive and considered the things he did for me down payments on the right to control me. No, thanks! Besides, there's nothing a man can do for me I can't do for myself."

"Your former fiancé was an idiot. And, there is one thing a man can do that you can't do for yourself." He paused. "No matter how many batteries you buy."

She could hear the laughter in his voice. "Now who's trying to be funny?" She flashed back to the feel of Michael Remington's generous package rubbing against her and, though she'd never admit it out loud, knew her brother was oh so right.

"Look, I know I sound like a broken record, but just because you're not in LA anymore doesn't mean you don't have to be careful. Even here in the Midwest, we have our crazies and lowlifes."

"Brandt, you don't have to worry. I wasn't alone. My boss was still at the office tonight, and he made sure I left when he did." She skipped over the part about not knowing Michael was there at the time. Her brother didn't need to know that part. "In fact, he insisted on walking me to my car and made sure I left the garage in one piece."

Her phone signaled an incoming call. Checking the screen, she groaned.

"What's the matter?"

"That's my boss beeping in. He made me promise to call and let him know when I made it home, and I forgot."

"Good for him."

She rolled her eyes again. "Whatever. Look, bro, I gotta go. Talk to you tomorrow."

She tapped over to the other line. "Hello."

A deep voice drawled, "Well, hello, Ms. Morgan. I trust you're safe and sound at home and not stranded somewhere on the side of the road?"

A shiver tingled along her spine. He had an über sexy phone voice. "Yes, I'm home. I'm sorry. I really did mean to call you, but my brother called. We got to talking, and it sort of slipped my mind."

"Okay then. I just wanted to make sure you were fine before I turned in for the night."

"Thanks for checking on me." Through the phone, she heard his refrigerator door open and close.

"You're welcome." He took a sip of something. "You know, Jordis, we do have remote access to the network available. I'll have Technology set you up tomorrow. You shouldn't be alone at the office that late."

"Here we go again."

"Excuse me?"

Jordis sat down on the couch. "Michael, I'm really not in the mood for this lecture again tonight."

"Again?"

"I just got the whole 'you shouldn't be at the office this

late' and 'why don't you just use remote access' speech from my brother."

"Ah. I understand. Big brother's protective of you."

"Actually, he's my younger brother. By four years. A fact he seems to keep forgetting."

"He's not forgetting. It simply doesn't matter to him. He's a man and you're his sister. It sounds like the two of you are close, which means he considers it his job to protect you and make sure you're taken care of."

"Is that the macho in you talking or are you speaking from personal experience as a sibling?"

An odd thunk, like the sound of a glass or bottle hitting a kitchen table, resounded through the receiver right before Michael's deep laugh caressed her ear. She'd never heard him laugh before. She liked the sound.

"Macho in me, huh? So, you think I'm macho?"

"Oh, in the worst way."

His chuckles tapered off as he continued, "Well, I don't know about that, but I do have two sisters. One's older than me and the other is younger, but I don't think I treat either of them differently because of our birth order. I'd certainly chastise either of them if I found out they stayed at their offices late into the night with no one around but a few security guards."

Jordis got up and strolled into her bedroom while he talked. She left the lights off and used the light from the hallway to see. She pulled off her skirt, laid it neatly over an overstuffed chair, and unbuttoned her blouse before plopping herself on her queen-sized bed. She lay on her back, with her head at the foot of the bed, staring blankly at the ceiling with one foot flat on the bed and the other dangling in the air at the end of her crossed leg. The fingers of her free hand absently caressed her abdomen as she continued their conversation.

"So, what you're saying is because I wasn't born with a *Y* chromosome, I need you or my brother . . . or some man . . . to protect and take care of me."

"No. What I'm saying is because I *was* born with a *Y* chromosome, it's my nature to want to protect and take care of the women in my life whether you actually need me to or not. It sounds as if your brother's of the same vintage."

A long silence followed his comment. A slight thrill ran through her at his use of the word *you*. She understood he spoke generally, but something inside her liked the idea he could consider her amongst the women entitled to his protection.

"You still there?" Michael asked.

"Yeah, I'm here."

"Well? No comment?"

What could she say to that? He hadn't spouted the usual male propaganda about women being the weaker sex or no matter what advances women have made in the workplace, it's still primarily the man's job to bring home the bacon. Because his argument wasn't based upon finding her somehow lacking or less capable than him, Jordis really didn't have a retort.

"Well, I guess if that's who you're telling me you are, there's really not much for me to say. But, I'm wondering, how do your sisters feel about your attitude?"

The line went quiet before he admitted, "Pretty much the way you seem to feel about your brother's."

They fell into an easy conversational flow, and he told her more about his sisters. Jordis hit the speaker button on her phone. Laying the phone on the bed beside her head, she continued the discussion in hands-free mode and allowed his voice to surround her in the darkened bedroom.

His voice rolled over her. She loved the sound, deep and smooth like one of those late night radio announcers who played only love songs. Unexpectedly, Spartacus flashed through her mind. He'd had a deep, sexy voice as well. She needed to stop comparing the two men, but the sound of Spartacus's voice in her head mixed with the resonant sound of Michael's oozing through the phone. Her nipples puckered.

Her hand moved up to rub against a nodule plumped under her satin black bra. The sexy tickle made her wish for large male hands to take over. She took a deep breath trying to control a tension she hadn't meant to rouse.

"You okay over there?"

She startled at the question, afraid he could guess exactly what she'd been doing.

"You aren't falling asleep on me are you?"

She could hear the humor in his voice and immediately relaxed. "Of course not." Without thinking, she added, "What woman could ever fall asleep on a man as enthralling as you?"

Almost as soon as the comment left her mouth, she realized the implications that could be taken from what she'd intended as a joke. Luckily, Michael didn't take it the wrong way. He simply chuckled and continued with their chat. He asked, and she answered, a few questions about what had drawn her back to the Kansas City area. Although she responded to his questions easily, explaining the city's proximity to her brother as one of its key selling points, she wondered if he sensed she was holding something back.

After a while, he brought the conversation to a close. "It's late. I better let you get some rest. Something tells me you like to get into the office early."

Jordis glanced at her digital clock, which glowed one fifteen in red. They'd been talking for almost an hour. She hadn't felt the passage of time. "Yes, I'd better go. I have a deposition first thing in the morning."

"Ok, I'll see you at the office."

They both hesitated before hanging up at the same time. Jordis laid in the dark for a while contemplating why she suddenly felt like a teenager who'd gotten a call from the star quarterback of her high school football team.

℘ ℘ | ℘ ℘

Jordis slept fitfully that night. The recurring dream she'd thought done slipped into her subconscious. The gladiator came to her. His tongue danced inside her mouth, and his hands explored and pressed until an exquisite ache between her legs made her moan in her sleep. Her buttocks ground into rumpled black Egyptian cotton. The top sheet slid languorously against her thighs. The sensuous friction heightened her senses. Dampness pooled in intimate places, bare beneath a flimsy, white silk negligee.

This time she didn't stop his touching. His fingers slid

inside her, taunting until intense heat burned inside her flesh and caused her to kick tousled sheets off the bed. Her negligee rucked up her hips. Her bare buttocks pressed harder into the mattress, and even in sleep, her pelvis began to tuck and release in an erotic rhythm generally shared by two. Her REM mind fixated on him, that beautifully bronzed and intoxicatingly muscled stranger.

A whimper pierced her sleep state. Jordis began to float towards consciousness, but the dream gripped her tightly and lulled her back down. In her dream, a different part of his anatomy took over her pleasure. A slow methodic rocking bounced her gently up and down the beige flat paint of a bedroom wall. Loud breaths and soft groans punctuated the staccato rhythm. Her grip tightened on the hips of her dream gladiator, and she rocked him back. The tempo built and she urged him harder, faster. Then it came, a coital explosion so intense a real mewl of satisfaction escaped her lips and startled her awake.

She laid wide-eyed, staring up at the ceiling and panting. She'd heard his voice call her name in her sleep. This time, she recognized the voice, and when he'd looked into her eyes, the once amorphous, indescribable eye color appeared in Technicolor gray. Her dream gladiator's eyes had been unmistakably gray.

Jordis squeezed her damp, sticky thighs together. She'd come in her sleep, but the edge wasn't completely off. She lingered in a state of semi-arousal. Although she had the mechanical means beneath her mattress to relieve her discomfiture, she wouldn't go there. She couldn't go there, because the face she'd seen in her sleep was . . . *Michael Remington's!*

"No," she complained audibly to no one in particular, but hoped the universe and her uncooperative subconscious would hear and heed.

She'd already been over this with herself. She would not—could not—embrace a sexual fantasy about her boss. She rolled onto her stomach, pulled a pillow over her head, and groaned. *Ugh!!* He'd ruined a perfectly good dream. Now, she wouldn't be able to separate her gladiator fantasies from the olive-skinned, gray-eyed counselor.

She hadn't had the gladiator dream in days. She'd had it almost daily for a straight week after New Year's. Her midnight rendezvous with the costumed Lothario had played over and over, night after night, as clear as a high definition movie. Somehow, in this morning's version, her anonymous suitor—previously safe fodder for fantasies of illicit sex—had morphed into Mr. Macho. She didn't even want to begin to analyze the Freudian implications of that.

His voice had rolled over her like a sensuous massage, the deep tone arousing her as much as the naughty imagery conjured by her dreaming mind. She surmised Michael had crept into her fantasy because his nectarous voice had been the last sound she'd heard before going to sleep last night, and it had made her think of Spartacus. Nothing more to it than that . . . she hoped.

Even as she rationalized the provocative dream, the glutinous feeling between her thighs told another story. She'd never reached physical fulfillment during her previous dreams about the gladiator. That she'd done so this morning implied a burgeoning attraction for the svelte partner she'd been loath to examine closely. In fact, she didn't want to analyze the *how comes* and *what fors* or anything else about the situation even now. Nothing good could come of it.

Her goal was partnership, her focus billable hours and finding a way, other than sleeping with Remington, to get appointed to the Metra Pharmaceuticals case. She needed to execute a serious display of mind over matter or, more aptly, mind over libido. Like their elevator tryst from the night before, Jordis intended—no, she *needed*—to put this and him out of her mind.

Determined to do exactly that, she rolled out of bed and headed for the bathroom.

❧ ❧ | ❦ ❦

Across town, Michael Remington slept in the buff with morning wood to rival the trunk of a hundred-year-old redwood. Her moans haunted him in his sleep. Juliet. Luscious breasts pressed against his bare chest and her golden skin looked good enough to eat. He pressed his lips against her throat and in his dream, she emitted that sound that made him hard as concrete. His fingers under her dress, he caressed her intimate folds in a steady rhythm. Feminine sounds of pleasure intensified a tumescence he yearned to push deep inside her.

For the first time, the Sandman took pity on him, allowing him to alter his body position and consummate his desire. The dream Juliet grabbed his hips and pulled him to her. He tucked his face into the curve of her neck and slid home, dipping in and out of her warmth until he felt her begin to spasm around him.

When she succumbed to her release, the *en rêve* orgasmic pulses took him to the brink. He looked into her face and this time, the mask had vanished. Hazel eyes stared back at him, beautiful kaleidoscope hazel.

"Jordis!" The shout shattered his soporific haze.

Breathing hard, he came awake disoriented and on edge. As his dream came back to him, he threw his legs over the edge of the bed, placed his elbows on his knees, and dropped his head in surrender. Even his subconscious mind wanted her. Looking down at his lap, he rose and headed for the bathroom.

He stepped into the shower and stood under the spray with his head down, hands pressed hard against the tile beneath the showerhead. Warm water sluiced through his hair and down his body, frustration raining off him with each rivulet pouring down his skin. He'd grabbed and squeezed hard on the base of his shaft as he'd shouted himself awake this morning, but it'd been to no avail. He'd ejaculated all over himself.

He hadn't had a wet dream since his teen years and having one today didn't please him. The combination of his encounter with his mystery woman superimposed over his encounter last night with Jordis had been too much for him to handle. Those exotic eyes of Jordis's—that seemed to shift color with the light, her wardrobe, and her emotions—were wreaking havoc on his equilibrium. He didn't understand it. He'd dated plenty of women with beautiful eyes. He didn't remember any of those eyes turning him inside out or tripping into his dreams until he practically pleasured himself in his sleep.

As the dream played over in his head, he groaned. Was he truly losing all self-control? Ms. Morgan had gone from simply screwing with his concentration at work to affecting his ability to sleep.

He lifted his face into the water then reached over and pumped two squirts of shampoo into his palm. He rubbed his hands together then ran them through his hair. A slideshow played in his mind as he worked his hair into a lather. *Juliet. Jordis. Jordis. Juliet.*

What was it about this woman, embodied in her two personas, that appealed to him on such an intense level?

He remembered his confusion over Juliet's eye color. He'd been perplexed about whether they were green or brown. He hadn't thought much about it after he'd realized he'd met two different Juliets that night. Although, part of him had wondered how he could have confused light brown eyes with green ones, even with being a few sheets to the wind. After meeting Jordis, he didn't feel like such an idiot. Her chameleon eyes covered that color dichotomy at various times of the day, plus the spectrum in between.

How had it taken him days to figure out his mystery woman and Jordis were one and the same? Because his encounter with Juliet had been shrouded in dimness, he'd assumed he'd fixated on Jordis as a way to compensate for not being able to find his mystery woman, a simple case of transference. Jordis had served as a temporary substitute for something—someone—out of his reach.

Now, he knew better. His hope for avoiding an office romance had turned into his greatest temptation to succumb to one. He couldn't allow that to happen. Jordis was off limits, and he possessed enough strength of will not to let her sensuality lure him into another office romance mistake.

He rinsed his hair and slathered in some leave-in conditioner. After washing with his favorite scented body shampoo and getting dressed, he headed to the office. By the time he got to work, he'd come to terms with the whole Jordis situation. He'd concentrate on solving the mystery of the vanishing discovery documents. Once he got focused on the case, his attraction to Jordis would wane.

So as not to tempt fate, however, he'd avoid Ms. Morgan today. He had a boatload of work to do, no sense pushing his self-control unnecessarily. He needed to leave that walking temptation alone.

CHAPTER 7

*I*mmediately upon arriving at his desk, Michael delved into dissecting his opponent's motion for summary judgment. He managed to focus for a few hours and stay away from Jordis, but she slipped into his thoughts before lunchtime. By two o'clock, he needed a serious testosterone detox and headed for his fifth straight two-hour workout of the week.

When he returned to his office, he threw down his duffel bag, frustrated with himself. He circled his desk and stared at the annotated papers he'd abandoned earlier. He needed help to prepare a response to the pending motion. A disturbing correlation existed between facts relied upon in the motion and confidential Metra Pharmaceutical information to which the opposing side should not have been privy. The mysterious disappearance of a box of privileged case documents no longer struck him as a mere filing issue.

Something didn't add up, and he could use co-counsel input to determine what.

Chase pressed him daily to quit dragging his feet about bringing in Jordis, but this case was too important to risk a slipup because his brain was in his pants instead of on litigation strategy. How could he possibly work closely with a woman who gave him wet dreams? He was beginning to think—asshole or not—Covington would be the better choice to back him on this case.

Twenty minutes later, he was still pondering the issue when his mobile phone vibrated the receipt of a text message. He checked his phone. A text from his younger sister queried whether he wanted to join her for dinner on the Plaza. Michael smiled to himself. As a graduate student, Raina rarely had any money and when she did, it went exclusively towards school materials or her wardrobe. What she really meant was did he want to buy her dinner, and since she had selected the Country Club Plaza, she likely counted on dining at a really nice restaurant.

He typed, *Sure. Ur treat?*

Her response made him laugh out loud: *ABSOLUTELY! Mickey Ds ok? :D.*

After texting Raina his acceptance of her dinner invitation and instructions her to meet him by the Bronze Boar statue on West 47th Street, Michael stepped away from his desk with a much lighter attitude. He looked forward to having dinner with his sister. He couldn't be around her unpredictable energy and stay in a mood for long. She was exactly what he needed to keep his mind off a certain leggy lawyer.

❧ ❧ | ❧ ❧

Jordis's mood soared with positive energy that mirrored the beautiful winter sunshine. She'd had a productive day at work. The deposition she'd taken in her trademark infringement case had gone her way. She expected to receive a nice settlement offer from opposing counsel sometime next week. On top of that, she'd managed to avoid Michael Remington. By the time the deposition had wrapped up, it had been late afternoon and Michael had been in meetings of his own.

She'd made it a point to leave the building early. She hadn't wanted to run into him today. The last thing she needed was to be alone with him again—in her office, in an elevator, or anywhere else—so soon. She still hadn't come to grips with his appearance in her dream. Whenever she'd had a moment of respite today, her mind had drifted to him, alternating between their encounter in the elevator last night and her erotic dream from this morning. It was unnerving.

Those gorgeous eyes of his had haunted her. Wondering where he'd gotten them from, she'd slipped into the Board Room before lunch to peek at the portrait of his father. She'd found her answer there. Austin Remington had been quite the looker. Although he'd been surfer blond and suntanned, his eyes were steely gray. Michael had his father's eyes. His olive skin tone must have come from his mother.

After her Board Room visit, the warning bells she'd ignored last night renewed their clang of impending danger where Michael Remington was concerned. Needing to quiet her troubled psyche, she chose to use her early exodus to visit her favorite bookstore. One of the last of a dying breed, the humongous chain store on West 47th Street constituted a four-level book palace and in-house café that romanced the bibliophile in her.

She wandered the largest print book collection in the city, idly browsing new releases, picking up selections here and there, and reading back covers until her frazzled nerves calmed. Two hours later, she decided to buy something that would totally engross her but wouldn't contain any romantic underpinnings. She opted for a thousand-plus page horror thriller about a small town that gets sealed off from the rest of the world by an invisible dome. The novel had been out a while, but she hadn't had time to read it. She managed to snag a hardcover copy off the clearance table, which ended the outing on an added note of delight. Sliding the novel into her reusable book tote on top of several other purchases, she exited the mega bookstore with a buoyant step and nearly collided with a laughing twenty-something hanging on the arm of . . . *Michael Remington?*

The look of shock on his face mirrored her own.

"Excuse me." The twenty-something smiled at Jordis. "I wasn't paying attention."

Jordis deftly covered her acute surprise and smiled back at the girl. "That's okay."

The young lady was quite beautiful. Long, naturally curly coffee-brown hair hung loose about her shoulders. The fall of hair framed a heart-shaped face from which peered laughing gray eyes. Jordis looked back at Michael. The young lady's eyes matched his shade almost exactly.

"Jordis," Michael said with a nod. "What are you doing here?"

Jordis kept her smile going, trying to mask her unease at her failure to avoid him for a full day. He wore black jeans and a black turtleneck sweater under a wool coat, but the casual attire in no way detracted from his overall appeal.

She lifted her book tote. "Gathering some new reading material and enjoying the last few days of the Plaza Christmas lights. Some of us do actually get out of the office at a decent hour from time to time." Hiding behind sarcasm, Jordis added with a pointed look, "The question is what are you doing away from your desk at only . . ." She glanced at her watch. "Oh my, six fifteen on a work night?"

Michael's lips lifted halfway when she made a fake gasp of surprise while checking the time.

"You two obviously know each other." The young lady looked back and forth between them.

"Yeah," Michael replied. "Raina meet Jordis Morgan. Jordis, this is my sister Raina."

That would explain the matching gray eyes. Raina didn't have her brother's deep olive coloring, however. Her skin was fairer, with only a slight olive undertone.

"Nice to meet you." Jordis extended her hand.

Raina grasped her palm and shook. "Likewise."

Continuing to look between Michael and Jordis with an inquisitive stare, Raina asked, "So, how do you two know each other?"

"Jordis works with me at the firm."

Raina gave her a once over. "You're a lawyer?" Blessed with the unshackled honesty of the young and the not-yet-jaded, Raina didn't bother to mask her incredulity.

"Um, yes." Jordis had dressed more LA today, but the doubtful look on Raina's face gave her pause. "Is that a problem?"

"No, but are you sure you work at my brother's firm?"

Jordis looked at Michael, who could no longer conceal his grin. His eyes surveyed the outfit she had on under her open winter coat. She wore a short black jean skirt with brocaded pockets and seams over black opaque tights that disappeared into black knee-high patent leather spiked-heel boots. A silver chain with several charms attached looped around the right boot at ankle level. A cropped, baggy loose cable knit sweater in coral layered over a shiny silver long-sleeved tee that showed through the holes in the sweater. Medium-sized silver hoop earrings dangled from her ears. Each bangle held two loops linked together so they revolved in opposite directions when she moved her head.

"You certainly don't dress like any of the lawyers I've met from my brother's firm."

Jordis laughed. "Well, I don't usually dress this cool for the office. I try to tone it down so they think I'm as straight-laced as they are. I took a few liberties today with casual Friday, knowing I wouldn't go home right after work."

Raina laughed. "I like her," she said to her brother. She looked back at Jordis. "Have you had dinner yet?"

"No, I was about to grab something and head home."

"Why don't you join us? We were just deciding where to eat."

Michael looked uncomfortable with his sister's invitation. Jordis suspected he didn't fraternize with his associates outside the office. He didn't really socialize with them in the office. She'd take the hint and put him out of his misery.

"Thanks for the offer, Raina, but I don't want to intrude on your evening. It was nice—"

"Don't be silly. You wouldn't be intruding. Would she, Michael?" Raina eyed her brother expectantly.

"No, of course not." His voice held an edge that, to Jordis, made him sound less than sincere.

"Besides," Raina explained to Jordis in a mock whisper, "you'll help keep me sane. I love my brother, but sometimes he can be a bit grumpy."

"Hey, you do remember who's paying for dinner tonight, right?" Michael reminded her with a frown.

Raina grabbed him around the waist and hugged him from the side. "Why you are, brother mine." She batted her eyelashes at him and dripped sweetness from her voice. "You wouldn't begrudge me a decent meal because I speak the truth now would you?"

Michael fought a smile through an indulgent shake of his head. The siblings were obviously close. Raina had her big brother wrapped firmly around her little finger, and she knew it.

"You know you haven't exactly been the best of company lately. Ever since New Year's Eve—"

"Raina," he interrupted in a stern voice.

"What happened New Year's Eve?" Jordis eyed Raina then Michael.

"Nothing," Michael interjected in a tone that left no doubt he considered the line of questioning closed. "How 'bout we head to a restaurant so we don't have to wait in line forever for a table?" Michael removed Jordis's bag of books from her hand and shouldered them himself. "Steakhouse okay with everyone?"

Michael and Jordis both looked at Raina. She shrugged. "It's fine with me unless Jordis would rather have seafood."

"Nope. Steakhouse works for me."

Raina hooked her arm through her brother's, and Jordis fell in at his other side. They meandered a few blocks west of the bookstore then headed south towards the *Plaza III* restaurant on Pennsylvania Avenue. Once the threesome reached the restaurant, the hostess seated them immediately at a U-shaped booth. Raina slid into the center of the *U*. Michael and Jordis took positions on the wings, sitting opposite each other.

ॐ ॐ | ॐ ॐ

Michael watched Jordis smile at the waiter and give her order. He tried not to be moved by her smile. He wasn't succeeding. He couldn't believe he'd spent the day avoiding her, and accepted a dinner invitation from his sister to get his mind off her, only to end up across the dinner table from her. To make matters worse, she looked absolutely stunning. Someone upstairs had a sick sense of humor.

When Raina had voiced her surprise earlier that Jordis worked at his firm, Michael had known immediately what his clotheshorse of a sister was thinking. The fashion diva in Raina had coveted Jordis's outfit. It wouldn't exactly fit in at RHM. The lady's personal flair equaled her professional chic, although the two personas sat on opposite ends of the fashion spectrum. She'd completed the black skirt and knee-high boots ensemble with a high ponytail that rode the back of her head and made her sculpted cheekbones standout. A few loose chestnut tendrils fell about her temples and gave the hairstyle a feminine edge. She looked like she'd stepped off a runway or out of the pages of a fashion magazine.

He thought about her boots. They conjured up visions of whips, chains, and leather bustiers over lace teddies. Not that he'd ever been into that sort of thing, but he had a sudden inkling of the possible appeal.

As if reading his thoughts, his sister said to Jordis, "Tell me about those boots. And where can I get a pair just like them?"

"You can't," Jordis replied. "They came from a little boutique on the Santa Monica Promenade in LA. The owner is a friend of mine. She specializes in finding unique fashions she imports in small quantities from all over the world. When customers shop at her store, they know they aren't going to run into a dozen or more ladies in the city wearing the same thing."

Jordis took a drink of water. "These boots she discovered somewhere in Europe. She refuses to say where, even to me. What she did tell me was she immediately thought of me when she saw them, and she acquired only one pair—in my size."

"Cool. They must have cost a fortune."

"Actually, they didn't cost me a dime. My cousin Narisa bought them for me last year. She and Lindsay, the boutique owner, conspired to make the acquisition as a special birthday present."

"Wow. I wish I had friends like that." Raina sipped her lemonade then gave Jordis a speculative look. "What size shoe do you wear?"

"Don't even think about it." Jordis's expression stayed serious though she appeared to be fighting a smile.

Michael chuckled as he watched his sister pout. "My sister fancies herself a budding designer. She's been addicted to clothes since the age of three when mom let her pick out her own outfit for the first time."

"Do you study fashion design now?" Jordis asked Raina.

The food arrived. Raina waited for their meals to be served before she responded. "I graduated two years ago with a degree in fashion design, but I'm still studying at the Art Institute. I'm focusing on art classes right now. I need to improve my drawing skills and work with textures some more. I want to be able to draw my own creations, not simply come up with ideas I have to pay someone else to draw."

"That sounds like a wise decision." Jordis picked up her fork and started on her entrée.

Raina and Jordis chatted about Raina's studies, fashion, and art. Raina got excited when Jordis mentioned she had a cousin in Los Angeles who ran her own fashion house and agreed to make an introduction. After a while, Jordis looked over at him, perhaps realizing he hadn't said much. He quietly stared back at her, his hand wrapped around the beer bottle on the table in front of him.

"Raina, I think we're boring your brother."

"Nah. Trust me." Raina cut into her steak. "If he were bored, he'd definitely say something."

The corner of Michael's mouth turned up at his sister's words.

Jordis's eyes shifted, and she twisted her left wrist a couple of times out of habit before she rubbed it absently.

"Is that right?" Jordis said, still looking at Michael.

Michael didn't respond. He lifted his beer and took a long, slow drink as he watched her over the bottle.

After a moment, Jordis heard Raina add, "Besides, my brother is never bored when he has a beautiful woman to look at it."

Jordis's eyes narrowed. Her gaze shifted to Raina when she sensed the young lady settle back into the booth. Raina glanced between Michael and Jordis a few times. Michael could see the wheels spinning behind those gray eyes so much like his own. She was getting the wrong idea about him and Jordis. He would have to set her straight when he got her alone. He didn't need her speculating to their older sister or, heaven forbid, mom about what was going on between the two lawyers—which was a definite nothing. Okay, maybe parts of him wanted something to be going on between them, but the parts above his waist were determined to keep the lower parts from getting their way.

About the time Michael was getting squeamish under his sister's perusal, a commotion at the front of the restaurant drew her attention. A group of five young men entered the restaurant. When they passed the table, a khakis-wearing young man with shaggy blond hair and big brown eyes looked at Raina and winked.

Michael caught Raina's reserved smile though she tried to act nonchalant about what had occurred. "Who's he?" Michael asked his sister.

Raina flinched, reaching for her drink to cover her reaction.

"Raina?"

"What?" she answered in an irritated voice.

"Who was that guy who winked at you?"

"No one."

"No one, huh?" Michael took another sip of his beer. "That's why he keeps looking over here every chance he gets. If he keeps that up, the boy's going to have a crook in his neck by the time he gets his meal."

Raina huffed out a breath. "Leave him alone, Michael. It's just a guy I know."

"Know from where?"

"Nowhere in particular."

"I see." A slow tick pulsed in Michael's jaw. "No one, from nowhere in particular. Sounds like a guy I should meet since he's so interested in my sister." Michael put his beer down and pushed on the table to rise.

Raina shot out a hand and grabbed his forearm. "Don't you dare!"

"Then start talking."

Raina glanced over at Jordis.

"What are you looking at her for? She can't help you."

Raina looked embarrassed by his words and heavy-handed tactics, but he didn't care. Their father had died when Raina was in high school, and Michael had always felt it his responsibility to be the protector their father didn't get the chance to be.

Jordis placed her hand on Raina's arm. "Raina, I know what it's like to have an overprotective brother meddling in your love life." Ignoring Michael's scowl, she suggested,

"Maybe if you give your brother some background information on the young man, he'll relax."

"Or, he'll take it and run a full background check then call the guy and make sure he's so afraid of what will happen if he makes one wrong move the guy won't even ask me out." Her words poured out in a rapid-fire gush.

Jordis laughed. "Okay, that's a bit of an exaggeration don't you think?"

"Humph." Raina snorted and flopped back in her seat. "Ask him."

Jordis glanced at Michael who met her gaze with a blank expression. "Michael, you didn't?"

He simply shrugged and finished off his beer.

Jordis returned her attention to an unhappy Raina. "Raina, what's the gentleman's name?"

Raina glared at her brother then gave an exaggerated sigh. "Christian."

"Christian what?" Michael demanded.

"Let's leave it at Christian for the moment." Jordis gave him a closed-mouth smile when he shot a glare at her.

She knew why he wanted the boy's last name, and she was intentionally blocking for his sister. He didn't like it. Raina, however, visibly relaxed.

Turning back to Raina, Jordis asked, "How do you know Christian?"

"His brother Jon attends the Art Institute with me. They share a car so sometimes, Christian drops him at school and sometimes when we all go out after class, Christian and his buddies are there, too."

"Wait a minute." Michael leaned forward. "Is he the clown who honked for you last week at mom's instead of coming to the door to pick you up?"

Raina blushed. "It's not as if he was picking me up for a date. He and Jon were giving me a ride to class."

"It doesn't matter," Michael insisted. "A man doesn't sit outside in his car and honk for a woman to come out. You should expect better than that."

"Don't be such a dinosaur," Raina groused.

Jordis coughed and picked up her sweet tea to mask her urge to laugh.

Michael gave her a warning look, but Jordis ignored him. "I may be a dinosaur," he said to his sister, "but I guarantee you after being out with me, a woman wouldn't give a bozo like him a second thought."

Raina rolled her eyes.

Continuing with her meal, Jordis changed the subject. "So, Raina, how did you get your brother out of the office so early?"

Raina laughed. "Easy. I just asked."

"You mean you just *texted*," Michael clarified.

"Same diff."

"You just asked . . . um, texted what?" Jordis asked her.

"I asked if he wanted to have dinner with me." Raina snagged the phone clipped to her brother's hip and typed in the code to unlock the phone. She clicked on their text message conversation and handed the phone to Jordis. "See?"

Jordis looked at Michael, hesitant to look at his phone log. His hand tipped up from his empty beer bottle as he gave a one-shoulder shrug, indicating he didn't mind.

She glanced at the text exchange and chuckled when she read the part about Mickey D's. "I see."

Jordis handed him back his phone, with an enigmatic smile he'd seen several times. The first time was the day she'd broken down Eric Covington's ass-backwards argument over the pro bono case selection. He'd surmised it usually foretold the pieces of some puzzle had fallen into place for her, and she had her analysis carefully delineated in her mind.

That she now gave him that look made him uneasy. "What exactly do you see?"

Jordis simply forked a piece of salmon.

He narrowed his eyes and gave her a don't-play-with-me look. "Jor*dis*?"

Her eyes went wide before she blinked them with a feminine flutter. "Mi*chael*?" She matched the lilt he'd put on the end of her name.

They stared at each other. She had no intention of backing down or giving in to him. He could tell by the set of her lips.

He wasn't used to women balking at his requests. They usually did exactly what he asked, too afraid a denial would cross them off his little black list. Women at his firm were particularly compliant. His position as future Managing Partner pretty much made his word their law. He didn't intentionally cultivate such behavior, but he had accepted and gotten used to never being challenged. Jordis must not have gotten the memo. She sat completely comfortable with her obstinate actions.

Despite his annoyance, Michael found himself fighting a smile at the deceptively innocent look on her face. He relaxed into his seat and placed his arm along the back of the booth. To hide his peeved amusement, he took a swig of the fresh beer he'd recently received from the waiter.

She was intentionally pushing his buttons. Maybe it was time he started pushing back.

CHAPTER 8

*J*ordis felt an unfamiliar contentment spread through her chest. Even when perturbed, Michael Remington managed to make her feel warm and playfully feminine.

He'd asked her what she saw. She saw that his prickly blustering and grumpy mood swings covered a man with a soft heart and a love of family. He had a hidden sense of humor and a depth of personality those who didn't know him outside the office never saw.

She liked the guy as a person. He'd already earned her respect as a capable lawyer, but for the first time, she could see the real man behind the Michael Remington mystique. He had a whole other side the professional façade and legal reputation masked.

As he watched her over his beer bottle, Jordis sat back. Raina temporarily forgotten, she returned his frank perusal. The clearing of a throat interrupted the mutual scrutiny. Their heads swiveled towards Raina. She rewarded them with a speculative smile.

Great, Jordis thought. Had her emotions shown on her face? Did Raina realize she was developing the hots for her brother?

She quickly returned her attention to her plate, and Raina graciously gave them a reprieve by turning the conversation to mundane topics. Michael drifted away, allowing the two women to get to know one another. They continued that way until the waiter brought the bill.

Jordis reached for the check to calculate her total.

Michael stopped her. He rubbed his fingertips along the back of her hand. "I've got it." His voice sounded intentionally seductive.

The pulsing physical awareness Jordis experienced whenever his skin made contact with hers sparked across the back of her hand. She jerked her hand back. He watched her with a challenging glint in his eyes.

"Don't be silly, Michael. You were supposed to have dinner with your sister. I got unexpectedly thrown into the mix. I can pay my own share."

"I'm sure you can, but that's not the point." He dug for his wallet so he missed Mr. Blond and Shaggy tilt his head quickly two times at Raina in a come-here motion.

The summons didn't go unnoticed by Jordis.

"Excuse me." Raina slid toward her, trying to take advantage of the exchange between her brother and Jordis to make a getaway.

Jordis put her hand on Raina's arm. "You are not going to respond to a come-hither-babe head shake. If he wants to talk to you, he should come over to the table."

"Like he's going to come over with Michael sitting here." Raina flopped back against the seat and crossed her arms.

"If he doesn't have the guts to speak to you in front of your brother, he's unlikely to be the kind of guy worth your time in the long run."

Raina made a face, but didn't respond.

Jordis sighed. "Trust me, Raina. I have one of him of my own." Jordis tipped her head in Michael's direction. "I learned the hard way that if a guy didn't have the guts to brave my brother to take me out, he ultimately proved himself without enough spine to keep my respect."

Raina's lips slid right, and she bit her lip in contemplation. The low hum of conversation pulsed from neighboring tables. A bus boy dropped a large plastic bin on the table left of Jordis and began to remove the abandoned plates, glasses and silverware. The clink of knifes and spoons hitting glassware tinkled while Jordis waited for Raina to make a decision.

"Okay," Raina finally whispered from the cocoon she'd folded in on herself.

"Good." Jordis sensed Michael watched her, but she ignored him. She didn't want him to sway her from encouraging Raina to garner her young man's attention, despite Michael's desire she do anything but.

Christian and his four buddies hovered in various stages of departure. Some stood by their chairs, others tossed dollar bills onto the table, and Raina's blond slid his wallet into his back pocket.

Jordis coached Raina. "Smile when he makes eye

contact with you then wait for him to make the next move."

The young lady looked at her doubtfully, still in a slouched position.

"And you might want to sit up straight so he can see you," Jordis added with a slight smile.

Sure enough, once he settled his wallet into his back pocket, Christian's eyes slid towards Raina. Raina repositioned herself in her seat and smiled at him. Jordis watched Christian's pleasured surprise transform slowly into the cocky grin of a guy who'd figured out he'd finally gotten the attention of the girl he wanted. He turned and murmured something to his buddies. Although they had a clear shot to the front door from their table, the group detoured to pass the booth Raina shared with Michael and Jordis.

"Hey, Raina." Christian's eyes never left Raina's face. "A bunch of us are headed over to the movie theater to catch the new sci-fi flick. Want to join us?"

"Sure." Raina scooted across the bench in the direction of her brother as she responded.

Begrudgingly, Michael rose to let her out. He stood next to Christian, who eyed him warily. Raina introduced the two men.

Thinking Michael preoccupied with his introduction to Christian, Jordis reached for the bill lying next to Michael's empty dinner plate.

Ever aware of his surroundings, Michael placed his left hand atop hers and chastised, "Nice try." Still grasping Jordis's hand over the check wallet, Michael grabbed his sister around the waist with his other arm and kissed her on the temple. "Thanks for having dinner with me. Even if you are leaving me hanging."

Raina laughed. "Somehow, big brother, I don't think you're going to miss me." She darted a quick glance at Jordis.

The hug Raina bestowed on her brother hid his answering expression from Jordis. He squeezed Raina. "Have a good time, but be careful. Call if you need anything." He looked at Christian before he finished. "Anything at all."

"I'll be fine. Stop worrying." Raina fairly skipped out of her brother's arms as she joined Christian and his exiting entourage. At the last minute, she turned. Dipping her head towards the battle of hands over the restaurant check, she called to Jordis, "Good luck with that." Although she smiled as she said it, Raina's voice held a doubtful tone that made it clear she had no confidence Jordis would succeed in her attempt to pay any part of the dinner bill.

After his sister walked away, Michael replaced the hand he held over Jordis's with his other so he could slide into the booth facing the right direction. Once seated, he adjusted his hand so he held Jordis's instead of merely pressing it down on top of the check. He turned the full force of those gray eyes on her. "Now that you've managed to get rid of my sister, explain to me why you refuse to let me do something as simple as buy you dinner."

❧ ❧ | ❧ ❧

Jordis slid past Michael while he held the restaurant door open. She'd given in and let him pay for dinner. When he'd slipped his hand under hers and began rubbing the back with his thumb, explaining she didn't want to owe him anything hadn't seemed important. She'd looked into his eyes and had one thought: *retreat* and retreat immediately.

Michael still had her bag of books. She extended her hand for them and thanked him once again for dinner.

He angled the bag out of her reach. "Take a walk with me." His eyes slid down to her boots. "That is, if those boots are conducive to strolling."

With her hand on the book bag handle resting on his shoulder, Jordis looked at her boots then back up. She gave him a sexy, flirty smile. "What's the matter? Don't you like my boots?"

"*Cara mia*, I like your boots just fine." He had a wicked look in his eyes. "But trust me, the last thing I think about you doing in those boots is taking a stroll."

"Hmm, really?" A tremor shimmied down her spine. "That sounds . . . interesting." The words purred out before she could censor them.

Michael's eyes flashed and the provocative nature of her comment hit her after the fact.

What had possessed her to say that out loud? And what had he called her?

"*Cara mia*?" She repeated the phrase in a flat voice, as if simply trying out the phrase, but her expression made it a question. "Is that what you called me?"

"Did I?" Michael grasped her upper arm and turned her to walk beside him without answering her question.

"Was that Italian?"

He glanced at her quickly. "You speak Italian?"

"No. I spent my junior year of college in France and the

summer after in Spain, but I never made it to Italy. What does that mean?" From her residual knowledge of French and Spanish, she had an inkling of what the expression might mean, but her intuitive guess didn't make sense to her.

"It's just an Italian expression." When she continued to stare at him, he added, "Don't worry. It's nothing bad."

Her bicep flexed under his grip. His refusal to answer caused naughty speculation to titter along her already hyperaware nerve endings.

He'd placed her so he walked closest to the street. An unexpected thought pushed aside the rampant speculation. Until Michael Remington, she hadn't paid attention that most men didn't follow such simple rules of gallantry anymore. Now, being around a man who behaved in a chivalrous manner regularly and without conscious thought, his actions stood out like a lighthouse beacon through heavy fog. She couldn't miss the subtle nuisances of care it suggested, and surprisingly, she liked the way it made her feel—special and . . . womanly.

Attractive, gallant, and he spoke Italian? Was he kidding her? "You speak Italian?"

"Yes."

"Fluently?"

"Yes."

"And where did you learn to speak fluent Italian?"

"At home." He let go of her arm and continued walking at a facile pace.

Without breaking her stride, which effortlessly matched his, she stared sideways at him waiting for him to elaborate.

"And my grandparents' place." He glanced at her before adding, "In Milan."

"Milan?" She stopped walking. "Your grandparents live in Milan?"

"My maternal grandparents, yes. I—"

"Jordis! Jordis Morgan is that you?" The familiar masculine voice made Jordis's skin crawl.

She turned towards the interruption. The tall, well-dressed man from her past advanced, his almond complexion and dark-brown fade flawless as ever. His eyes roved over her boot-clad feet then back to the front of her sweater, lingering a bit too long. *Keith.*

Counter to the cheerfulness of his voice, Jordis replied in a substantially less welcoming tone. "Keith." She expelled a slow breath. "What are you doing in Kansas City?"

"I'm in town on business. I'm consulting with the Sprint Center as they work through the viability of bringing a WNBA team to the City of Fountains."

"That's nice. Well, it's been good seeing you." She whipped around to head the opposite direction.

"Hey, wait." Keith touched her arm. The chafing look she gave his hand led to its quick removal. He cleared his throat and looked from Jordis to Michael.

She reluctantly introduced the two men. "Keith Wilson meet Michael Remington."

"Mike, it's nice to meet you." Keith extended a hand towards Michael.

Michael accepted the hand. "Likewise. And the name is Michael."

Keith shot Michael what Jordis considered his charismatic smile. The look usually charmed everyone he met. Guys wanted to be his buddy; business associates wanted to do his deals; and women simply wanted to do him. At the moment, the look made her sick to her stomach.

"No disrespect meant, man. Figured we could cut through the formalities. Any friend of Jordis's is a friend of mine."

Michael replied in a smooth, even tone, "My friends call me *Michael*."

Keith hesitated then chuckled awkwardly. "Well, sure. No problem." Keith shifted and stuck the hand he'd shook with into his pocket. His gaze moved back to Jordis. "I thought maybe we could have dinner together while I'm in town."

"Keith, we've said everything we need to say to each other. Dinner won't be necessary."

He stepped forward as if to touch her again. "Look, Jordis, I'd like a chance to clear the air. We both said some things last time I know we regret."

Jordis's tension mounted. She tried to play it cool, but she was having a hard time managing the emotions assaulting her with Michael standing by as a witness.

At some point, Michael positioned himself closer to her. Jordis hadn't sensed him move, but his warmth now radiated along her side. His hand rested above the small of her back. The touch wasn't sexual. After a brief glance at his face, she intuited it also wasn't meant to be possessive.

He glanced back at her, eyes soft and concerned. His expression told her he wasn't acting out of ego or a need to mark territory in front of another male. His thumb rubbed in light waves against the layers under her sweater. The tension building inside her loosened.

She wasn't used to this kind of unequivocal support from a man—other than her brother. She'd always faced her battles alone. She'd cultivated internal strength and an indomitable spirit through hard knocks ever since her parents split up when she was nine. Michael's silent offer of support was as irresistible as it was unexpected, making Jordis do something completely foreign to her independent spirit. She leaned into him to accept and relish in that support.

A flicker in Keith's eyes conveyed he'd seen the unspoken bond transpire. The bristle to his male ego telegraphed from the flash of barely controlled anger he directed at Michael. Michael's expression didn't change. He stared straight back at Keith, sending the message he wasn't impressed or cowed by his presence.

Jordis regained Keith's attention. "I think the air is plenty clear. I meant every word I said when I called off our engagement. Whatever your regrets, they're irrelevant to me now."

Keith's head tilted. "Michael *Remington*," he said slowly. "As in, Remington Hager & McCormick?" Keith looked right at Jordis as he finished.

She could almost see the dirty thoughts dancing through his brain, and it pissed her off.

"Yes," Michael replied.

"I see." Keith directed a condescending I-was-right-about-you smirk at Jordis.

"No, you don't see—"

"Oh, yeah, Jordis. I see you wasted no time. How long have you been at the firm now? Has it even been two months?"

Jordis bit back the obscenity that threatened to burst from her mouth in response to Keith's veiled personal dig. She didn't bother to correct him about the length of her employment at RHM. "No, you don't see." She took a step forward. "He lied, Keith. He lied to cover his own ass." Her voice dropped to a dangerously calm tenor, but her body still communicated aggression. "Then he used you to make sure his story stuck."

Keith's eyes flashed a momentary look of doubt.

She pressed her point. "Think about it. When a woman's own fiancé doesn't trust her integrity, it makes it pretty easy to get others to doubt her word."

"Is that what you told him?" Keith gave a mirthless laugh. "He bought that line?"

Something in Jordis went cold. "If that's how you feel, Keith, why are you standing here claiming you want to 'clear the air'?"

He switched tactics. "Look, babe, I miss you." He reached for the hand not pressed against Michael's side, a bold move considering Michael's expression. "I thought maybe you were ready to talk about what really happened. Maybe we can finally get past it, get back to being a team." His hand eased towards a loose curl dangling across her forehead.

Michael's hand blocked the move. "You need to keep your hands to yourself."

Keith bristled. "Look, man, could we have a moment alone, please?"

"No," Michael and Jordis said at the same time.

Michael adjusted her body in a way that made it

awkward for Keith to continue holding her hand so Keith released her.

She glared at her ex. "What do you want, Keith? What's this really about?"

Keith's eyes flicked towards Michael.

"Whatever you want to say to me, say it. Trust me, he's not going anywhere." Jordis focused her attention on Keith, but out of the corner of her eye, she caught the look and tilt of head Michael gave him at her comment.

Keith's jaw tightened. The familiar tick revealed his mounting anger. "Clearly, this isn't a good time." He pulled his wallet from his pocket and retrieved a business card. He placed it in Jordis's hand. "Here's my card. I'll be in town for two weeks. Give me a call when you're ready to talk."

Jordis read the card in her hand.

Keith looked past her at the man standing at her shoulder. "*Michael.*" He laced the farewell with a macho inflection.

Michael's smile stayed as nonchalant as his tone, and he nodded his head in dismissal. "*Keith.*"

ॐ ॐ | ॐ ॐ

Michael watched Jordis squeeze Keith's business card into a wadded ball.

"He just ruined a perfectly good day." Her voice held a tense edge that affected Michael in a strange way.

He didn't like her change in mood. Stepping behind her, he placed his right hand on her waist and leaned around her to open her fist with his left. "No, he didn't."

When her hand unwound, he removed the wadded card. "Because we're not going to let him." He dropped the crumple into a neighboring trash receptacle.

Jordis looked over her shoulder at him.

"You still owe me a stroll, Ms. Morgan. Come with me." He took her hand.

"Where are we going?"

He pulled his phone from his pocket and sent several text messages using only his thumb. Satisfied, he nodded before placing the phone back in his coat. "You'll find out soon enough."

He guided her towards the street. As his mystery woman, she'd said they would be hard pressed to do dinner-and-a-movie or getting-to-know-you drinks after their steamy first encounter. He disagreed. They'd done dinner. While a movie wasn't in the cards, they could certainly take advantage of one of Kansas City's favorite couple spots. Their first kiss had been above the backdrop of the Plaza lights. It seemed fitting that their first date also occur on the Plaza—even if she didn't know it was their first date.

They strolled several blocks hand-in-hand and stopped at a corner where passengers commandeered horse-drawn carriages for a fee. Several people waited in line for carriages to return. Jordis looked at him with a question in her eyes. He gave her that smile often used by parents to keep children in suspense when planning a surprise.

Soon, the clip clop of horse hooves against frigid concrete drew Jordis's attention to an approaching carriage. Unconsciously, she squeezed Michael's hand. Open steel bars shaped like a pumpkin sat atop a carriage bed to create the ambience of the popular Cinderella carriage. Drawn by a speckled white stallion, the glow of the white Christmas lights wrapped around the pumpkin cage made the coach appear almost magical.

"I used to love riding in that carriage at Christmas time when I was a kid." Jordis's voice softened with the pleasure of her memories. "I wonder who has the next ride."

The carriage pulled to a stop at the curb. The father of a family of four approached the driver of the carriage intending to purchase the next ride. They watched the driver shake his head negatively indicating the carriage was unavailable.

"It looks like someone has it reserved." Regret tempered her nostalgic cheerfulness. "Too bad. It would have been fun to take a ride."

Michael squeezed her hand back. "Then let's do that."

"You brought me here to take a carriage ride?"

Her baffled expression made him want to laugh. He drew her along by their still joined hands. "Yes. In fact, I brought you here to take a ride in this carriage." He motioned towards the Cinderella carriage.

Jordis stopped moving. Her expression turned from bafflement to disbelief. "But . . . the carriage is reserved."

Michael tugged her close and lowered his voice. "It's reserved for us."

"But, how did you—?"

"The wonders of modern technology." Michael patted the breast pocket of his coat.

"That's what you were doing? Making reservations for a carriage ride?"

"Yes."

A soft breeze blew more loose tendrils of hair around her face. "Why did you do that?" She shivered beneath her wary expression.

With the sun down, the temperature had dropped. He pulled her scarf from under the collar of her coat and wrapped it around her neck. "Because I heard you tell my sister that when your mother brought you and your brother to the Plaza for carriage rides, you selected this carriage whenever it was your turn to pick. No matter what had happened that week or that day, a ride in the Cinderella carriage made you happy. After Mr. Wilson, I thought a little carriage therapy was in order."

He brushed the hair off her face. "Now, stop questioning me and get in the carriage. You're wasting the night."

CHAPTER 9

*M*ichael offered Jordis his hand and assisted her into the carriage. When he settled beside her, the carriage driver looked back. "All set, folks?"

Michael nodded and the renewed clip clop of hooves announced their departure.

Jordis angled her body toward him. "You were listening the whole time."

Apparently, she hadn't realized he'd been paying attention when she'd talked with his sister about her memories of carriage rides on the Plaza. "Yes, I was listening."

Her face lit up, and he almost wanted to thank Keith Wilson for inspiring him to charter a carriage ride to make her feel better. Her delight made the astronomical fee he'd agreed to pay to guarantee the last minute availability of the carriage worth every dime. Of course, he'd still find a way to get back at his old high school buddy, whose family owned the carriage service, for taking advantage of Michael's predicament to jack up the price. For now, however, he was glad his friend had come through for him so he could counteract the negative effect of Jordis's interaction with her ex.

When Wilson approached Jordis, the force of Michael's immediate dislike of the man had surprised him. He wanted to know more about their relationship. He'd gleaned the two had been engaged and the relationship hadn't ended well. He wanted to know why, but he wouldn't risk a renewed downturn in her mood by asking. He'd broach the subject some other time.

Jordis hunkered into her coat.

"Are you cold?"

"A little. I guess I spent too many years in LA, and my blood hasn't thickened back up yet."

Michael leaned towards the driver and asked him to pull over up ahead. He turned back to Jordis. "I'll be right back."

He jumped out of the carriage and walked purposefully into a coffee shop. A few minutes later, he returned with two tall cups of steaming liquid. Climbing back into the carriage, he handed her a cup.

Jordis took a sip. "Mmm. What is this?"

"Good?"

"Delicious. It tastes almost like gourmet hot chocolate, but it clearly has some coffee in it." She took a long swig and a look of ecstasy crossed her face.

Michael chuckled. "I noticed you always drink tea. So, I told the barista you're not really a coffee drinker, but I was trying to corrupt you. She came up with this. It's a milk chocolate turtle mocha. Do you like it?"

"It's incredible. What's in it?"

"Two types of gourmet chocolate—including chocolate shavings—real cream, flavored cappuccino, nuts and something secret I can't get the owner to tell me."

"I wouldn't tell you either if I had a hot chocolate recipe like this. I'd be a millionaire from hot chocolate sales alone." She adjusted in her seat. "Have you talked to them about possible trade secret protection for their recipes?"

His brow furrowed. "Actually, no. I never thought about it. But you're right. Dana should be taking precautions with her recipes."

"Dana? You know the owner well?"

"Yes, she graduated from high school with my sister, Liliana. She was always at the house for some reason or another."

"I'd love an introduction. Some intellectual property protection with a targeted social media campaign and we could make this shop the place to come for gourmet beverages. Then, Dana and her staff could upsell their other goodies."

He'd never thought about a business pitch to Dana. He rarely got involved with clients until they had a dispute they wanted to squash or litigation they needed to win. Jordis's brain seemed to work on a proactive basis all the time. He admired that. The transactional team led by his Business and Finance partner had been after him for some time to work on a targeted cross-marketing campaign with the Intellectual Property Litigation group. Maybe he needed to put Jordis to work on the project as a liaison between the two departments. He filed the thought away for later consideration.

His attention returned to his carriage companion. The tension in her shoulders from the encounter with Wilson had started to ease. The calming motion of the gliding carriage and the hot beverage appeared to have relaxed her. He placed his arm along the seat behind her head, letting his fingers slide through the hair of her ponytail from time to time.

After a while, Jordis asked, "So, your grandparents live in Milan?"

His head bobbed. "My maternal grandparents."

He didn't usually talk about his family. People, especially women, had a way of taking personal information and using it like weapons in warfare. His ex had. She'd gone so far as to pretend to share his interest in motorcycles by buying one of her own. She'd taken a rider training course and gotten her motorcycle license, but the woman didn't actually like to ride. Whenever they made plans to ride together, something always came up. Too distracted by work, and convinced her wedding planning kept her equally busy, he didn't put two and two together until he uncovered the little schemer's plot to fawn her pregnancy by another man off as his. She'd scoped him out and planned his seduction like a professional mercenary staging a coup. The devastation she'd wreaked on his faith in women and belief in romantic love still lingered.

Somehow with Jordis, he didn't feel the tight pull of angst that usually accompanied a woman's inquiry into his personal life. In fact, he felt compelled to tell her about his Italian roots.

"My parents met the summer after my father graduated from college. He embarked on a summer tour of Europe. On his jaunt through Milan, he spied a beautiful Italian girl coming out of a gelato shop with a group of friends one day. According to my father, she'd been breathtaking. He couldn't take his eyes off her. Eventually, she noticed him staring and smiled at him before disappearing from the piazza.

"My dad always chuckled when he described how, try as he might, he'd been unable to stop thinking about the Italian beauty. So, he returned every day for four straight days to the same spot at the same time of day hoping she would show up again. On the fourth and final day, he resolved that if she didn't show, he would relent and move on to the next city on his seat-of-the-pants itinerary."

His fingers slid through her ponytail again. "My father sat outside the gelato shop that day for five long hours. As dusk began to filter over the piazza, he gathered his disappointment and rose to leave. That's when he spied my mom walking alone. She'd come specifically to find him. From that moment on, the two spent every possible minute together. They decided to make it permanent after knowing each other for only two weeks."

"Wow. That's very romantic."

"My grandfather didn't think so."

"No?"

"Nope. Apparently, he was dismayed when the 'smooth-talking American'—" He made air quotes with his hands. "—requested permission to marry his daughter. Grandfather had expected my mom to marry a nice Italian boy and raise tons of children in Milan, not abscond to another continent with an Anglo."

"Ah." She nodded her head. "Same story. Different country."

He stared at her for a moment. "Is it?" Those expressive eyes of hers watched him closely, waiting for him to explain his question. He caressed her cheek with a bent finger. "How do you feel about Anglos, Jordis?"

Jordis fumbled the coffee cup in her hand. She tried to grab it, but shaky hands and marked surprised weren't a good combination, and the cup tilted from her grasp. Michael managed to grab the cup before leftover chocolate mocha filled her lap. He tucked it aside.

"I . . . um . . . What do you mean?" Her soft voice contrasted with the look of amazement on her face.

Her eyes darkened slightly, the way they had last night when he'd kissed her. The realization that she wasn't wholly immune to him sent a jolt of testosterone pulsing through every cell of his body. He'd initially been reluctant to bring up the topic, but the more attracted to her he became, the more he ached to know her preference in men. Her reaction told him a lot, but he needed to hear her say the words.

Enjoying her discomfiture, he leaned back in his seat and undid the sole fastened button on his coat to counteract the sudden rise in his body temperature. "I think you know what I mean."

❧ ❧ | ❦ ❦

Jordis's eyes slid over him from head to toe in the few seconds it took her to adjust upright after the coffee scare.

Michael Remington had sex appeal in spades, and she suspected he knew it. His posture oozed confident masculinity. An odd set of contrasts comprised his persona. Staunchly proper and GQ in the office, he came off as conservative and straight-laced. Here, on a carriage ride wearing black jeans and a black sweater, he looked edgy and even a little dangerous.

He was quite yummy . . . for a white guy. Hell, who was she kidding? For any guy. The last thing she needed, however, was for him to know she thought so. So, she tried to keep her expression unreadable.

Holding her gaze, Michael pressed for an answer to his question. "There's that old cliché that women like their men tall, dark, and handsome." He was sporting a smile she'd bet a year's salary made women of every persuasion want to drop their panties. "I'm just curious. What's your perspective?"

Responding to the flirtatious mischief in his eyes, Jordis gathered her aplomb. "My perspective is there's usually a basis for most clichés." She positioned her back into the corner of the carriage bench farthest away from him. "I'd have to say tall, dark, and handsome always worked for me." She flashed her own mischievous grin.

He angled his body towards her. "Just how *dark* does your tall and handsome have to be?"

They stared at each other for five seconds that, to Jordis, felt more like five hours. "Are you . . . asking me . . . ?" Her voice trailed off. She dared not voice what she thought he was asking.

She was riding through the Plaza with the heir apparent to one of the most successful law firms in the city. Everyone knew he, as the only attorney amongst the living relatives of the founders of the firm, reigned as crowned prince and soon to be managing partner. He'd been labeled the most eligible bachelor at the firm. He was probably one of the most eligible bachelors in the city. Yet, no matter how many women threw themselves at him, he managed to avoid office interludes and serious relationships. Why he sat asking about her preference in men as if interviewing her to be his potential paramour, she couldn't fathom. Surely, she was missing something.

"What I'm asking, Ms. Morgan," his voice dropped half an octave, "is if you've ever had a white guy before?"

Her mouth fell open. Her nipples tightened under her shirt. The rousing image evoked by his question—having her way with this particular white guy—made her hormones dance. Her hand tightened into a ball on the seat.

He leaned closer, placing a hand on the side of the carriage beside her shoulder. The scent of his cologne—*that* cologne, the one that made her salivate and think of Spartacus—filled her. The aphrodisiac quality of the fragrance, marked with patchouli and sandalwood, made this interaction so much more troubling than the conversation alone. Her eyes closed.

His other hand gently touched her face. She opened her eyes.

"Well?" he asked softly.

"No." She hadn't. But, if she were ever going to have one, he'd be at the top of her list. He was easily the sexiest man she'd ever met. She hesitated, struggling against the loaded question she knew better than to ask, but she couldn't help herself. "Why?"

He smirked. "Do I really have to spell it out?"

She stared into his eyes, not asking the obvious question of whether he'd ever been with a woman like her before. It didn't really matter since he'd made his interest in her clear. How much of that interest was genuine and how much stemmed solely from curiosity, she didn't know. What she did know was she needed a change of topic before they ended up crossing the line again, a line that kept getting blurrier by the second.

"Michael, I think we need to talk about something else."

"Do we?"

"Yes." She pulled her coat tighter around her.

He studied her movement. "I tell you what. If you slide over here so I can keep you warm, I'll drop my line of questioning, and we can just enjoy the rest of the ride."

Step into my parlor said the spider to the fly. The nursery school line popped into her head as she considered his offer. She *was* getting cold again, but sidling up next to him didn't seem like a smart move.

"Come on, Jordis." He reached for her. "I promise to be on my best behavior."

Her posture stiff and unnatural, she allowed him to pull her close. After a few minutes, snow flurries began to fall. She raised a palm and caught a few flakes. She glanced at Michael as they melted in her hand. "It's starting to snow."

She didn't think anything was quite as beautiful as a carriage ride in the snow through the Country Club Plaza Christmas lights. The night fell around them in an enchanting flurry too beautiful to waste on worries. It wasn't as if he was going to jump her in public. She relaxed and they rode in silence, enjoying the view.

The evening got late. Reluctantly, Jordis broke into the snowy fantasy with a voice of practicality. "We should call it a night. I think we've monopolized the carriage enough for one evening."

"It's up to you. We have the carriage reserved for the rest of the night if you want to continue." He glanced at his watch. "Granted, they only run for another thirty minutes, but the thirty minutes are yours if you want them."

She struggled to resist the tempting offer, but she lost the battle. After a moment, she adjusted her coat in a way that covered her knees and placed her more firmly against his side. "Why don't we have him make one more loop around Seville Square and drop us by the bookstore? I parked in the garage right next door."

"Okay, sounds good." He instructed the driver as to their final run and tucked her tighter against him. As they approached the bookstore, Michael took an interest in her bag of books. He glanced in and pulled out the mega book on top. He checked the cover and glanced at her. "Stephen King? I never would have pegged you for a horror fan. You seem way too upbeat and Girl Scout for that."

"Guilty as charged." She flashed the Girl Scout sign. "But there's probably a lot about me you wouldn't suspect."

Made curious by that statement, Michael dove into the bag for her other treasures.

"Hey," she cried, grabbing for her bag. The movement placed her across his lap. Her hand squished the top of the bag closed. "A woman's reading material is private unless she offers to share."

"Umm, is that all I had to do to get you in my lap tonight?"

She straightened as if she'd been prodded with a poker.

Michael chuckled at the look on her face. He lowered his voice to a tease. "You know, you didn't have to come up with an excuse. You're welcome to climb into my lap anytime."

She tried not to smile at his comment, but she couldn't help herself.

A few seconds later, the carriage driver reined in the white stallion pulling the carriage and parked in front of the bookstore. Michael replaced her book and exited the carriage. As he helped her down, he paid close attention to the legs covered by her knee high boots. He pulled her close and whispered in her ear, "Especially, if you're wearing those boots."

Her grip on his arm tightened, and her heart pounded.

Tearing his eyes away from her, Michael released her long enough to tip the driver. When they stepped away from the carriage, they nearly bumped—literally—into Eric Covington escorting a tall, blue-eyed blond.

"Well, well. Small world," Eric clucked.

"Eric." Michael's jaw tightened.

"What brings you two here tonight?" Eric glanced at Jordis.

"I ran into Jordis coming out of the bookstore. We decided to grab a beverage and enjoy what's left of the Plaza lights."

Well, he'd given most of the truth, Jordis thought.

Eric's expression said he suspected there was more to the story. His eyes flicked to the carriage pulling off behind them. "Sounds good." He gave Jordis an ungracious smile before focusing back on Michael. "Anyway, I guess I'll see you in the morning. Usual time?"

"Yes. Same court as last time."

She looked between the two men. "What's going on tomorrow morning?"

The superior tilt of Eric's smile got more pronounced.

Michael answered. "Basketball. Some of the guys get together on a regular basis to play a few pickup games."

"Some of the guys?" Now she understood the superior glint in Eric's eyes. He wanted her to know he had an ace up his sleeve. Nothing like sports bonding to keep the good ole boys network strong and woman-free. "Only the guys in the firm are invited to play?"

"Well, Jordis, I doubt any of the women would really want to play with us," Eric said.

"I would."

Eric laughed. "Yeah, right. This isn't HORSE we're playing. We play a serious ball game. We don't want to have to take it easy because we've got girls on the court."

"So you're saying only men are allowed to play in the firm pickup game?"

Michael interrupted. "Of course not." He looked at Jordis pointedly. He'd surmised, correctly, she'd intentionally played the gender card. "Anyone is welcome to play, but no woman has ever decided to join us."

"Has one ever been invited?"

Michael didn't answer her.

She looked back at Eric and smiled victoriously. "Where's the game being played? I'd love to join you guys in the morning."

After going over the particulars of the game, Eric

walked away with his date and Michael shepherded her towards the parking garage. Coat collars turned up against the deepening cold, they strode quickly with Michael's arm firmly around her waist.

They entered the garage and approached her Charger.

Michael frowned. "You don't have another car?"

"No. There's nothing wrong with this car."

He glanced outside the parking garage at the snow flurries falling heavier now then glanced back at her. "Except it's useless in snowy weather. This model doesn't even have front wheel drive."

"I know. I've thought about that. I keep thinking I ought to get a four-wheel drive SUV or something, but I can't bring myself to part with the Bee. So far, the weather's been mild enough it hasn't mattered."

"Jordis, you make enough money to have more than one car. Why not buy a second car to drive in the winter?"

"I don't know. It just seems wasteful for a single person to have multiple cars, particularly if I'm only going to drive one of them a few months out of the year."

He cleared his throat and looked away.

"What?" she asked.

"Nothing."

She considered his expression. "Michael, exactly how many cars do *you* have?"

"Well . . ." He hesitated, as if reluctant to discuss the subject then he grinned. "If you don't count the Ford F350 I use to haul around my motorcycle, I have three."

Her face mirrored the incredulous tenor of her voice. "You own three cars, a truck *and* a motorcycle?"

"Yes, Ms. Do-Right. And maybe I should drive you

home in my weather-appropriate SUV."

She retrieved the bag of books he carried, opened her car door, and shook her head. She placed the books in the car. "I'll be fine. The snow isn't even sticking to the ground."

He glanced towards the wet street once again. No snow had accumulated. If she went straight home, she shouldn't face any challenging roads.

When he looked back at her, she couldn't help but smile. "You really are a dinosaur. I don't know whether to be flattered by your gallantry or insulted you think so little of my driving skills." She brushed a light dusting of snow off the shoulders of his coat.

"Be flattered." He grabbed one of her hands and kissed it.

Her heart did a little flip. The warm tingling sensation she'd been feeling since he'd charter a carriage ride to cheer her up ramped to a hotter setting.

"Make sure you go straight home. Kansas City weather is temperamental. This could turn heavy without warning."

She leaned into him without removing her hand from his. "Relax, Michael. I've got your number. If I run into any trouble, I promise I'll call."

"Unless you get a call from your brother."

She laughed. "Touché." She crossed her heart with her other hand. "I promise. No distractions. No diversions. If I need assistance, I will call." Before he could say anything else she added, "And I'll call to let you know I made it home safe."

He nodded, satisfied. "Okay." They stood staring at

each other. His hand wrapped around hers. He pressed their joined hands against his chest and pulled her closer. His voice dropped to a husky whisper. "I want to kiss you."

"I know."

"You know?" His lips curved and his other hand moved to shift loose hair behind her ear.

"Yeah, I know." She sighed. "And I want you to kiss me." She stepped back. "But you're not going to."

"I'm not?"

"No. You're not. We agreed that wasn't going to happen again."

"Did we? I don't remember that." He pulled her back against him.

"Michael . . ." She pulled away and stepped into the enclave created by her open car door. "I'm going home now. Thank you for dinner and the lovely carriage ride. I had fun."

"You're welcome." Michael slid his hands into his pants pockets.

She got into her car and started the engine.

After a moment, Michael turned and walked towards his SUV. Jordis watched his retreating back, regret strong in the pit of her stomach. Why did the sexiest man on the planet have to be her boss?

That thought had barely crossed her mind when Michael turned around and strode purposefully back towards her car. He yanked the car door open, reached in and pulled her up against him. With one hand inside her coat, firmly wrapped around her waist, and the other against the back of her head, he kissed her like the world was coming to an end.

She melted, completely.

Her hands grasped the lapels of his coat, and she kissed him back, releasing the pent up sexual frustration she'd fought all day. He pressed her against the side of her car, pushing his tongue deep as he devoured her mouth.

She responded in kind, pulling him tight against her so she could feel all his hard body parts with every thrust of his tongue. When they finally came up for breath, they were both panting.

He placed his forehead against hers. "For the record, I never agreed not to kiss you again. *You* were the one who stated we were both in agreement it would never happen again. I never conceded the point."

Such a lawyer, she thought, but didn't say. Her mind reeled. Standing with Michael's forehead pressed against hers reminded her of the last time she'd kissed a man on the Plaza: a man who had smelled just like Michael, a man who had rubbed his thumb along the base of her neck just like Michael, a man who had used his tongue . . . *just . . . like . . . Michael*.

Spartacus? She stood frozen, eyes fixated on his chest.

From somewhere outside herself, she heard her voice say, "You don't have to concede the point, counselor. You know we can't continue this given our work relationship."

With his hands bracketing her head, he lifted her face and stared into her eyes. "I can't seem to get you out of my system. Work relationship be damned. I'll find a way to handle this." He tapped a kiss against her lips and folded her back into her car. Right before he shut the door, he ordered, "Lock the door this time."

Inside her car, Jordis sat motionless except for her shaking hands. *Spartacus.* The thought assaulted her again.

Michael rapped a knuckle against the widow, making her jumped. He pointed to the lock and repeated, "Lock the door."

She complied. He was halfway to his SUV before she recovered enough presence of mind to put on her seat belt. When she looked up, he sat watching her from the seat of his Navigator. He wouldn't pull off until she did.

Shifting the Charger into *Reverse*, Jordis backed out of her parking space and exited the garage. Michael followed her to the highway, merging onto the northbound lanes of I-35 behind her and taking the interchange for I-169 North when she did. Her pulse sped up when she thought he might follow her all the way home. Then, he turned off at the exit leading to the ritzy Briarcliff West neighborhood.

Relief slid over her, easing her elevated blood pressure. She shuddered out shaky breaths, and her agitated mind finally registered Michael's comment before he'd ordered her to lock her door: *Work relationship be damned. I'll find a way to handle this.*

What was that supposed to mean?

CHAPTER 10

*J*ordis sat in the dark in front of her gas fireplace when she got home. She had the blower up high so it mimicked a roaring log fire. She'd wrapped herself in a fleece throw and her hands around a mug of hot chocolate. Her mind wandered back to New Year's Eve.

What she remembered about the gladiator included olive skin, large hands, a seductive voice, and odd colored eyes. She thought about how the gladiator had followed her out to the taxi. He'd been persistent about wanting to see her again to pick up where they'd left off.

Juliet, Michael's voice whispered in her head.

Last night in the elevator, she'd thought she'd heard him breathe that name. She'd dismissed it as her imagination. But had it been?

When they'd gotten carried away tonight, Michael had done something she'd never experienced before except when Spartacus had kissed her. No two men kissed exactly alike. She'd recognize that passionate, unique mixing of lips and tongue blindfolded. She'd certainly dreamed about it enough over the last few weeks.

Lady, you pack one hell of a kiss, he'd said that night.

Yeah. So did he.

The thought that Michael Remington had intruded on her midnight rendezvous dream had upset her this morning. Turns out, he'd always been a part of it. He'd thrown her off with that subtle, romantic kiss in the elevator. But even then, somewhere in the back of her mind, she'd known. Everything about him had been too familiar, right down to the way he smelled. She'd let her brother's call distract her from thinking it through last night.

"Crap!" She sat up, thunking her half-full mug down on the coffee table.

Michael was her gladiator. Those odd colored eyes she hadn't seen quite clearly, she now knew were gray. He'd cut his hair and traded his sexy costume for designer suits, but how could she not have seen it before? A haircut—is that really all it took to throw her off? Wasn't that as bad as Lois Lane not being able to tell Clark Kent was Superman because of a dorky pair of dark-rimmed glasses? Color her lame and stick her in a clichéd romantic comedy.

Did he know who she was? Had he known this whole time?

Surely, if he had connected her to the masked ball and his New Year's Eve kissing partner, he would have said something to her.

Unless his current pursuit was just a game to get to finish what he'd started that night.

The thought made her melancholy.

Whatever his awareness of her identity, that he was her gladiator made an already difficult situation more challenging. If he hadn't figured it out already, she didn't want him to. She didn't need him to connect her with the woman who made out with strangers on open balconies. She had a hard enough time dealing with her intense physical attraction to him and getting him to accept personal boundaries where she was concerned. Letting him know they had a shared history stemming from a steamy, anonymous encounter wouldn't help her cause.

She couldn't believe she'd been so obtuse about the matter. All the signs had been there. She simply hadn't wanted to see them. She hadn't wanted to spoil the fantasy her gladiator represented. She'd embraced her New Year's Eve memory not simply as naughty entertainment, but as a sign she might ignite that kind of passion someday in someone confident enough in his manhood to handle and accept all the facets of her personality.

Men tended to be attracted to women like her—smart, independent, financially secure—but ultimately, the glamour wore off. At some point, they began to expect her to be less in control and more needy. If she made advances in her career, they eventually felt threatened. It got real old real quick.

Keith had been a perfect example. The more her career advanced, the more pressure he'd exerted for them to attend his business functions at the exclusion of hers. Slowly, every bunch of flowers, gift or special dinner presaged some obligation he felt she should fulfill at his request. If she never heard the expression "with all the things I do for you" again, it would still be way too soon.

She'd never been one of those females who spent her formative years fantasizing about babies by a high school sweetheart or white picket fences or knights on white chargers. Like the heroine in that *Cheetah Girls* song her goddaughter used to love—what was it called? *Cinderella?*—she'd rather rescue herself.

Her father had disappeared shortly after the court finalized her parents' divorce so the vision of a man as protector and provider wasn't one she'd fostered. She'd always been driven and career-focused. Understanding it was up to her to provide for herself, she'd pursued a law degree with single-minded determination.

Last year, she'd learned how tenuous her sense of security really was. A horny senior partner who wouldn't take no for an answer, a late-night work session used as an ambush, and a he-said she-said scenario that left her on the losing side had nearly cost her everything. Luckily, a partner at her prior firm who'd believed her side of the story had known the hiring partner at RHM, and she'd quickly found a new job.

Talk about your double irony. This time, it wasn't just the senior partner who was horny. She wanted him right back. She wanted him right back, but she couldn't have him because of their work relationship. And now, she couldn't even hold onto her fantasy suitor because he was that same untouchable senior partner.

In some ways, knowing the man who had unleashed her inner vixen under a starry winter sky was the same man who'd turned her inside out in a firm elevator and in a public garage reassured her. At least she wasn't a complete harlot; she only lost control—and all sense of propriety—with one man.

The ring of her telephone interrupted her thoughts. Jordis lifted the phone from the arm of the couch, read the caller ID then hit *Ignore*.

Narisa.

She didn't feel like talking to her cousin right now. Although, Narisa would certainly get a kick out of this current twist of fate.

Her phone beeped a notice. Looking at her phone again, she saw Narisa had sent her a text message: *Stop avoiding me. You can't still be mad about New Year's Eve! Answer my calls, you witch!!*

Jordis shook her head. That was Narisa for you. When she'd stopped by her cousin's to chew her out for leaving her stranded that night, she'd made the mistake of telling Narisa about her run-in with the gladiator. Instead of being chagrined, Narisa had told Jordis to be thankful she'd been unavoidably detained.

Whatever. Her cousin getting laid—even by her gorgeous, professional football player new boyfriend—wasn't exactly unavoidable. Nevertheless, in Narisa's opinion, if not for her no-show, Jordis would have missed what Narisa considered the best part of Jordis's evening. Not only had Narisa thought the whole story exciting and sexily romantic, but she'd also encouraged Jordis to find the man and take him up on his date offer.

Well, Jordis had found him. Now that she knew he was her boss, no way could she take him up on his offer.

She'd allowed herself to get way more comfortable with the man tonight than she should have. He was quite charming and gallant when he wasn't in his brooding or domineering mode.

Thinking about how he'd handled Keith brought a smile to her lips. She'd thought Keith headed for an aneurysm when Michael told him to keep his hands to himself. Then, Michael had chartered the Cinderella carriage to make her feel better. His thoughtfully sentimental gesture had instantly grabbed her heart. By the time they'd finished the carriage ride, all she could think about was how much she wished they'd met under different circumstances.

His kiss at her car had practically curled her toes. Why couldn't she remember Keith ever kissing her that way? Brandt had always claimed she'd settled when she'd agreed to marry Keith, that he'd been expedient and comfortable—someone to present the power couple image prevalent in her social circle without the emotional investment of true soul mates.

There was nothing comfortable about Michael Remington. His blatant masculinity evoked heat and desire and consistently made her edgy, but it didn't matter. She couldn't have a liaison with him. She needed to keep her libido in check if she didn't want to face some pretty nasty and dire professional consequences.

Time to put her focus squarely back on partnership. Playtime with Mr. Remington was over. *Well*, she smiled again, *except for the ball game scheduled for tomorrow.*

৵ ৵ | ৻ ৻

All heads turned towards Jordis when she walked into

the gym the next morning. She had her hair pulled back in a high ponytail and wore an Under Amour workout suit in red with a white stripe down the side of the pants. The pant legs, unzipped at the bottom, showed a hint of white Nike hightops with a red *Swoosh*. She carried her own basketball under one arm and a duffle bag strapped over the other shoulder.

That she'd come dressed to play didn't surprise Michael, but her air of total confidence as she walked towards a court full of men did. This wasn't the lady who wore Michael Kors suits, three-inch heels, and French manicures. Those Nikes had seen court action. She hadn't put together some new outfit to impress the boys. She'd played ball before. Where and how well, they'd soon find out.

"Who's the lady?" Jackson Montgomery asked Michael. Due to his wife's advancing illness, Jackson had been holed up in the hospital so long it had taken a near act of Congress to convince him to come blow off some steam.

"That's Jordis Morgan," Eric Covington volunteered. His tone revealed exactly how perturbed he felt about her presence.

Chase followed with Royal McCormick, the partner in charge of the Business and Finance practice group.

"What's the big deal gents?" Chase asked. "The lady came to play. Since we have an uneven number of players today, Jordis will help even out the teams."

Only five guys had made it to the court that morning. Jordis made six. They would have to play three-on-three.

"Which team gets stuck with her?" Eric asked.

"I say the former college basketball stars get the girl." Royal slapped a hand on Eric's shoulder and grinned at his partners.

Chase and Michael looked at each other. Generally, the group tried to divide them, feeling they had an unfair advantage having played ball together at Michigan State. Today, the group apparently figured having a woman on their team would be such a handicap they wouldn't be much of a threat. Chase and Michael smiled at each other. Woman or no woman, they intended to wipe the floor with these guys.

Jordis stepped up to the group. "Gentlemen, how's it going this morning?"

"Just fine, lovely lady." McCormick advanced and shook her hand. "It's a pleasure to meet you. I'm Roy McCormick, Business and Finance."

"Hello, Roy." She smiled at the tawny-haired lawyer. "Jordis Morgan, Intellectual Property." She glanced around the bunch, introduced herself to Jackson Montgomery then turned back to Roy. "So, it's a pleasure meeting me, Roy, but not playing with me?"

"Um, well . . ." Roy looked to Michael for help.

Jordis laughed at his fumbling. "Don't worry, Roy. I won't hold it against you that you chose to pawn me off on the 'former college basketball stars.'"

"You heard that, huh?" McCormick smiled at her, non-apologetic.

"Yeah, I heard." She moved closer to Roy and smoothed the front of his shirt in a flirtatious gesture. Her eyes widened slightly in appreciation for the play of muscles under her hand. She left her hand resting over his heart when she looked deep into his eyes. "You sure you want to give me away, Roy, without even knowing if I can play?"

Roy licked his lips. "Darling, I'd love to take you on, but I don't think here's the right time or the place."

Michael's jaw tightened at McCormick's double entendre, and he fought the urge to pull Jordis away from his colleague. Watching her paw Roy's chest was breaking him out in hives.

Chase took one look at Michael's tense posture and grabbed Jordis by the arm, pulling her away from McCormick. "Well, then, Jordis, it looks like you're with us."

She looked over at Michael. "That okay with you, boss?"

Michael gritted his teeth at the boss title. She used it to annoy him and keep distance between them, reminding him their relationship as supervisory attorney and associate made a sexual relationship taboo.

"No problem at all, Miss Morgan." He wouldn't let her get to him today. He motioned for her basketball, and she tossed it lightly. "Now, get those pants off so we can play some ball."

He put extra schmooze on the "get those pants off" portion of his command. Her eyes flashed. She hadn't missed his intentional taunt.

She eyed him as she slid her athletic pants down her legs. His eyes followed the slow, deliberate movement of her hands, and his eyes narrowed. He had a weakness for her legs. A weakness she knowingly used to taunt him back. The lady was playing with fire. Her striptease and fierce attitude lured him to an edge he doubted she was prepared to handle.

When her pants and jacket finally came off, Jordis wore black spandex biking shorts with a red Nike basketball tank edged in white and stenciled with the number 23. The tank hung to her hips, but did little to hide her shapely backside. Michael's mouth went dry. He noticed the other men checking her out. He immediately wanted her to put her pants back on. It dawned on him having her on his team meant someone from the other team would be guarding her. Some other man would be putting his hands on her hips and backside to guard against her offensive moves on the court. The thought made him want to rescind her invitation to play.

When they lined up on the court, Michael consciously squared up against McCormick. He still had some residual angst from the flirtation that had gone on between the partner and Jordis. He wasn't giving McCormick any excuse to get up close and personal with her. Roy would enjoy that way too much. Chase took Jackson, which left Jordis and Eric guarding each other.

Eric tossed the ball to Jordis. "Ladies first. Take the ball out."

"Why thank you, Eric," Jordis said with a faux smile. She let him check the ball. When he stayed back, playing her loosely, she dribbled once and immediately put up a jumper for a three-point shot.

"Ho!" McCormick exclaimed, raising his hands above his head in the universal touchdown gesture. "Nothing but net." McCormick turned to Jackson and Covington. "Boys, did we just get played?"

Jordis winked at him, and McCormick eyed her with a little more heat.

Eric eyed her with a little more venom.

The game was about to get interesting.

Eric began to play more aggressively. Every time he touched Jordis defensively, Michael's teeth clenched. At the rate things were going, he would need a set of partials before the game ended.

Midway through the competition, Chase, Jordis and Michael led by ten points. Jordis got the ball again. She'd taken the last four shots over Eric and his expression showed exactly how he felt about that. When she went up for a jumper this time, Eric hammered her hard. Jordis hit the ground with a grunt.

Michael moved quickly, but Chase got to her first. "Foul, Covington! What the hell was that about?"

"What? All I did was block the shot. If she can't handle playing with the guys, she needs to get off the court."

"Bullshit, Covington. That was a cheap shot." Chase shoved him out of the way. "Don't let it happen again."

Chase turned as Michael stepped over, watching to see if he'd need to intervene between Michael and Covington.

Lucky for Eric, Michael only had eyes for Jordis. He squatted beside her. "You all right?"

"Yes. No harm done." She sat up and looked over at Eric, mumbling a curse under her breath.

Michael noticed the direction of her gaze. "I've got Covington from here on out."

"No. You don't."

Fury settled in Michael's chest. Fury he intended to use to put Covington in his place despite Jordis's determination to do this her way. He sensed another battle of wills coming. "Look, Jordis. That was intentional. He's trying to make a point, and I've had enough of these games between you two."

"Me too, and I'm about to put a stop to it." She held out a hand. "Help me up, please."

Michael gave her a tug up, and Chase moved in to huddle with them. "What's the plan? Michael, you taking Covington?"

Chase knew him well. "Yes."

"No," Jordis contradicted. "Covington's mine, Remington."

Chase looked between the two. He gave Michael a sympathetic look, but took the decision out of Michael's hands by asking Jordis, "What do you want us to do?"

She put out her hand. "Give me the ball and clear the field."

"Jordis—" Michael started, but she interrupted him.

"Michael, you interfere in this, and I'll turn that Jag parked outside into a crushed aluminum can. Let me handle Eric. Pick up your man and keep him out of my way."

Michael's brow creased at her reference to his Jag, but he nodded and stepped over to McCormick.

"Your lady all right, Remington?" McCormick asked.

"She's not my lady," Michael ground out.

McCormick chuckled. "Maybe not, but you sure want her to be."

Michael narrowed his eyes at his partner, wondering why he'd said that.

"Dude, it's written all over your face. I'm surprised Covington can still walk."

"If it were up to me, he wouldn't be able to."

McCormick watched Jordis check the ball for Eric. "Feisty one, huh?"

"You don't know the half of it."

Roy eyed Jordis pensively. "She wouldn't happen to have a sister?"

Michael stared at McCormick's grinning face. The man was a flagrant flirt and hopeless womanizer. "No. No sister. Just a younger brother."

Royal made a tsking sound. "Pity." When Michael gave him a discerning eye, Roy—who at an even six feet was several inches shorter than Michael—patted him on the shoulder. With laughter still in his voice, he soothed, "Easy, big guy. You can't fault a man for appreciating the scenery."

The men's focus went back to the game. Eric made a move to get around Jordis, and she swatted the ball away. Throwing her whole body into the move, she knocked him on his ass in the process.

"Oh, sorry. My bad. You okay, Eric?" She offered a hand to help him up.

He stared at her hand for a few seconds before extending his to let her assist him. "I'm fine. Let's go again, counselor."

This time Jordis had the ball. When Eric pressed her, she dribbled behind her back, slid past him and went for an easy layup. They kept at each other basket after basket. Eric would shove. Jordis would shove back. For every basket Eric made, Jordis made two. When she had an opening, Jordis drilled the ball to Chase or Michael for an easy shot, but for the most part, the other men accepted the rest of the game was the Jordis and Eric show.

By the final minutes of the game, Jordis had sunk nine baskets to Eric's five and Eric's frustration showed. His deteriorating attitude affected his performance. Jordis set up for the last shot. Eric crouched to guard her.

She kept her dribble out of his reach, adding some fancy footwork for good measure. Each time he tried for the ball, she outmaneuvered him. She toyed with him, dribbling the ball between her legs and behind her back a few times for show.

She dribbled left then right a few feet, Eric on her heels the whole time. She spun backwards, letting him trail her but not get a drop on the ball. After she'd dribbled around him a few times, she passed the ball behind her back, headed out of the paint towards the top of the key. Stepping theatrically outside the three-point line, she pivoted towards the basket and released the ball. Her hand hovered in the air, wrist bent in homage to her follow through.

Swish, nothing but net.

"I believe that's game, boys," Jordis purred before going for her towel and wiping her face.

Roy fisted his hands on his hips. "Okay, give. Where did you play?"

She smiled. "Stanford. Lady Cardinal. Conference champs three years in a row. National champions my senior year."

Nodding, Roy grinned back at her. "Ah. That explains the red jersey."

Smile still in place, she picked up her belongings and headed for the locker room.

Behind her, Eric hung in half, hands braced against his knees while he tried to catch his breath.

McCormick stepped to Covington and patted him on the back. "Damn, son, the lady took you to school." He glanced at Jordis's retreating back. "And looked mighty fine doing it." With a smirk in Remington's direction, McCormick grabbed his bag and headed for the men's locker room.

Chase placed a hand on Michael's shoulder. "I think McCormick's in love." He laughed at the predatory expression Michael gave him and lifted his hands. "Don't shoot the messenger." He bent to snatch up their duffle bags. "Just saying."

Michael took his bag from Chase and followed after Roy. "Did you know she could play ball like that?"

"Nope." Chase walked alongside him. "That tidbit wasn't included in her resume, *boss*."

Now the joker was intentionally screwing with him. Michael's nerves had had enough. As they entered the locker room, Michael leaned his shoulder into Chase and shoved hard.

Chase landed with an echoing thud against the lockers and laughed. "Tsk. Tsk. Someone's awfully touchy this morning." His jovial mood not shaken in the least, Chase headed for the showers.

❧ ❧ | ❦ ❦

Twenty minutes later, Chase and Michael strolled towards the gym exit. When they hit the sidewalk, Michael paused. Jordis's car sat in the parking lot under a shade tree. "She's still here."

"She who?" Chase feigned ignorance.

"You know, Chase. You keep messing with me, and I'm going to kick your ass."

"You and what army?" Chase jumped aside with a

laugh when Michael dropped his duffle and grabbed for his head. Skirting Michael's grasp, he conceded, "Okay. Okay. Sorry man. You're just such an easy target these days. You need to take care of that."

If it had been anyone but Chase, Michael would have pretended not to understand. Chase knew him too well. They'd been friends since they were twelve and Chase's mother had joined the firm as his grandfather's secretary. "If only it were that easy."

"It's that easy if you let it be." Chase turned serious. "Not every woman is like your ex, Michael. You've got to stop looking for gold diggers and schemers around every corner and let yourself relax around a woman.

"I spent a lot of time with Jordis when she helped me with my last case. I can guarantee you the woman in there—" He tilted his head towards the gym. "—isn't impressed with your position and doesn't need your money. And, given her comment on the court earlier, we can also conclude she's not even impressed with your ride."

They both glanced at his 2010 silver Jaguar XF, with plates REM ESQ, remembering Jordis's aluminum can threat.

"If you're not sure you're interested, McCormick looked like he'd be more than happy to step in."

"Not. Gonna. Happen."

"I don't know, man." Chase chuckled. "After watching that lady play ball, I have to tell you if I didn't know you were already hooked, McCormick would be the least of your worries."

Before Michael could comment, Jackson exited the building and approached them. "Well, that was quite a game." He chuckled. "Certainly full of surprises. Any chance Jordis will want to play with us again?"

"After the crap Covington pulled, I doubt it," Michael replied.

Jackson shrugged. "She seemed to handle him well enough. She doesn't impress me as a woman who backs down from a challenge."

"And you'd be right." Chase looked pointedly at Michael.

"Well, one of you should ask her. We've got the Metropolitan Bar Association basketball tournament coming up in a couple of months. We could use her. Maybe we could win the trophy back from Shauke, Hardeman and Lowe." Jackson turned towards his car. "See you guys next week."

Michael and Chase waved him off then Michael checked his watch, wondering what was taking Jordis so long. Soon the parking lot on this side of the building would empty. The private court at the back of the facility cost more to rent and generally only got reserved for nighttime events and fundraisers. Michael gladly paid the higher fees to have a private court uninterrupted by youth league practices and female patrons more interested in picking up guys than working out. Other than their firm games, this court didn't see much activity during early weekend hours.

Michael picked up his discarded bag and told Chase he was going back in to check on Jordis. Chase gave him a fist bump and walked away. McCormick and Covington exited the building, said their goodbyes to Michael, and strolled towards two of the remaining five cars in the lot. Michael reentered the gym to search out Jordis.

Chapter 11

*J*ordis lay with her back against the locker room bench, legs straddling either side, feet on the floor. Her side hurt where Eric had elbowed her dozens of times, and she could feel the wrist on her shooting arm cramping up. She hadn't played ball in a while. She certainly hadn't expected to go at it this hard during what was supposed to be a friendly pickup game.

The effort to get her tank off had been excruciating. Bruises had started to form along her side and rib cage. They wouldn't be pretty come tomorrow. She lifted her arm over her eyes and winced at the painful tug along her side. She needed a shower, but the thought of trying to pull off her sports bra made her cringe.

A knock sounded on the locker room door.

"Jordis, you in there?"

Michael.

"Come on in."

Michael rounded the corner and saw her laid out on the locker room bench.

Jordis dragged herself to an upright position, her legs still straddling the bench.

"You all right?"

"Yeah. Just a few bumps and bruises. Nothing a hot shower, some ibuprofen, and a nap won't cure."

Michael looked down at her midsection and cursed. He dropped his bag and squatted beside her. "Good, Lord." He ran his fingers lightly over purple and blue blotches along her right rib cage.

She flinched at his touch. "It looks worse than it is. I bruise easily."

His fingers traced across her midsection. The pain of her bruises scattered, leaving a slow boil in its place. He smelled good. It wasn't the woodsy fragrance he usually wore. This scent smelled crisp and clean, with a bit of citrus. His sporty fragrance, she thought. It made her want to get physical with him in a way that had absolutely nothing to do with sports. His fingers caressing her skin didn't help. His touch, his smell, his words were messing with her equilibrium. She couldn't think when he touched her like this.

She scooted back along the bench, breaking their skin contact. The movement freed her ribs from his touch, but he dropped his hand to a thigh covered by black spandex.

"Maybe I should take you to the emergency room for x-rays."

"No. Trust me. I've had much worse than this."

He looked into her eyes as if trying to judge her

forthrightness. "Yes, maybe you have." Absently, he rubbed her thigh as he spoke. "Doesn't mean we should ignore it. That push and shove match got intense. Covington came at you pretty hard. You should have let me take him."

Jordis placed a hand on top of his to still its movement and quiet the tremors he'd set off in her nether region. "I fight my own battles, Remington. You need to remember that."

"I gave you the lead today, *Morgan*, because you insisted, but I'm not a man who stands by and lets his wo— . . . people be bullied. One day, Covington's going to cross a line with you that he finds me standing on the other side of. *You* need to remember *that*."

He looked down at her hand. He frowned before running an index finger over a polished nail. No French manicure graced her nails today. She wore only clear polish over her natural nails. He seemed fascinated by that.

"Something wrong?" she asked.

He looked into her eyes, searching for something. "No." He took a deep breath and rubbed a hand along the back of his neck.

She recognized the move as a sign something bothered him. Whatever it was, he pushed it aside.

He placed his other hand on her opposite thigh and changed back to the topic she thought she'd escaped. "If you're all right, why were you lying in here half dressed?"

Her leg flexed beneath his touch. The movement made him look down. Jordis became conscious of her legs spread wide over the bench. Feeling exposed, she started to swing her far leg over so she could close her legs. Michael stopped her.

He shifted his position so that he knelt on one knee, one hand on each of her thighs. "Answer my question, Jordis."

Hyperaware of his hands on her thighs, she found it difficult to speak. "I had a hard time getting my jersey off. I couldn't bring myself to try for the rest."

Michael's gaze dropped to her sports bra, lingering long enough for her nipples to pebble under his gaze. His voice deepened. "I could help you with that."

When his eyes returned to hers, they were that smoky gray that reminded her of storm clouds. The color of lust, she decided. The color, the look, the man, all combined to make blood rush through her veins and pool in her sweet spot. She swallowed, fighting the dryness in her throat. With his hands so close to the apex of her thighs, all she could think about was letting him help her with that and a whole lot more.

She fought the urge.

She'd resolved to take a stronger stance on this whole lust thing. Right now, she silently questioned whether that resolve would hold.

ৡ ৡ | ৵ ৵

Taking her silence as encouragement, Michael slid his hands up her legs. When they neared the crease where her legs joined her torso, she said his name in a breathless whisper. The sound of her longing tapped the adrenaline in him that hadn't yet dissipated from the ball game. The desire that had bombarded him earlier when she'd stripped off her sweats filled him. The chemically-charged emotion churned together with the jealousy he'd felt when she'd flirted with McCormick and overlaid the possessiveness unleashed by Covington's manhandling of her.

He wanted her.

He'd wanted her since the moment he'd seen her standing across the conference room that first day. No, he'd wanted her since he'd touched her for the first time New Year's Eve. The complication of their work situation had done nothing to chill his craving. That, in itself, told him this wasn't some passing hormonal attraction. Denying himself what he wanted only prolonged a turmoil that wouldn't dissipate until he'd made her his.

His thumbs angled down towards the bench. As they crested, he slid his hands into the crease of her legs and rubbed both thumbs against her center. A gasp escaped her lips, and her hands went immediately to his wrists.

He ignored her hands and circled his thumbs against their prize. Without ceasing the motion of his thumbs, he leaned into her neck and kissed it. Her skin tasted salty after her workout on the court. The natural taste of her ratcheted up his desire. He swiped the tip of his tongue against her skin then nipped the spot with his teeth.

She shivered and satisfaction rushed through him. She wanted him. She may not want to want him, but her body craved his touch as much as his craved hers.

He pulled back to check her eyes. He would know for sure when he saw her eyes.

Yep. They were that dark foresty green of desire she couldn't hide even when she could mask her emotions in other ways. Triumph mixed with the hunger he nurtured, and he moved one hand from the damp heat he'd created between her legs to grasp her by the neck. He kissed her deep and with longing. Gone were the gentle, seductive, courting kisses. This kiss said I want you, all of you, and right now.

Jordis pulled back from him, her chest rising and falling rapidly as she tried to catch her breath. "What are you doing?"

"If you have to ask, I'm not doing it right."

"Michael, you can't possibly . . . I need a shower."

He couldn't suppress the lusty smirk that tilted his lips. "Yeah, let me help you with that." His hands went to her midsection. "Who knew you were hiding all these muscles under those designer clothes?" He rubbed a palm against the slight indentations outlining her abdominals. "It's damn sexy."

She gave a nervous laughed. When his hands moved to the elastic bottom of her sports bra, her breathing stopped.

He began to move the fabric up. "Why don't we get this off so I can see what else you've been hiding under your Michael Kors?"

Jordis's eyes widened, and she placed her hands on top of his to stop him. Her gaze darted towards the shower stall then over to the locker room door. Though furtive, her glances told Michael everything he needed to know. She might be wondering about the wisdom of getting in a public shower with him present and was probably calculating the chances of them getting caught. She didn't, however, seem opposed to his presence per se.

"You shouldn't be in here, Michael. I've got this."

"You couldn't do it alone before. What's changed?"

"I'll take a shower later."

"Don't you have to meet Miss Gardner at the office soon?"

Jordis closed her eyes and sighed. She clearly hadn't factored in the client appointment.

He removed her shoes and socks then stood and offered her his hand. "Come on."

They stared at each other, motionless, his stubbornness bouncing against her will.

"Let me help you, Jordis. I won't do anything you don't want me to do."

Without saying a word or breaking eye contact, she took his hand and stood. Her head dropped as she mumbled under her breath, "Maybe that's part of the problem."

Michael stifled the grin that threatened his face, not letting on he'd heard her hushed admission. He led her to the shower stall, leaned in and turned on the water, careful to adjust the temperature so it wasn't too hot. He turned her so she faced the shower, her back to him. "Raise your arms."

A grunt of pain escaped when she got her arms all the way up.

"Easy." He pushed the stretchy material up her sides, using all his will power not to brush her full breasts with his fingers as he lifted the sports bra to free them.

After he pulled the bra up and off, Jordis dropped her arms across her chest. He could tell she had some discomfort, but she hid it well, exhibiting the classic stoicism of a trained athlete. Knowing she'd had a college basketball career shed additional light on her personality. The drive, the discipline, the ability to take hits from an opponent but keep pressing forward were skills she'd mastered playing ball.

"Now the bottoms."

She looked over her shoulder at him. "Don't be crazy. Those I can definitely manage by myself."

He slid his hands to her waist and pressed himself fully against her back. His arousal nested at the juncture of her buttocks and lower back. "You sure about that?" His hands traveled around to her abdomen, gliding through drops of water splattered on her skin from the shower spray. "I'd be happy to help. Maybe I could wash your back."

Her defined abdominal muscles flexed beneath his palms. Her eyes closed. "Michael, enough."

"Enough? I haven't even started yet." He dropped his lips to her neck, alternating between nipping and nibbling. His large hand eased down her stomach and wayward fingers pushed inside the band of her spandex.

Jordis pressed a hand firmly over his from the outside of her shorts and instinctively pushed her hips back to avoid his touch. The movement rubbed her behind against his erection. The thin layer of spandex shielding her buttocks taunted the bulge beneath his athletic pants. He grew firmer against her, and Jordis's knees released as she tried, but failed, to stifle a moan.

He dipped behind her and grasped her securely around the middle with his other hand. Her shapeliness nested over his erection, bursting the fount of lust he'd heretofore been able to keep under a tight lid.

His cheek leaned against the side of her head, and he placed his lips so his breath could tickle her ear. "I want you."

The hand beneath the waistband of her spandex moved

lower, undeterred by the pressure of her hand. He smoothed past soft curls and fingered her lightly. The sound she emitted fell somewhere between a startled breath and a whimper. Her hand clamped tighter over his.

"You're wet for me," he choked out in a gruff voice. "Why do you keep fighting this? Let me show you how great it could be between us."

He stood wrapped around her moving nothing but the middle finger of the hand between her thighs. Jordis, tight with tension, radiated indecision. Her shallow respiration betrayed her arousal, and her hand squeezed down on his as if she intended to stop him, but she didn't push his hand away.

After what seemed like an eternity of silence, Michael braced himself to have to let her go. He sighed out her name questioningly.

Her desperate reply rasped through her vocal cords. "M-Michael, what are you doing to me?"

Instinctively, he understood the psychological import of the question. They stood in the middle of a public locker room where anyone could walk in on them. Under normal circumstances, he had no doubt this would be the last place Jordis would ever consider entertaining a man's advances, but the sexual tension between them denied rational thought. He couldn't think beyond the immediate feel of her in his arms. Apparently, neither could she because to his astonished relief, she slowly relaxed her restraining hand and slid it up to rest lightly on his forearm.

A thrill rippled through him. He fought for control. Losing it like an inexperienced adolescent would do little to advance his long-term plans. He wanted to take this woman to a place that left her totally weak for him. With that thought in mind, he let his fingers dabble languidly, taking a detour now and then at the nodule of nerves that comprised her pleasure point.

Jordis writhed against him. When she let out a long, deep moan, he filled her with two fingers. Her vaginal walls flexed around the intimate entry, and her legs began to tremble. She dropped the arm she'd kept over her breasts and braced her hand against his thigh.

Michael's fingers played rhythmically inside her, and he raised his free hand to an exposed breast. Dropping his lips to her neck once more, he tortured her with lips and tongue all the while stroking with one hand and stimulating a nipple with the other.

Jordis's pelvis began to rock against his fingers. She dropped her head back to his shoulder, opening her neckline to greater attention. Soon, the urgent gyrations of her hips communicated the intensity of her need for fulfillment. She pulsed then constricted around his fingers. The compressions announced her impending release.

Michael squeezed a nipple and slid a third finger inside her. "Come for me, beautiful."

With a loud keening moan, Jordis shattered. His erotic command pushed her right over the climatic edge. His hand continued an easy rhythm between her thighs, and he supported her while she rode out the spasms rocking her body.

Spent, she collapsed loosely against him, breathing deeply. Her eyes closed.

He removed his fingers and rested his hand against her *mons*. "Your shower's ready," he whispered. "Invite me to join you."

She shook her head in the negative. She turned in his embrace, forcing his hand to vacate her shorts. Sliding inside his open athletic jacket, Jordis pressed herself against his chest, her forearms bent between them so her breasts were covered once again.

Her head landed against the crook of his neck, tucked beneath his chin. "I shouldn't have let you do that." When she finally looked at him, those kaleidoscope eyes revealed more than they ever had before. "I shouldn't have, but I can't seem to find the decency to regret it. How screwed up is that?"

"It's not screwed up, Jordis. We're consenting adults. What we do is nobody's business but ours." Placing his hand at the base of her jaw, he lowered his head and kissed her softly.

She pulled away. "It's not that simple and you know it. You can't be objective about my work if we're . . ." Her voice trailed off.

"Having mad, passionate sex?" he finished. His lips curved into a wicked smile.

She shivered. "Yes, that." Her voice trembled. Her hands slid around his waist, her breasts now flush against him. "Please, Michael. You've proved I'm not as good at resisting your full-court press as I thought I was. I need you to back off."

He sighed and hugged her close, pressing a kiss against her forehead. He recognized her entreaty for what it was— fear. She felt the pull between them like he did. They both knew where this was headed. It seemed almost inevitable. The only question was when. She'd told him to back off, but in that moment, he heard the truth. She was afraid. She was as afraid of her attraction to him as he was unnerved by his feelings for her.

Something loosened inside him. The knots he'd been tied in for the past two weeks slid free of his gut and disintegrated. He didn't want her to be afraid—not of him, not of anything ever again, because he truly cared for her. He didn't just need to scratch an itch. He needed her in particular.

Today, he wanted to set them both free, but this wasn't the right time or the right place. The first time he made love to her shouldn't be in a public gym shower or across some locker room bench. He intended to take his time and love her thoroughly, which deserved a bed or at least a rug in front of a fireplace.

He squeezed her. Her forehead rested against his chin. Through his cotton T-shirt, he could feel the peaks of her naked breasts. A powerful gush of déjà vu ensnared him for the third time in three days. Memories of New Year's Eve overtook him: *Juliet, on the balcony. Her dress drooped to her waist. His arms braced around her as he shielded her from view by pressing her naked breasts against his bare chest.*

As Jordis stood in his arms, her height matching that of his Juliet, Michael couldn't believe he'd been so preoccupied with finding differences between the two women he'd initially overlooked Jordis always wore heels. Until today, he'd never stood next to her in anything other than stilettos or platform pumps.

The first time he'd held her like this, he'd wrapped his arms around her to shield her from wandering eyes. The same feelings of protectiveness came over him now, even though he was the one from whom she currently needed protection.

He moved his hands to her waist and turned her towards the shower stall. Guiding her in and drawing the curtain closed behind her, he said without thinking, "Wash up, milady. I'll wait for you in the gym."

A loud clunk resonated from behind the curtain.

"Jordis, you all right?"

"Y-yes. I'm fine. Be done in a jiffy."

Her voice sounded shaky. She'd obviously knocked something over, but he decided to let it go. He needed to focus on a solution for this ethical dilemma. He was her supervising attorney, but last night, he'd gotten a glimpse of what they could be together, and he wanted it. He wanted a chance to spend more time with her, to take more carriage rides with her, to make love to her. How could he get her to stop pushing him away?

Should he tell her he was the gladiator from New Year's Eve? Part of him wanted to, but the other part didn't want to risk it. She'd made it clear, as Juliet, she didn't want to see him again.

That was no longer an option. In approximately forty-eight hours, they'd be spending every workday together.

One thing he knew for sure. This time, he had no intention of letting her walk away.

He glanced back at the shower curtain on his way out of the locker room. He had two days to come up with a plan.

ॐ ॐ | ॐ ॐ

On the south side of the city the next evening, Eric Covington stood outside his parents' Mission Hills estate and took a deep breath. Sunday dinner at the Covington house—that sacred weekly tradition—was not to be missed. The ever-dutiful son, he arrived right on time, promptly fifteen minutes early.

Eric rang the doorbell. He had a key, but Covington decorum dictated he never let himself into his parents' home unless they were away and the servants had the day off. He heard the tumblers disengage. His parents' housekeeper swung open the heavy oak door.

"Mr. Eric, it's nice to see you," Maggie said in English flavored with a heavy Mexican accent. Her name was short for Magdalena, but no one in the Covington family ever used her given name.

Eric stepped into the foyer, removed his suit coat and handed it to Maggie without a word.

"Your parents are in the sitting room."

"Of course. Where else would they be?" He headed to greet his parents.

In a lilting tone, Maggie mocked under her breath, "Of course. Where else would they be?"

Eric stopped and narrowed his eyes, watching Maggie hang his jacket in the coat closet. He'd caught the sound of her murmur.

Unaware he watched, she continued in a whisper, "A 'thank you' would have sufficed, *mierdita*."

He didn't know what the Spanish word meant, but he surmised it wasn't complimentary. He raised a brow when Maggie turned and spotted him. She gave him a blank look, hands still at her sides.

"Anything you want to say to me, Maggie?"

"No, sir."

Eric gave a smug nod. "I didn't think so."

He left Maggie and entered the sitting room. His mother, Georgina Covington, stood by the fireplace with back reed straight, hair flawlessly coiffed, and makeup applied with the precision of a Hollywood makeup artist. She looked like a walking Barbie doll, right down to the blond hair. In her case, the color had come with birth, although it had been enhanced by a talented salon artist's application of lowlights.

The perfect businessman's wife, his mother had advance degrees in keeping up appearances, making her husband look good, and being the proper hostess. Impeccably groomed as ever, in her navy Chanel sheath dress with the proper hemline just below her knees, she made an elegant picture. She chatted with his father, who stood at the bar pouring what Eric suspected was his second or third scotch of the evening.

Georgina and Blake Covington made quite a pair. A throwback to the days when old-monied families made sure to marry their offspring to each other to keep the haves having and the have-nots from sullying the bloodlines.

Eric was their only child. He wasn't surprised by this. His mother was a cold fish, but then she probably had to be to remain married to Blake Covington for over thirty-five years. Eric was only surprised his mother had ever given his father the opportunity to assume the copulation position long enough to ejaculate the sperm it took to make him.

Georgina Covington looked up as her son entered the room. "There's my sweet boy." She spread her hands, which had been positioned in a double-handed hold around a glass of red wine, and opened her embrace to him.

He dutifully approached and placed a bland kiss on each cheek. "Mom." He glanced over at his father. "Dad."

"Eric. Come on in, son. Drink?" Blake gestured with his half-empty tumbler.

"Sure." He could use a drink. Sunday evenings with his parents were usually not to be taken straight. Sure enough, his father hadn't even finished pouring Eric a scotch—knowing Eric preferred whiskey—when the drill started.

"I understand you'll be taking over as second chair on the Metra Pharmaceuticals case. That'll be quite a feather in your cap, son. Even more so, if you get Remington to let you argue a few motions before the court."

"Dad, a decision hasn't yet been made as to who will be the new second chair."

"I thought Chase Hager was all set to take over the Werner case from Jackson Montgomery. There's no way he can handle both. What's to decide?"

"There are several other senior associates who stand a good chance of receiving the appointment."

"There's no one in your class with the credentials or pedigree you have. Remington would be foolish to pass you over."

"I agree, but with Jordis Morgan at the firm now, nothing is a given."

"Jordis Morgan? What kind of name is *Jordis*? It's a woman?"

Eric nodded.

"Pretty?"

"As a matter of fact, yes."

"I see."

"No, dad. It's not like that. Remington likes to win too much to let his libido drive his case strategy." Eric said the words, but after yesterday, he wasn't so sure he believed them.

Blake guffawed. "Son, there's not a man on the planet who hasn't been ruled by his dick against his will at one point or another."

"Blake!" his mother chastised from across the room, taking exception to her husband's graphic language.

"I'm sorry, Georgie, but the truth is the truth. Remington puts his briefs on one leg at a time like the rest of us." His father turned back to him. "You need to make sure that girl's not an issue."

"How, exactly, do you suggest I do that?"

"Son, if you're not capable of revealing an adversary's incompetence, then you have absolutely no future in high-stakes litigation." His father turned and headed for the dining room. "Let's be seated. Dinner should be ready."

Eric glanced down at the unwanted scotch in his hand and started to take a drink. Thinking better of it, he dropped the tumbler on the sideboard as he followed his parents into the dining room. He'd need a drink by the time his father finished maligning his legal skills and detailing his shortcomings over dinner, but he'd wait until he got home and drown out the memory of his father's voice with the fifty-year-old Tennessee whiskey he had stashed beneath his bar.

The movement of his feet slowed on the way to the dinner table. At the moment, he'd rather be anywhere other than about to sit across the dinner table from the old man. His father never tired of rehashing the same old story: Eric should have come to work at the firm in which his father was a partner. If he had, Eric's future would have been guaranteed.

His father never understood the last thing he wanted was the man looking over his shoulder every minute of his career. He'd thought signing on with a firm as large and reputable as his father's would give him the same opportunities for advancement and a chance to show he could make partner without riding his sire's coattails.

Jordis Morgan flashed through his mind. He pondered the coincidence of her and Michael being together on the Plaza Friday night and then being the last ones left in the gym yesterday morning. He was still stewing over the ass whipping Jordis had given him on the court. The thought of her alone with Remington inside the gym only pissed him off more.

From what he could see, his dad was right. He was losing the bid for second chair in the Metra Pharmaceuticals case for all the wrong reasons. If Jordis got the Metra assignment and handled it successfully, he'd be hard pressed to win the IP litigation partnership spot up for grabs this year.

He needed to find a way to take Jordis Morgan out of the picture, especially with Remington seemingly making case decisions with his privates. If he let her skirts outmaneuver him, his father would never let him live it down. He was through taking a back seat to the leggy sextress. He had no intention of conceding this case appointment without a fight. Time to get proactive and find out what Jordis was really made of.

Eric smiled for the first time since entering his parents' home. Monday morning, the games began.

CHAPTER 12

*J*ordis got to the office early on Monday and sat at her desk finalizing notes from her Saturday conference with Miss Gardner. The conference had gone well. They'd made a lot of progress and covered a lot of background information. During the meeting, Jordis decided to help the young lady get current and back child support in addition to helping with her landlord-tenant issue. She figured it did no good to fix the housing issue if the young woman continued to struggle to make ends meet and feed her child.

She made a final notation on her memo to file then let her mind drift to the past weekend. Michael Remington had called her "milady." She'd been leaning against the body wash dispenser in the locker room shower as she tried to remove her shorts when he'd let the word slip. Her shock had been so severe she'd accidentally pulled the dispenser off the wall.

He knew who she was. She didn't know when he'd figured it out or why he hadn't said something to her, but she'd spent all weekend wondering what to do about the matter.

Confront him?

Continue to play clueless?

Neither approach boded well for her desire to second chair the Metra Pharmaceuticals case.

She took a deep breath to calm herself. Maybe she'd jumped to conclusions. Perhaps Michael didn't know for sure she was the anonymous Juliet. Maybe he hadn't confronted her because he simply suspected and hadn't found a way to confirm it. She had to be careful not to tip her hand until she knew for sure what he knew one way or the other.

A movement at the corner of her eye made her look up. Eric Covington strode into her office dangling a file folder in one hand. He shut the door and propped himself against it.

Curious, Jordis laid down her pen. "Eric, to what do I owe this unexpected pleasure?"

He gave her a charming smile. "It seems I underestimated you." He glanced toward the file on her desk with its label color-coded to indicate a pro bono matter. "Again."

"Really?" Sarcasm laced her voice. "In what way?" She stood and gathered her paperwork into a neat pile.

"You're good. I'll give you that. I never thought you'd be able to play the sex card with Michael Remington. He's known to be immune. Alyson certainly hasn't had any luck throwing herself at the partner. But I guess every man has his weakness."

Jordis step around her desk and leaned her butt against the front edge. "Excuse you?" She crossed her arms and stretched out her legs, crossing one foot over the other.

"No need to feign ignorance with me, Jordis. You and Remington looked mighty cozy together on the Plaza last Friday night." Eric pushed himself off the door. "To think, last week, I'd actually considered apologizing for my behavior towards you. We got off on the wrong foot. Granted, we both want the partnership appointment at the end of the year, but I didn't think that meant we had to act like adversaries."

He stopped in front of her.

"I've never considered you an adversary, Eric, except, of course, when you've made yourself one."

He dropped his folder on her desk, and his hands went up in that gesture of truce he was famous for. "I know. I know. *Mea culpa.* I tend to be very competitive. You shouldn't take it personally." He stepped closer. "Especially since it seems you and I are cut from the same cloth."

Unease shimmied all over her at his invasion of her personal space. "I'm nothing like you."

"No? So, you're saying I shouldn't be congratulating you on your new case assignment?"

She smiled, but her demeanor remained cool. "Why, Eric, I didn't think you were that broken up about my assignment to the Gardner case, but thanks for the congratulations."

Eric chuckled and glanced casually around her office. Something on the wall caught his attention, and he walked over to where her diplomas and awards hung. His eyes stopped on her certificate for Order of the Coif, the prestigious legal national honor society for the top ten percent of a graduating law class. He frowned at the certificate. He gave her a curious look before he glanced back at the wall and her Stanford Law School diploma. He noted the date. "You're two years older than me?" he asked, his voice incredulous.

She shrugged. She'd caught his expression at her Order of the Coif certificate. He was surprised all right, but she suspected it had less to do with her age and more to do with his befuddlement in the face of evidence to contradict his arrogant assumption she was less qualified than him.

His question about her age didn't surprise her, however. People frequently thought her younger than her true age. Most people guessed her age at an average of five years off the mark. Many thought her eight to ten years her junior—at least based upon looks.

With law firms' penchant for docking lateral associates a year or two of seniority upon transfer, she'd lost a year of seniority with each of her firm moves, making her older than any other associate on her team. Among his other off-base opinions, Eric apparently had assumed she was younger than him.

Leaving his perusal of her credentials, Eric returned to stand in front of her. "What were we discussing? Oh, yeah." He slid his hands into his pants pockets. "You know I wasn't congratulating you on the Gardner case."

"No? Then what were you talking about?"

"I'm asking if you used your considerable feminine assets," his eyes scanned down her body, "to stack the deck in your favor for the Metra Pharmaceuticals second chair assignment."

"Don't insult me. I don't trade sex for professional advancements."

"No?"

"No." Her brain flashed the memory of her and Michael in the gym locker room on Saturday, but she pushed it away. That's not what that had been about.

He studied her for another minute. "So, it's just a coincidence you and Remington happened to come out of the gym together Saturday morning?"

Jordis's jaw clenched. Knowing Eric had waited outside to see when they'd left annoyed her. "He was being a gentleman, Eric." Her hands dropped to the desk beside her hips, her fingers grasping the edge. "He didn't want me to come out to an empty parking lot. I was slow getting dressed. Seems I had some sore muscles and bruises from being pounded on the basketball court." She looked pointedly at him.

Eric made a face at her mention of bruises. "If that's really the case, then I apologize for that . . . and for my insulting insinuation." He stepped closer. "Let me make it up to you."

"Make it up to me how?" Skepticism moved in to dance with the unease still racing along her spine. Was he being sincere or was this a case of keep your friends close and your enemies closer? Her instincts shouted he was up to something.

"Why don't you let me buy you lunch?"

She uncrossed her legs to stand, but he moved so his feet straddled her ankles, preventing her from rising. She stared at him blankly, incredulity making her momentarily speechless.

"I'm serious." He reached for her face. "I'd like us to start over."

Her hand went up automatically. "Eric, what are—"

The opening of the door sounded behind him. Eric jumped away, the action and the expression on his face making him look guilty.

Michael Remington paused in the doorway, his hand on the doorknob. He considered Eric. "Sorry to interrupt." He glanced at Jordis, a hard look in his eyes. "Eric, I need to borrow Jordis for a meeting. It doesn't appear you two were in the middle of anything important."

"Just making plans to go out." Eric retrieved his file off the desk and headed for the door.

Jordis frowned at his misleading comment. She stood to correct him, but he interrupted her before she could.

"Jordis, I'll catch you later." He left, but not before giving her a smug glance and a wink behind Michael's back.

When Eric was gone, Jordis focused on Michael. He watched her with an undecipherable look on his face.

"Was there something you wanted to talk to me about?" She moved to put her desk between them.

"Meet me and Chase in the East Conference Room in ten minutes."

"Okay. What's up?"

"We'll talk about it in the conference room." He turned abruptly and walked out, the trademark Michael Remington brood gracing his face.

The residual testosterone level in the room from the Covington-Remington back-to-back encounters surged a little high for her liking. Eric Covington's moves had caught her off guard. Of all the behaviors she expected of him, making a pass at her wasn't one of them. She could imagine what the scene must have looked like from Michael's perspective.

And Michael. What was with him? He'd seemed upset about something.

Was she in for an unpleasant surprise when she walked into that conference room?

She decided not to put off the inevitable. She grabbed the Gardner file and dropped it on her secretary's desk on her way to the conference room. A ways down the hall, she noticed Alyson and Eric chatting outside Eric's office. They stopped talking at her appearance and stared at her quietly.

The gossip has started already, she thought. Feeling like a goldfish in a bowl, Jordis nodded and walked on.

She entered the East Conference Room to find Michael at the table in rolled up shirtsleeves. The light dusting of hair over his forearms made him look masculine and capable. His olive skin mimicked the perfect tan. That she noticed all this annoyed her. She hadn't been summoned here for the Michael Remington Admiration Society. She was here for . . . Well, she didn't know what she was here for, but she was about to find out.

"Jordis, have a seat." Chase motioned her to the conference room table.

Michael's eyes dropped to the gold stilettos she'd donned today. His lips curved up momentarily as if he were thinking of something amusing.

"Something wrong with my shoes?"

"Nope." The look he initially gave her could have melted ice in the Arctic. Then, his eyes shifted. "No boots today?"

Trust me. The last thing I think about you doing in those boots is taking a stroll. The memory of his words, combined with the sweltering look in his eyes, made her pulse pound. If she didn't know better, she'd think he was intentionally baiting her. But why?

She kept her face and emotions neutral. She wouldn't think about his large hands playing idly with his stylus or about how they'd felt against her skin this weekend. She was a professional. She would behave professionally . . . for now. Then she'd head straight home and have a date with BOB while she fantasized about olive skin and gray eyes.

Screw that boss crap. She needed to get this lingering itch scratched mechanically since she had no intention of letting him scratch it in the flesh. Eric's accusation had reinforced what she already knew. She didn't have the luxury of—and certainly couldn't risk—indulging in any more hands-on activities with Mr. Remington.

Chase took the lead in the conversation, oblivious to her mounting discomfort. Distracted by her wayward thoughts, she almost missed him say they wanted her to take his place on the Metra Pharmaceuticals case.

She gave a mental fist pump.

"I'll need you to work late tonight," Michael said. "We need to sort through the key issues of the motion and divvy up the work to get our response done quickly."

The imaginary fist pump died. Apprehension replaced elation. The last time a partner with a sexual attraction to her asked her to work late, the performance he'd demanded had nothing to do with her mental prowess. She'd put Michael off Saturday. Was this his way of making sure she went all the way with him? She hadn't anticipated he'd be one of those partners who passed out assignments then expected some late night appreciation.

Jordis looked at Chase. "I'm happy to step in. I'd like some time to get up to speed on the documents before I start strategizing on the case. Tomorrow afternoon would be better for me."

"You'll be working closely with Michael. I'll let the two of you sort out the details. I just wanted to make myself available in case you had any initial questions I might be able to answer."

"No questions at this time. I'll spend some time with the file today and let you know if anything comes to mind." Jordis finally looked at Michael. "Why don't we convene tomorrow right after lunch? That'll give me plenty of time to get up to speed on the facts and history of the case."

"I'd prefer to start tonight," Michael responded.

Jordis hesitated. In the silence, a buzzing phone announced one of them had a call. Michael and Chase both checked the phones clipped on their belts.

Chase stood. "Excuse me." He freed his phone as he stepped into the hall and closed the conference room door behind him.

As soon as the door closed, Michael asked, "Jordis do you have plans tonight?"

Plans? How was that any of his business? "Um, no. Why do you ask?"

"I'm trying to figure out why you're trying to avoid

work tonight. I'd think after a key case assignment of this nature, you'd be anxious to prove yourself."

"Prove myself how?" The question popped out before she could check herself.

Michael's brow creased. "What's that supposed to mean?"

Jordis glanced at the door. Chase was still outside. She dropped her voice to a half whisper. "Is this your way of 'handling it'?"

"Handling what?"

Jordis took a deep breath. She didn't know whether to call him on his ploy to give them an excuse to work together or simply be smart about avoiding situations that placed them alone at late hours. She really wanted this case, but it stuck in her craw that she'd gotten it because Michael Remington wanted to sleep with her. She had no doubt that's what had given her the edge when word around the firm had Covington pegged as shoe-in for top pick.

She wasn't slinking quietly into another *quid pro quo* situation where she'd be expected to put out to advance her career. "You know, Michael, I expected different from you. Friday night when you said you'd find a way to handle things between us, this isn't what I thought you had in mind."

His jaw flexed. "Why don't you stop talking in riddles and say what you mean?"

"*Fine.*" She shot from her seat, abrupt momentum forcing her chair back and nearly over. Pressing her hands flat on the conference table, she leaned towards him. "Just how are you expecting me to prove myself, Mr. Remington?

With my brains or on my back?"

His eyes flashed with sudden understanding. He rose slowly from his chair, an evil look on his face, and said in a low mocking voice, "I don't know, *Ms. Morgan.* Which one are you better at?"

Jordis had the good sense to move away, but he stalked her retreating figure. He backed her into the antique buffet holding the coffee setup, leaving her nowhere to go. Refusing to be intimidated, she slid to her right.

He reached out and pulled her back in front of him. "Where are you going, Jordis? You didn't answer my question." With his hand firmly on her hip, he held her imprisoned by placing his other hand on the antique close enough to her body she could feel the heat from his forearm radiate along her side.

Shallow, labored breaths pulsed from her lungs, fed by her building temper. The woodsy scent of his cologne bombarded her senses. She couldn't smell it without thinking of that kiss in the elevator or the feel of his hands under her coat in the Plaza parking garage.

That her body reacted physically to him despite her fury intensified her mounting rage. The ever-present sexual tension between them affected her more than his looming presence. By the smirk on his face, he knew it. Her emotional gears shifted from angry to pissed. Two could play that game.

She drew a finger down the line of buttons under his Armani tie and said in a sultry voice, "Lucky for you, I'm great at both." She leaned into him, both palms flat against his high-thread-count designer shirt. She let one wander languidly against the fabric. "Which one were you planning to take advantage of?"

Satisfaction speared through her when his hand flexed on her hip and he sucked in a sharp breath.

It was short lived.

He countered immediately. "Which one are you offering?" He pressed his hips against her, making the high edge of the buffet bite into her lower back.

The twinge at her back barely registered due to the feel of his arousal throbbing against her pelvis, but it wasn't lust in his eyes. He looked like he wanted to throttle her.

"And are you planning to put out right here or do I have to take a number behind Covington?"

She flinched. "Bastard!" The word burst from her mouth and her hands shoved hard against his chest. "Get off me!"

He grabbed her wrists. "You know, sweetheart, I've been at this game a long time. No one calls into question my integrity without being able to back it up. Make no mistake. I want you. I want you bad. But I don't make professional decisions with my dick. So, the next time you think you're currying favor with me because I want to stick mine in you, remember this. I'd never risk my reputation or the future of this firm on a piece of tail, not even one as mouthwatering as you."

"Michael!" Chase stood in the doorway, a look on his face comprised of equal parts horror, surprise, and ire.

Michael released Jordis's hands abruptly, and she tottered to the side before regaining her balance. She glared at him, fists balled tightly at her sides, using all her energy not to punch him and to swallow words that would likely end her career at RHM. She turned to leave, back straight, fists still clenched.

Before she reached the door, Michael called after her. Jordis stopped, but didn't turn around.

"You have all afternoon to review what you feel you need to review. I'll expect you back here at six o'clock. Don't worry about dinner. I'll have something brought in."

She exited, shutting the door with a force only a few decibels below a slam.

∾ ∾ | ∾ ∾

"Dammit!" With one swipe of his hand, Michael sent the silver tray holding coffee condiments flying off the buffet onto the floor. Sugar packets fluttered listlessly to the carpet and blanketed red plastic stirrers lying in a pick-up-sticks pattern. Mini creamer cups bounced and rolled.

Chase surveyed the mess. "Did that help?" He shook his head. "What the *hell* is wrong with you?"

Michael stormed over to the windows, not happy that his partner had witnessed him becoming completely undone. "It's her."

"Jordis? Well, duh, Sherlock."

"No. Juliet."

"Juliet? Michael, don't you have enough to worry about with your feelings for Jordis? You really think you need to hang on to this fixation on Juliet?"

He turned to face Chase. "She *is* Juliet."

"What? You don't honestly believe Jordis Morgan is your mystery woman?"

"Yeah." His shoulders dropped. "I do."

"Um, Michael . . ." Chase crossed his arms. "You have

noticed that's not a suntan Jordis is sporting, right?"

Michael gave his buddy the evil eye. "Don't be a smart-ass."

Chase chuckled. "I'm just saying. That's a pretty funda-mental characteristic to overlook."

"I know, but it was dark. I was focused on her dress. Well, actually, I was focused on how she *looked* in that dress. I was so wrapped up in the way she made me feel I didn't think about the possible nuances of her complexion. I just assumed . . ." He shoved his hands into his hair, paced a step and then stopped. "How 'bout you cut me some slack, huh? What difference does it make what color she is? If we're talking skin tone, I'm probably as dark as she is."

Chase's head bobbed at the comment. "True. And you know her color doesn't matter to me, of all people, but the info would certainly have changed the nature of our search." A wide grin spread across his face.

It was true Chase wasn't one to draw color lines. Be-neath the blond hair and blue eyes, there was more to Chase than met the eye. At the moment, however, Michael didn't give a crap about the man's elevated psyche. His hands found his hips as he glared at his friend.

Still grinning, Chase backed off. "Okay. Okay. Let's put that aside for a minute. What makes you think she's Juliet?"

"It's been driving me crazy from the moment I met her, this nagging feeling that I knew her from somewhere. Then I . . ." Michael's voice trailed off.

"Then you what?"

He took a deep breath. "I kissed her."

One side of Chase's mouth twitched. "You kissed her?"

Michael was glad someone found this funny. "Several times."

Chase stepped over the coffee service mess and leaned against the buffet. "Let me get this straight. You believe Jordis is your elusive mystery woman. You've kissed her. More than once. And then you called her a 'piece of tail' just now as your way of moving this budding romance to the next level?"

Right. Stupid. Michael shook his head. "No, I—" He dropped into a conference table chair. "Ugh! That woman is driving me out of my mind. I dream about her. I start out dreaming about Juliet, but by the time the dream is over, she's changed into Jordis."

"And because of this morphing dream, you believe Jordis is Juliet?"

"It's more than that."

"All right." Chase walked over and sat down perpendicular to him. "Tell me about it."

He ran Chase through his encounters with Jordis thus far.

Chase nodded his head then glanced at the door through which Jordis had exited. "How does Jordis feel about all this?"

He leaned back in his chair, somewhat relieved Chase didn't think he was nuts. "I don't know. We haven't discussed it."

"Why not? Until you verify it with her, this is all supposition on your part."

"If you remember, as Juliet, she didn't want me to know her real name. Given her absolutely-not stance on a relationship with her supervising attorney, I'm doubtful she'll be thrilled to learn the truth." He drummed his fingers against the table. "I've come up with another way to check her attendance at that party New Year's Eve."

"How?"

"I realized I could remember the number on the side of the taxi she left in. I sent the information to our investigator this morning to check out."

"So you really can't be sure she's your Juliet until you get a report back from Rodriguez."

"I'm sure. I've never been so sure of anything in my life. Whatever Rodriguez finds during his investigation will only be confirmation of what I already know in my gut."

Chase nodded. "Okay. Then she's right to be concerned about the supervising attorney issue. You need to get that resolved if you're serious about pursuing this."

"I can't ask her to pass on the Metra Pharmaceuticals case because I'm attracted to her."

"No, but if you both want this relationship to continue, you could mutually agree Jordis take a different case assignment or transfer to another department. She's got as much transactional experience as litigation. She'd be great in Business and Finance. I'm sure Roy would love to have her." Chase laughed loudly at the look on Michael's face. "Down, boy! I didn't mean it *that* way. Roy is a lot of things, but he would never step on another man's toes, especially not a friend. Boy, you've got it bad!"

He had it bad all right. When he'd walked in on Jordis with Covington this morning something vicious and green had crawled onto his back, and he hadn't been able to shake it loose. "You don't understand."

Chase rose and put a hand on Michael's shoulder. "I understand better than you think. I once dated a woman who turned me inside out like that." Chase headed for the door.

Michael swiveled his chair towards his friend's departing frame. "What did you do?"

Chase stopped and turned. A slow grin crept up one side of his face. His eyebrows peaked as he cocked his head. "Think about it for a minute." When Michael's eyes finally widened in a startled face, Chase laughed. "Yeah, I married her."

CHAPTER 13

*M*ichael stopped outside the East Conference Room a few hours later and stared through the open door at Jordis working silently at the conference room table. Chase's comment about marrying the only woman to turn him inside out weighed on Michael's mind. He'd stumbled into unknown emotional territory, but he was nowhere near that quagmire of male dysfunction.

He'd been stewing over his run-in with Jordis all afternoon. His actions had gotten out of hand. He'd never behaved that way with a colleague, especially not a woman. That Jordis thought him one of those guys who felt entitled to collect special favors from his female employees had angered him. He normally flicked off others' opinions of him—good or bad. For some reason, this woman's opinion of him mattered, a lot. Perhaps her opinion mattered too much.

She was hiding something. More than being close to her brother had brought her back to Kansas City. When he'd returned to his office this afternoon, he'd logged into his voicemail and received a heads-up from an unlikely source. The unexpected message had caught him by surprise: "Remington, Keith Wilson here. It seems you and I have something in common."

Michael had moved to erase the message when something in the man's tone had caught his attention. The animosity came through in a harsh sneer: ". . . so before you get too attached to our Miss Jordis, you might want to ask her why she really left LA."

Part of him understood Wilson had left the warning expressly to cause trouble for Jordis. From the bad blood he'd witnessed between the two, Wilson wasn't exactly a reliable source of information. Nevertheless, Wilson's insinuation Jordis had left LA for some nefarious reason had him curious.

He took a deep breath as he considered how best to proceed with her. He'd been adamant about starting their strategy sessions tonight. During his analysis of the plaintiff's motion for summary judgment, he'd discovered some troubling factual information relied upon by the other side. He wanted to talk through his suppositions and theories about how the plaintiff had obtained some of that factual information, but he needed to clear the air between them first and now the mystery of LA nagged at him.

He stepped into the conference room and closed the door. He leaned against it. His eyes wandered to the Chinese food on the credenza. It hadn't been touched. "You're not going to eat?"

Jordis didn't turn around or speak.

"Jordis?"

"I'm not hungry. Let's get to work."

She leaned over the table and sorted through a pile of folders on the far side of the table. Her tight, firm bottom drew his attention. The enticing image made him want to step up behind her and lift her skirt. He closed his eyes briefly to gain some control. He needed to make peace with her. That wouldn't happen if he let his baser emotions get the better of him.

"Jordis, we need to talk." He moved to her side and reached for the stack of folders in her hand. His palm brushed the back of her hand, and hot energy rippled through him from that simple touch. He went still, hyper-aware of the feel of her skin against his palm and the curve of her hip pressed against his. His hand trailed slowly past her wrist, up her forearm. Jordis pulled back, but Michael rested his hand against her far hip to keep her close.

"Michael, don't. We're at the office. We need to focus." She broke his hold and placed herself out of his reach.

He blew out a long breath. "Yeah. Focus." He stepped away from the table. "I can't focus very well when I'm around you."

Jordis scowled at him. "Well, you need to get over it."

"And you need to get a clue!" His brows bunched into deep creases.

Her widened eyes lit instantly with fury.

He drove a hand into his hair. He hadn't meant to bark at her, but how could he get over this if he couldn't even talk with her about it. "We can't stick our heads in the sand. This spark that ignites every time we're in a room together isn't going to go away just because we work together and I happen to be your supervising attorney."

"Maybe. Then again, we're adults not children. We understand sometimes there are things we want that we can't have. A simple case of self-control, mind over matter, and we manage to get along without them just fine."

"Mind over matter? Really? That's your answer?" His arms crossed over his chest. "Is it really that easy for you to turn it on and off?"

"Yes, it's that easy." She looked away.

He couldn't see her eyes to judge her truthfulness.

She stepped around the table to where she'd spread out her case notes and sat down. Michael watched her pull over a folder and primly open it, purposely avoiding eye contact. Minutes passed while she fiddled with two pens and a highlighter. He didn't move.

Eventually, she looked up. "I thought you ordered me here to work on the case, not discuss our personal issue."

He raised a brow at her use of the word *ordered*. "Well, now, I want to address both."

Jordis sighed. "Since we're on the client's time at the moment, how about we stick to the case?" Impatience and disinterest lived on her face, but those eyes—those extremely expressive eyes—revealed what she'd hidden from him moments before. She'd lied about how easy it was for her to turn off her emotions.

He slid his hands into his pockets, satisfied he wasn't in this alone. "You're right. We have work to do. So, I'll table the personal discussion—*temporarily*." He leaned onto the table, palms flat. To match his mood, his voice modulated to the unyielding tone he used when cross-examining a hostile witness. "Make no mistake, however. When we're through here, Ms. Morgan, we're having that other conversation."

Butt dropped into a chair, he snapped open his own folder, took a deep breath to center himself, and buckled down to focus on the case. "Our opponents have taken a pretty aggressive stance on their motion for summary judgment. Something has made them think they have the upper hand, and we need to figure out what it is." He snatched up a group of folders piled to his right. "Take a look at these. They were in the last batch of documents adverse counsel sent over. Interestingly, the file room managed to misplace the box they came in for over a week."

"A week?" She flipped open the top folder of the stack he'd handed her without missing a beat. Apparently, she was better at this mind-over-matter thing than he was. "Where were they finally located?"

"In the file room, misfiled a few cases over. I thought it rather suspicious when they turned up basically in plain sight. And, they weren't the only documents missing. A box of our client's confidential, attorney-client privileged documents went missing at the same time."

She leaned her forearms on the table. "Let me guess. The box of confidential documents managed to show up at the same time as the missing discovery documents."

"Exactly." He grabbed a document from the stack of pleadings his secretary had left for him and tossed it across the table at her. "Here's a copy of the motion. I highlighted some factual allegations and legal theories which appear to be based upon confidential information."

Jordis's head snapped up. "You think opposing counsel

had improper access to the attorney-client privileged documents?"

"Or they've had access to the database where we store electronic copies of all case documents. I've asked the IT department to look into whether the firm database has been accessed by any unauthorized users, but it will take a couple of weeks for them to do a thorough evaluation."

"We don't have a couple of weeks." Jordis stood and commandeered the conference call setup in the middle of the table. "I think I can do better than that."

She dialed a number and pulled a microphone/speaker satellite towards herself and slid one towards Michael.

A deep voice answered on the other end. "Brandt Morgan."

"Hey, bro. I need your help with something, and I have you on speakerphone with my boss. So, behave."

"Which boss is that?" Brandt asked. "The arrogant, domineering jerk or the prince of a guy with the great sense of humor?"

Staring at Jordis's mortified face, Michael responded, "Michael Remington here, Brandt. I believe I would be the arrogant, domineering jerk."

Jordis bit her lip as she tried to hide a smile. Michael continued to watch her, and she shrugged at him.

Brandt laughed. "It's a pleasure to meet you by phone, Michael. What can I do for you guys?"

Jordis leaned towards the speakerphone. "Michael thinks someone may be tapping into our case database and accessing privileged documents."

"I think it may be more than just case documents, Brandt," Michael added. "I don't keep my strategy notes or work product on the main database. I have a separate electronic system for those, but I believe our opponents may have had access to those as well."

"Oh, so we're going on a spy hunt." Brandt's voice dripped with glee.

Jordis shook her head at the excitement in her brother's voice. "You're such a geek."

"And proud of it. Jordis, do you have your laptop handy?" Brandt asked her.

"Sure." She leaned over and pulled her laptop out of her tote.

"I have remote access set up on your laptop. Let's get down to business."

They worked through issues with Brandt as he scouted around the firm network. After a couple of hours of troubleshooting, Brandt discovered a gateway that allowed back door access. An unknown external ISP had used the gateway several times. Michael made arrangements for Brandt to liaise with the firm's IT group so he could gather more detailed information on the breach and run a trace.

"Once I get set up with your people, Michael, it should only take me a few hours to track the unknown ISP and figure out whether your backdoor was left open by an insider or pried open by a trespasser. Sis, I'll talk to you later." Brandt clicked off.

Jordis made a show of checking the time on her mobile phone. "I think we've covered enough ground tonight. I need a break and some dinner." She gathered her notes from the table and stood. "I'll look at everything some more tomorrow and let you know if I find anything else of note."

"Jordis, now that we're off the client's dime, let's talk. We can heat the Chinese food if you want to eat."

She shook her head and shouldered her tote. "I'm not in the mood for Chinese." She headed for the door.

"*Stop*." At the sharp crack of his command, she froze. "Maybe you have nothing to say, but I do. At least, let me apologize for what I said earlier."

"Apology accepted. Now let's move on."

He reached for her, but she yanked her arm away. "Don't."

"Jordis, talk to me. I . . ." He huffed out a breath.

She stared at him, waiting.

He felt like an imbecile having to admit what had been going through his mind. "I was angry."

"I figured that much out on my own."

"No, I mean, when I walked in and saw you with Covington, I—"

"You assumed I was making out with him only days after my interlude with you."

His lips pressed together at her directness.

"What's the matter, Michael?" She gave him a skeptical look. "Were you jealous at the thought I might not be completely bowled over by your charms?"

"Yes!" he snapped.

Her look of surprise took the edge off her smart-aleck remark.

"I'm not usually a jealous man. I don't get possessive over women. But for some reason with you, I feel both. I don't know what to do with that."

"There's really nothing for you to do with that . . . except maybe let it go." She took a step towards him. "We're colleagues, Michael. Nothing more. I've been handed a case that will pretty much make my career here as long as we don't screw it up. I'm not jeopardizing that for a fling with a man who can have any woman in this firm he wants." A shrug hitched her tote strap higher on her shoulder. "Do us both a favor. Pick someone else."

"You don't mean that."

"Let's be clear." Her eyes narrowed. "I want you, too. Bad. But I want this partnership more than I want your d—... *member* in me. So, this piece of tail is going home so we can both keep our integrity intact." She strode towards the door.

This time he let her go, afraid if he put his hands on her, he'd try shaking some sense into her or find a more sensually demonstrative way to prove the bluff behind her words. Neither action would be a wise way to handle their impasse, especially not at the office. He'd accumulated enough marks against him for one day.

She'd made her position clear. She prioritized using this case to cement her selection to partnership. Her career took precedence over any personal relationship with him. The one time it would have been to his benefit to have a woman use him to try to further her career, he ended up with an ambitious associate with ethics.

She was stubborn and combative. How he could be simultaneously annoyed and turned on by that baffled him, but he was done questioning his feelings. Somehow, he had to show her that surrendering to her passion was as important as advancing her career.

Tomorrow he'd start the full-out campaign to thaw the deep freeze she'd placed around her heart. They'd settle this matter between them and then he'd find out what happened in LA. She'd thought he'd been arrogant and domineering before. She hadn't seen anything yet.

❧ ❧ | ❧ ❧

A sealed manila envelope waited on Jordis's chair when she got back to her office. She picked up the pouch and opened it. The handwritten note she slid out made her cringe.

> *You little slut!*
> *We need to talk about that elevator kiss!*
> *Meet me at Delilah's in Zona Rosa.*
> *9 pm sharp.*
> *Come alone.*

Someone had seen her and Michael Thursday night. How was that possible?

She plopped down into her chair. The day kept getting better and better. First, Covington. Then, the row with Michael. Now this. She wanted to scream.

She looked up from the note to find Alyson McGovern leaning against her open office door watching her.

"Well, well, well," Alyson crooned. "Word is you were assigned second chair in the Metra Pharmaceuticals case today. Congratulations." She sounded anything but congratulatory.

Jordis crumpled the note in her hand, her fist tight around the wad of paper. "Thanks, Alyson. What can I do for you?"

"Oh, nothing in particular. I just wanted to stop by and be amongst the first to say well done." Her grin conveyed irritation rather than amity. "You know, I'm rarely outdone in getting something I want." Alyson sauntered into the room. "No worries though. I always have a backup plan."

Placing her hand on the back of a guest chair, Alyson gave Jordis a once over with her eyes. "I guess I just wasn't exotic enough for Mr. Remington."

Jordis's eyes narrowed. "Just what are you trying to say, Alyson?"

Alyson gave a catty laugh. "No sense playing coy with me. Eric may have bought that drivel about why you and Michael took so long leaving the gym last weekend and given you the benefit of the doubt about your carriage ride on the Plaza, but we women know exactly what was going on."

Jordis stood. "Exactly what are you accusing me of?"

Alyson's eyes widened in feigned innocence. "Me?" She touched her hand to her chest. "I would never *deign* to accuse our senior partner's pet associate of anything untoward." Alyson's hand swept the room. "At least, not here where I could be overheard and lose plausible deniability."

She laughed before heading for the door. Looking back, she advised, "You should be careful what you say and do at the office, Jordis. There are eyes and ears everywhere." She grabbed the door handle, but didn't exit. "And don't be foolish enough to believe pets can't fall out of favor. A man like Michael Remington enjoys a little variety. Who knows what will happen when he gets bored with the flavor of the month." With a gleam in her eye and a wicked curve to her lips, Alyson left, pulling the door closed behind her.

Jordis looked down at the crumple in her fist. Untwisting the wad, she opened the note and read it again. Had Alyson sent it? Had Eric? The two of them had obviously been talking.

She didn't have one jackal at her back, she had two. How could she have been so stupid as to forget about Alyson's sexual designs on Michael?

Possibly, Alyson's interest lay more in getting a prime case assignment than lust, but Alyson didn't have the experience of Eric or herself so the Metra Pharma appointment wouldn't have been an option for Alyson. *Unless, of course, she were sleeping with Michael Remington.* The thought put Jordis back in her seat.

She glanced at her desk clock, which displayed a quarter to nine. Her stomach churned. Out of principle, she hadn't eaten any of the dinner Michael had brought in. His orders had to be followed when it came to work, but she didn't have to eat his food. She placed one hand over her unquiet stomach and fingered the note on her desk with the other.

Soon enough she'd know what game Eric or Alyson had in mind. At least the slime had chosen a meeting spot unlikely to be patronized by the upwardly mobile clan of their firm. *Delilah's* was a trendy hole-in-the-wall for singles and artsy types. Whatever game her stalker wanted to play, she wouldn't have to worry about all those possible "eyes and ears."

❧ ❧ | ❦ ❦

Jordis arrived at Delilah's and sat in her car surveying the parking lot for a recognizable face or car. She didn't notice anyone she knew. As for the cars, she wasn't familiar enough with her coworkers' vehicles to easily pick out a particular ride.

Bucking up for the confrontation ahead, Jordis disembarked from her car. She stepped inside the eclectic scene. Low lights shadowed tables of differing heights and shapes. An acoustic guitar accompanied a plaintive female voice in a haunting rendition of Roberta Flack's *Killing Me Softly*. Bodies huddled together, a mix of casual acquaintances, friends, and obvious lovers—of all persuasions. Jordis's eyes glanced over two gentlemen in an intimate embrace before she caught a glimpse of a familiar face.

She tensed. She was never going to live this down. Stepping up to a round, bar-height table, she tossed down her purse. "Vivian, I'm going to *kill* you."

Her redheaded colleague's eyebrows shot up. "What did I do?"

Jordis hoisted herself into a high-backed chair and let out a deep breath. "When I got your note, I nearly had a heart attack. I thought the worst. I drove here expecting to find Eric or Alyson waiting for me."

Vivian noticed the tight look on her friend's face. "Oh. Sorry about that."

"You should be."

"Didn't you recognize my handwriting?" Vivian gestured to a barista and motioned towards her cup and then at Jordis.

"No, I didn't." Jordis saw the pantomime and shook her head. "You know I'm not a big coffee fan. They wouldn't happen to serve alcohol here? I need a real drink."

"As a matter of fact, they do." Vivian hopped down from her seat. "Be right back."

Jordis reached for her handbag.

Vivian waived her off. "Tonight's tab is on me."

Jordis threw her handbag back down. "No argument from me. It's the least you can do. And no froufrou drinks either. Bring me something that'll make my throat burn."

Her friend hesitated. "Are you driving tonight?"

Jordis leaned back in her chair. "No. You are."

Vivian disappeared and returned quickly with a tall glass that, with one taste, Jordis identified as a Tom Collins. Gin. That would work.

Vivian waited for Jordis to finish half her drink before she delved into the matter of the evening. "Well, clearly, you're not gay, but I see I was off base about you not doing white guys."

"I don't." Jordis sighed. "Or, at least, I didn't. That elevator kiss was a fluke." After this past weekend, Jordis knew that wasn't exactly the case, but she didn't want to talk about it. She downed more of her drink.

"Ah, I see." Vivian sat back with a grin. "An interracial virgin. Is that the problem?"

"W-what?" Jordis choked a bit on her drink at Vivian's use of the word *virgin*. "No, of course not." She'd pretty much barreled past that particular issue when she'd let Michael fondle his way through third base.

She gave Vivian an indignant look. "*Hello!* He's my supervising attorney. You are familiar with the Rules of

Professional Conduct?"

"*Hello!*" Vivian mocked. "The Rules are just guidelines to prevent certain unethical behavior."

"Exactly."

"So avoid the unethical behavior without passing on the phenomenal bedroom skills of your hunky managing partner."

"Phenomenal bedroom skills? How do you know the man has phenomenal bedroom skills?"

"That man is drop-dead sexy. Any man who looks like that, moves like that, and gets that much female attention has to be great in bed. Otherwise, the Lord is simply not merciful."

She chuckled at her friend's backwards Catholic reasoning.

Vivian sipped her latte. "So, how do we get you and Mr. Remington from liplock to horizontal mambo?" She made a sensual sound of pleasure while wiggling her eyebrows suggestively.

Jordis burst out laughing at the lascivious expression. "That is *sooo* not going to happen."

"Really?" Vivian eyed Jordis suspiciously. "We'll see about that."

Jordis shook her head, her laughter tapering off. "How did you know, by the way?"

"We'll get to that later. First, tell me all about that elevator kiss." Vivian leaned forward. "And don't leave anything out."

CHAPTER 14

*J*ordis looked up as Michael, dressed in a charcoal gray Armani suit she loved on him, strolled into her office two days later. He'd left his jacket off and rolled the sleeves of his baby blue dress shirt to mid-forearm. The blue of his shirt gave a silver glint to his gray eyes.

Except for an exchange of emails, they'd only spoken a few times since their evening meeting. Each time, he'd been completely professional. He hadn't mentioned their disagreement or made a pass at her once. She should be happy. That's what she'd wanted. Instead, because she was dealing with a known master strategist, she kept waiting for the other shoe to drop. No way he'd let her off this easy. He had to be up to something.

Michael sat down in one of the two guest chairs opposite her desk. "I sent you the preliminary arguments for my section of our response to the motion for summary judgment."

She sat back. "I got them."

"Did you have a chance to look them over?"

"Not yet. I'll take a look later this afternoon and let you know my thoughts."

"That'll work. Thanks." He stood and turned to go.

"Michael?"

He stopped and looked at her.

"Is that all you wanted?"

He shrugged. "Yeah. Oh—" He looked down at his hand as if with afterthought. "And this is for you." He placed a tall refillable beverage mug on the desk in front of her.

She glanced at the mug with a brown screw-on lid. On its beige front, a script *J* floated in the center of a painted ornate medallion and the word *tea* floated around the sides multiple times along with various words for coffee, like *java, latte* and *café*.

"What's this?"

"Just a little something to get you through the afternoon." He strutted to the door.

Her eyes fell to the drape of his slacks over his tight butt. He had a nice backside. The kind a woman would like naked and tensed beneath her hands while he . . .

She shook her head. *Enough of that.*

Regaining focus, she looked up and found Michael watching her, his hand poised on the handle of the open office door. His suppressed grin and look of amusement let her know he'd caught her eyeing his ass. He winked and exited.

Arrogant jerk.

If she didn't know better, she'd think he came by just to make her drool. Although she had no intention of acting on her lust for him, that didn't mean she'd found a way to get over it. To her chagrin, after what he'd just witnessed, he now knew it.

Her torso flopped against her high-backed chair, and she pondered the mug before her. The script *J* on the front made it obvious he'd bought it for her to keep. She didn't want to accept gifts from him, but how did a woman turn down something as simple as a travel mug—a personalized one at that—without seeming petty?

She lifted the mug, took a sip, and almost moaned out loud.

A milk chocolate turtle latte.

That snake. A little something to get her through the afternoon, indeed.

Without saying a word, he'd reminded her of their Plaza rendezvous. She should run to the break room and pour the beverage down the drain. But, she wouldn't, and he'd known she wouldn't. She liked them too much.

She berated herself for being a weak-willed ninny and took another sip, resigned to the Proustian effect unleashed by the burst of flavors across her tongue. By the time she finished the latte, she had to concede this skirmish in her battle to resist Mr. Sex Appeal. She couldn't concentrate on work. Memories from the first night she'd tasted the drink invaded her thoughts. A carriage ride in the snow and a makeout session against a parked car kept intruding on her concentration.

Exasperated by her unproductive morning, she gave up on work and went to find Vivian for an early lunch. She needed to regroup and find a way to win the next battle in this war of near-fatal attraction.

❧ ❧ | ❦ ❦

The following week, Michael sat at his desk twirling his stylus with a grin on his face. He'd decided his best offense with Jordis hinged on a covert operation. Her strong-willed personality wired her for battle. A strong offensive would have set her on a defensive path to fight off his every advance. By downshifting his play, he'd thrown her off balance. She hadn't been sure whether to trust his disinterest or steel herself for a sneak attack.

He'd never had to pursue a woman before. Who knew it would be so much fun?

He'd made sure to be a gentleman at every turn, but every once in a while, he'd stand a little too close to her or touch her absently and seemingly in innocence.

At first, he'd thought he wasn't getting anywhere. He'd feared despite his apology, her anger had doused any remaining embers of the passion she may have felt for him. Last night, he'd learned otherwise. He'd escorted her to her car after their evening of polishing the response to the motion for summary judgment. When he'd touched the small of her back to lead her out of the elevator, she'd jumped nearly a foot in the air.

He had her tightly wound, which meant he was getting to her. More than mere embers rested in her hearth for him. If he stoked just right, he had every confidence he could stir up a blaze.

They'd filed their response with the court this morning.

The opponents would have fourteen days to file a reply, but he and Jordis were banking on an ultimate decision in their favor. Tomorrow, they'd move on to the next phase of their case strategy, but right now he needed to figure out the next phase in his strategy to win her.

His phone rang. He checked the number on the caller ID and picked up before his assistant could. "Michael Remington."

"Yo, Remington, Battle Rodriquez here. I've got your preliminary report. You want to tell me why you had me investigate a member of your own firm?"

"No."

Battle laughed. "Diplomatic as ever I see, Remington."

A former marine with a law degree, Battle Newton Rodriquez was Michael's investigator of choice. He'd served as a Judge Advocate before doing a brief stint with the FBI's Behavioral Analysis Unit. He ultimately decided working hard to capture evildoers served no purpose if their crimes often went unpunished due to shortcomings in the case for prosecution. He now freelanced, putting together airtight evidence portfolios on varied matters for lawyers and law enforcement agents across the country. Not only was he thorough, he was unfailingly discreet.

Michael trusted no one else to get him the information he needed about Jordis and her prior life in LA. He'd been curious about Keith Wilson's relationship with Jordis since that night on the Plaza. He'd garnered from what she and Wilson had said to each other that their split had occurred over something involving her work. He hadn't gotten around to questioning Jordis about the relationship. The timing had never seemed right. When he'd thought about

Wilson's meddling voicemail message and what Jordis hadn't said whenever he'd tried to make conversation about her time in LA, Michael figured the story might hold the key to breaking through her current emotional blockade.

Battle filled Michael in on what he'd found out about Wilson and Jordis's relationship and the facts surrounding her departure from her prior firm. "The party line I got from her prior firm's administration was she'd had 'some case management issues' and 'irreconcilable personal conflicts' with a senior partner. I did some asking around and learned the story has a more scandalous version. Apparently, rumors of sexual impropriety between Jordis and a senior partner made the rounds."

Michael's ire rose when Battle detailed rumors of alleged sexual favors for which Jordis was supposedly rewarded with premium case assignments. A raw burn festered in his gut. He felt momentarily betrayed. The lady was being awfully self-righteous about a liaison with him for someone with a history of shenanigans with her superiors. Then, a twinge of guilt hit him. He knew better than to jump to assumptions without hearing both sides of a story. The allegations of poor case management didn't gel with what he knew about the woman. Not to mention that, according to Battle, the prior firm had paid her a severance package equal to three years' salary plus corresponding bonuses.

The size of her severance package alone gave him pause. Given what he estimated Jordis's salary level and bonus range would have been in LA, she'd walked away with upwards of seven figures. That was a hefty chunk of change to dole out to someone who'd been guilty of sexual impropriety. People paid that kind of money to keep someone from filing a suit they didn't want filed.

Michael thought about Chase's comment a few weekends ago that Jordis didn't need Michael's money. Had Chase known about the sex scandal and the severance package? If he had and hadn't said anything, Chase had some serious explaining to do. Pushing aside his growing desire to manhandle his best friend, Michael let this new information settle in.

Unless Jordis tended to pitter away her paychecks—something he doubted—with the payoff she'd received and her current income, she was sitting pretty. It didn't come close to his assets, factoring in his investments and real estate holdings, which included the office tower housing the firm. Nevertheless, for an independent woman like Jordis, her cashflow situation meant she'd never need, or want, to look to a man for financial support or gain.

Battle's voice lured him back into the conversation. "Now that I've given you an objective rundown of the basic facts, let me say, you know that's all bullshit, right?"

"Yeah. I'm thinking the same thing." At least, he hoped so.

"I did some checking with her first employer and asked around about the situation with her ex. The lady's had a pretty stellar career up to her prior position. Seems mighty suspicious that a woman who graduated in the upper percentile of her law school class and has a near perfect court record had to resort to sexual bribery to get ahead. From where I'm sitting, I suspect the partner involved . . ." Battle's voice faded and papers rattled, suggesting he was looking up something. ". . . a Lowell Bruner, has been caught up in this kind of thing before and probably failed to mind his manners. Only this time, he picked the wrong woman, and they had to either pay her off or risk a PR circus with the potential to negatively impact the firm's reputation."

Michael hummed in response. The picture Battle painted gave him new insight as to why Jordis had tried to avoid working late with him. Given the prior sexual advances he'd made, it was understandable she wondered if he might be after more than her legal expertise. His ego wanted to believe she should have known he wasn't that kind of guy, but if the situation had been reversed . . . *What would I have thought?*

"I'll get the written report to you in the next day or so," Battle said. "Oh, and before I forget. I'm faxing over right now the information you wanted on that taxi drop New Year's Eve. I also started working on that other matter you sent me concerning the prior expert witnesses of the opponent in your patent case. I'm beginning to think there may be something there. I'll let you know where things end up."

"Okay, Battle. Thanks for getting this done so quickly."

"You didn't exactly give me a choice." Battle chuckled. "I'm getting curious about this Ms. Morgan. Maybe I'll deliver the report personally so I can check out the lady myself."

"You stay away from my firm. I have a business to run. The women here haven't finished swooning from your last visit." Half black, half Latino, Battle's model-worthy looks sent the females at RHM into a tizzy every time he stopped by. Until Michael got a lock on Ms. Morgan's affections, he wanted Battle Rodriguez as far away from her as possible.

"I can't help it if the ladies love this *chocolate suave*," Battle cooed, overemphasizing the Spanish vowels. He laughed. "Talk to you later, man."

The connection clicked off.

Michael shook his head. Battle was an arrogant SOB. Good thing he was so damn effective.

Michael pulled Battle's fax off the machine. He'd specifically asked Battle not to email him an electronic report because he didn't want anyone else privy to this information.

In black and white, the address to which Juliet had been taken on New Year's Eve glared up at him. His gut twisted into a knot. Since their basketball game, he'd been acting on the assumption Jordis and Juliet were the same person. Now, he faced the possibility he'd been wrong.

He considered shredding the fax and letting the matter rest. At this point, it shouldn't matter who the woman he'd kissed on New Year's Eve had been. The woman he wanted was Jordis. Yet, a part of him needed to know if he'd truly imprinted on a woman after no more than a brief forty-five minute anonymous encounter.

He pushed the intercom. His secretary, Lana Davenport, answered. "Yes, Michael?"

"Lana, I need Jordis Morgan's personnel file, please. Right away."

"Okay. I'll take care of it."

Ten minutes later, Lana walked into his office and dropped the folder on his desk. "I hope there's not a problem with that young lady. I like her."

Lana's comment surprised him. "Really? Why?"

Lana wasn't the type to be easily swayed by people. A bit of a pillar at the firm, Lana had started out as his father's secretary when the firm first opened. She was practical, super-efficient and no-nonsense. If Jordis had impressed her, that was saying something.

"It's refreshing to meet a young female attorney who doesn't think she has to dress and act like a man to be taken seriously at her job. Plus, after the way she handled *Studly*, she's becoming a bit of a legend around here."

"You heard about that?"

"Of course." Lana headed for the door. "You know you can't keep anything from the staff around here."

After she closed the door, Michael stared at the file she'd left on his desk. His pulse raced. He sat quietly for several seconds before he forced himself to flip the file open to the sheet containing Jordis's personal information.

He flopped back in his chair. The address *wasn't* the same.

How could he have been wrong?

His jovial mood of earlier dissipated. He picked up his stylus and twirled.

If he'd been off base about Juliet, what else had his over-active libido blinded him to?

He wanted to believe the prior rumors about Jordis were false, but maybe she'd been playing with him this whole time.

Logically, he recognized she hadn't come on to him. He'd been the one to make the first move, and he hadn't backed off even when she'd asked him to. But, maybe she was better at playing hard-to-get than her predecessors.

She was certainly more intelligent than any of them.

He didn't want to consider the possibility another schemer had pulled him in, but old hangups died hard. Women invariably disappointed him. He couldn't keep the doubts completely silent. He needed to talk to Jordis.

The time had come to end their stalemate.

Michael found Jordis in the part of the firm gym that contained the basketball half court. She had a rack of basketballs beside her from which she repeatedly snatched balls and immediately took outside shots. Even sporting a casual ponytail, she looked beautiful. She'd dressed in athletic pants and a lycra Under Armour long-sleeved t-shirt. The form-fitting shirt accentuated her defined arm muscles and hugged all her upper curves.

Her body moved with an athletic grace he admired and which turned him on. So many levels existed to this attraction he nursed. The more he learned about her, the more he wanted her.

He stood out of her line of sight and watched in awe as she hit six shots in rapid-fire succession. Something, even in his college days, he would have been hard pressed to duplicate.

The seventh shot hit the back of the rim and bounced off.

Jordis put her hands on her hips and dropped her head forward. Her chest rose and fell with a huge breath. A few seconds later, her voice carried to him. "What do you want?"

She'd sensed his presence.

He wondered if she would have made that last shot if she hadn't. The betting man in him said she would have.

Jacketless and tieless, he strolled onto the court, the top two buttons of his dress shirt undone. "I just talked to my investigator. His preliminary research into the issue you raised about the expert witnesses shows there might be something there. He'll start his official investigation tomorrow."

"Great." She picked up a ball from the floor. "You didn't have to track me down to tell me that." Her voice was stiff.

"No, I didn't." His hands slid into the pockets of his slacks. "Jordis, we have to talk. We need to address this tension between us."

She propped the basketball against her hip and sighed heavily. "Okay, Michael. Talk."

She still had her defenses up.

"What are you afraid of?" That wasn't what he'd intended to ask, but once it was out, he sensed he'd asked exactly the right question.

"I'm not afraid of anything." She dribbled the ball she had in her hand and looked up at the goal. She took a shot. It hit its target.

Michael walked beneath the goal and retrieved the ball. He drilled her a chest pass, which she caught without thought. He maintained his position. "Come on, Jordis. It's time we were straight with each other. Tell me what you're afraid of."

She held the basketball in front of her balanced between her two hands. She gazed at the ball while she turned it a few times. When she looked up at him, the shield had lowered from her eyes. "Setting off a chain reaction of events that will cost me my career. This is my third firm, Michael. If I have to leave RHM before I make partner, my marketability will suffer and my reputation as a top-rate lawyer will be in serious question."

Michael weighed his words, understanding the significance of her revelation. "It doesn't have to come to that."

"It *shouldn't* have to come to that. That doesn't mean it won't."

He started towards her. "Jordis, your career here is in no way contingent upon what happens—or doesn't happen—between us." He stopped in front of her. "If that's what this is about, know I wouldn't do that to you."

"Can I get that in writing?"

He gave an amused grunt, but replied seriously. "If that's what it takes."

"What if I'm the one to break it off?"

He all but rolled his eyes, dismissing her comment as if insulted. "I'm a big boy. I think I can handle it."

"Unfortunately, it's not just about you, Michael. If we cross this line, the moment it gets out we're having an affair—and it would get out—my credibility at RHM will be destroyed. It's hard enough making it in this environment without having to live in the shadow of vicious gossip and slanderous epithets. I should know. I've been there before."

Michael stiffened. *Was she admitting she'd had an affair with that partner?* "What do you mean?"

Jordis studied him. He wondered if his apprehension showed on his face. She looked to be considering her words carefully.

Her eyes closed.

Michael waited patiently for her to open them.

When she did, she spoke softly. "At my prior firm, I was assigned a case with a senior partner named Lowell Bruner. After we'd worked together a while, he began to get a little touchy-feely." Jordis clamped tightly on the ball she held between her palms.

He removed the ball from her grasp.

She dropped her hands. "I rebuffed his advances. Politely. At first. I was naïve enough to believe a man of his position and reputation would accept my disinterest and move on. I was wrong." Her hands tightened into fists. "One night, we were working on deadline in his office and it got late. I didn't realize he'd told the staff not to disturb us. As a result, neither his secretary nor mine came by to indicate they were leaving for the day, but he knew exactly when everyone had left." She paused.

Sensing her hesitancy, Michael encouraged, "Go on."

"He decided to force the issue. One minute, we were discussing the case. The next, he was pinning me down on his office sofa assuring me it would be to my advantage to give in and my disadvantage not to. I tried to reason with him. I failed. When he started trying to unfasten my clothes, I fought him. I had just managed to knock him to the floor when another partner walked in. There I was with my blouse open, my skirt pushed up against my hips and Lowell on his knees in front of me with his pants unzipped. You can imagine the picture it made."

"Jordis, I assure you that other partner knew exactly what was going on."

"That's what I thought, but that's not the position the other partner took." She sighed, dropped her head and ran both hands over the gel-shellacked hair leading into her ponytail. After only a few seconds her head sprang up. "Wait. You believe me?"

This time, Michael spun the basketball. "Why wouldn't I?"

"Just like that? No questions?"

"What am I missing?" He stared at her through her silence then clarity dawned. "Keith didn't believe you."

"No. He didn't. He asked me a million questions about the encounter, and then he still doubted my word. He was in the middle of a deal with the partner who walked in on Lowell and me. Closing the deal turned out to be more important to him than putting his trust in me."

She looked into Michael's eyes. "How can you be so sure?"

"*Cara*, I've seen your fighting spirit on the basketball court over a few points. If you tell me you had to fight that man off, I have no doubt you both looked like you'd been in a fight."

"For all the good it did me. That didn't stop the funny looks or the talk around the firm or the constant sexual innuendos from male colleagues who openly propositioned me. I was considered easy and fair game."

"That wouldn't happen here." Knowing the partners at her prior firm had allowed that to go on angered him. They'd intentional shirked their leadership responsibilities and left her vulnerable to hazing because they'd wanted her gone.

"Of course, it would. You can't control what people

think."

No way would he allow bullying like that to happen at his firm. "No, but I can make damn sure they keep those thoughts to themselves if they want to continue working at RHM."

She gave him an incredulous look. "You can't be serious?"

"Of course, I am."

"*Riiight*." She stepped away from him. "I keep forgetting your name is in giant letters on the side of the building. It must be good to be the king."

The classic Mel Brooks movie line sent his lips into a smirk and his thoughts into sinfully inappropriate territory.

"Okay, conjuring up that particular image probably was not wise on my part." She couldn't stop her own grin.

"Probably not." He was relieved she'd volunteered what had happened at her prior firm. Now was probably a good time to tell her he'd found out about the scandal on his own, but she hadn't let her guard down like this around him in over a week.

Being this close to her made him want to touch her, to pull her into his arms, to press his mouth to hers until her lips were swollen from his kisses. If she found out he'd had her investigated, he'd never get the chance.

His decision made, he captured her hand and tugged her until she settled against him. He pressed the basketball into his side while his free hand found her ponytail and stroked. When she finally relaxed against him, he dropped his head and pressed his lips to hers.

Her mouth stayed closed initially, but it didn't take long

for her to open to him. He deepened the kiss.

They got lost in each other, and she moaned.

He grew aroused.

As soon as she felt him rise, she pushed away. "Dammit, Michael. After what I just told you, how can you possibly still think this is a good idea? Don't you understand the word no?"

"You've never actually told me *no*, Jordis. Why is that it?"

She started to protest, but he cut her off. "You've told me you can't. You've asked me to back off. You've consistently reminded me I'm your supervising attorney. But, you've never once told me no or to stop. Not even now."

Her eyes lost focus. He could see her mentally running through each of their encounters, trying to determine if what he'd said was true. Her brow creased, and her gaze focused back on him. Her mouth opened then closed.

He had her. "I understand you're conflicted. And now, I have a better understanding as to why. But I'm not Lowell Bruner."

She opened her mouth to interrupt him.

He held up a hand. "Wait. Let me finish."

She closed her eyes again. Her shoulders rose and fell, and she dropped her head.

The bent index finger of his left hand slid under her chin and tilted her head back up. He waited for her to open her eyes before he continued. "I don't appreciate you lumping me together with some lecherous lawyer who uses his partnership position to extort sexual favors from associates. I would hope you think more of me than that."

"Michael, I—"

He crowded further into her personal space. "I can't deny I think about stripping you naked just about every minute of every day, but here's the thing. I think I've gotten to know you pretty well. So, there's one thing I'm certain of. If you didn't want me as much as I want you, you'd have absolutely no problem telling me no."

Her eyes flickered. The tapestry of hazel shrunk as her pupils dilated. The tight pressure that had surrounded his heart since his phone call with Battle lessened.

His hand snaked around her neck, and he planted a soft kiss on her lips. When he pulled back, the clipped edge to his voice dissipated into a low rumble. "And, in case you have any doubt, I'm also not Keith Wilson. I'll *always* be your champion. Trust me to take care of you."

He released her and moved to leave. After a few steps, he realized he still held the basketball against his side. He turned. "This isn't over between us, Jordis." He dribbled once and put up a jump shot. The ball flew through the air in a graceful arc and drilled through the hoop with such power the net didn't move. One side of his mouth quirked. "Not by a long shot."

CHAPTER 15

$\mathcal{L}$ ate the next evening, Jordis entered Michael's office cranking her neck from side to side. She hadn't meant to work so late, but something didn't add up in the reports from the opposing side's current expert witness. She'd been determined to make sense of it before she went home. She'd compiled a few notes she wanted Michael to read when he first arrived in the morning so she dropped the papers on his chair where he couldn't miss them.

As she reached for the pull chain of his still-lit desk lamp, her eyes fell on a masculine body sprawled on the office couch. Unlit recessed lights left shadows that danced across the lithe torso. Jordis stepped to the brown leather sofa, her bare feet soundless on the plush Berber carpet. She'd abandoned her shoes in her office and hadn't bothered to put them back on for the short walk to Michael's office. She hadn't expected anyone else to be here.

She perused the coffee table adjacent to the couch and took in miscellaneous papers, various ballpoint pens, and several different color highlighters scattered about. She picked up a page from the table and glanced over the sheet. Notes in Michael's fluid, masculine cursive filled the margins, annotating the possible source of certain facts.

She studied Michael. He'd kicked off his dress shoes made of soft Italian leather and rested in black sock-covered feet. One foot was up on the cushions, his knee bent against the back of the couch, and the other rested on the ground. His head lay propped against the corner of the couch. One arm draped over his chest; the other was caught between his body and the back of the sofa. She allowed her eyes to travel the length of him, enjoying an unobserved opportunity to appreciate his physique.

Goodness, he was sexy. Even in his sleep, he radiated a sex appeal that made her long to climb onto the couch and stretch out on top of him. She'd always had a thing for tall, athletic men. Michael had that in spades, plus a confidence and intelligence that made him almost irresistible. But, resist him she must. Nothing was more important to her right now than making partner. She couldn't let anything distract her—not competitive colleagues, not worries about keeping a masked interlude secret, and certainly not an affair with a senior partner.

She hadn't spoken to Michael all day. She'd tried to hold onto her fury over everything that had happened between them. Avoiding a liaison with him would be so much easier if they were at odds with each other. The chemistry between them made it hard to resist the lure of a sexual tryst.

To make matters worse, over the weeks they'd worked together, her professional admiration for the man had grown and her personal interest had followed. She'd like to think she'd simply fallen for his charm, his innate charisma. She could dismiss that as a shallow offshoot of their mutual physical attraction. The emotional draw he now held for her, however, couldn't be dismissed as something trivial.

The playful side of him she'd glimpsed while he'd tried to cajole her out of her funk with him had made her smile—behind his back. She understood his end game, but she hadn't been able to completely resist the appeal of his overtures. After thinking through what he'd said during his apology, she'd been unable to hold on to her anger. Without the shield of animosity, her heart couldn't stave off the softer emotions.

Michael admitted he'd been jealous. Try as she might to ignore that, a part of her felt flattered.

While Michael's assumption about her involvement with Eric had been insulting, from Michael's position at her office door, it had probably looked like she and Eric had been kissing or were about to kiss. In hindsight, she figured that's exactly what Eric had wanted. What better way to eliminate competition from the boss's presumed paramour than to make the boss think she was two-timing him? In so doing, he would destroy the boss's motivation to give her preferential treatment.

She also couldn't ignore her own behavior. She'd let the

baggage from her prior firm affect her thinking. She'd accused Michael of using his position to pressure an associate into having sex with him. As he'd pointed out yesterday, her accusation hadn't been a very favorable comment on her opinion of his character. She'd painted him with the same brush as the lowlife that had harassed her. He hadn't deserved that.

She looked down at him. If she reached out, she could touch his hair. Reason told her she shouldn't, but her fingers itched to touch him. She leaned over the couch, checking to make sure he was still asleep. His chest rose and fell evenly. His closed eyes and relaxed posture evidenced deep slumber.

She lifted her hand, inched it towards his head, then hesitated. Could she touch him softly enough not to wake him?

Her heart pounded.

Walk away, Jordis. Walk away.

Despite the warning voice in her head, she inched her fingers the rest of the way. They flitted lightly over the hair at the top of his head. The thick silkiness called to her. Her touch grew bolder. She eased her fingers into the slightly longer hair at his forehead and stroked them to the tips of the strands.

Her breathing changed.

The tickle of his hair beneath her fingers set her blood pulsing and made her want to touch more than his hair. *Good Lord.* She pulled in a long silent breath. How could touching him so casually have such an intense effect on her?

She struggled for control, thinking she needed to get

out of here before he woke up. She glanced at his face and froze. His eyes were open, his gaze locked on her face. Slowly, as if inching away from a rabid wolf, she removed her hand.

In an unhurried move, he captured her wrist. "Don't stop now." His husky voice slithered over her and further stirred her roiling hormones.

"Sorry." Her voice was a whisper. "I didn't mean to disturb you, but it's late. Don't you want to go home?" She tried to play off her intimate ministrations with feigned concern for his wellbeing.

"I think things are a lot more interesting where I am." His grip tightened on her wrist as she sought to withdraw it from his hand. "Where are you going?"

"Like I said, it's late. I need to go."

"Do you?" A clear challenge reverberated in his voice. "I think you need something else."

Her breath caught, and every nerve in her body began to tingle.

"Come here, Jordis."

Slowly, he drew her the last few inches to the couch. He eased to a sitting position and placed her between his spread legs, releasing her wrist and sliding his hands under the hem of her untucked blouse. He rubbed his fingers along her lower back then up her spine until he reached the back of her bra. He looked into her eyes.

The prospect of his hands on her breasts made her lower parts dampen. Nevertheless, she made a half-hearted attempt to stop the madness. "Michael," she panted, "we can't do this."

He spread his hands wide along her back. Paralysis

overtook Jordis's muscles. She stood immobile, transfixed by the look in his eyes.

They remained in that position for several long moments, wordless, just breathing. Then, his thumbs moved in an arc, easing around her sides until they found the swell of her breasts. He mapped the undercurve of each breast, staring at the center of her chest as if he could see through the material of her blouse to the naked flesh below or make the buttons open with his mind.

"When you touched my hair, I could feel it all over." His voice remained low, husky. "It was as if you pulsed with electricity and sent a charge through my entire body." He glanced up into her eyes and rolled his thumbs across the front of her bra to caress her pebbled nipples. "What would it take for me to make you feel that way?"

She moaned and started to pull away.

He stopped her. "Don't run from me this time." His thumbs worked over her nipples back the other direction. "Let me make you feel that way."

She stifled a whimpered. She certainly felt the charge now. The excitement forced her to breathe through her mouth. "Don't play games with me, Michael."

"Trust me, the play I have in mind has nothing to do with games." He pressed a kiss above the first button of her blouse. One hand released a breast and began to unbutton the blouse from the bottom. "I need to be with you tonight. Tell me what you need."

Her hands went to his arms, squeezing his biceps. "You know this is a mistake, right?"

"It doesn't feel like a mistake. *You* don't feel like a mistake."

Intellectually, she knew she should stop him, but her mind couldn't suppress the building eruption of certain desire. She was a successful career woman, financially independent, sexually self-aware—everything women's magazines touted as the modern-day Superwoman—but Michael Remington was evidently her Kryptonite. She hadn't given herself to him yet, but it didn't matter. She was his.

Something about this man drew her. The lure of the words he'd uttered on New Year's Eve pulled at her: You *are my true Juliet.*

He hadn't spouted them as a come-on. He hadn't known she could hear him. He hadn't known who she was then or even her name, but he'd been inexplicably drawn to her, too. She'd replayed those words in her head for days after that night, and she'd craved him. She still craved him, and she now understood the craving was mutual.

"Jordis, tell me what you want."

She wanted him.

What would it hurt to give in to him this one time? People already thought she was sleeping with him. If she was going to be the subject of gossip, she might as well reap the actual benefits of the torrid affair she was supposed to be having. Right?

Wrong.

She was making excuses for herself, putting herself in a dangerous position. She was already on the verge of falling for the guy. How much more emotionally entangled would she become if she slept with him? And what about her reputation and her career?

He'd told her to trust him to take care of her. She'd

never trusted anyone to take care of her before. She didn't know how. This man made her want to try, and she understood the folly of that. Even the indomitable Michael Remington had limits to what he could accomplish. She, better than anyone, knew he couldn't protect her from small minds and petty behavior. But, she also knew without a doubt he'd try, and she loved that about him.

He pushed against her back, causing her knees to fall against the couch between his thighs. He released another button on her blouse and skimmed his tongue in light circles against her skin.

Small minds and petty behavior quickly lost their significance. She closed her eyes, unable to process her conflicting thoughts. Her hands eased up his arms, across his shoulders, and over the buzzed hair at the back of his head. Resistance loosened inside her, leaving her powerless to stop her heart from making a decision that plunged her headlong into a carnal abyss.

❧ ❧ | ❦ ❦

Michael took Jordis's touch as encouragement to abandon the sampling and head for the feast. The taste of her made him hard and needy. A woman had never made him needy before. He had to fill her with everything in him soon or he was going to explode.

He pulled her closer, turning her and laying her on the couch. His tongue eased into her mouth and touched the tip of hers. When she hummed into his kiss, he tilted her face so he had a better angle to plunder her mouth. He ran his hands down her sides, along her hips until he reached the hem of her straight skirt. He started pushing the skirt slowly up her thighs.

She flinched before grabbing his wrists. He looked down to where her hands gripped him. A knot formed in his stomach. If she stopped him now, he wouldn't survive it.

"We can't do this." She glanced over at his open office door.

His eyes followed her glance. "There's no one here but us."

"You can't know that."

"Yes, I can. I checked." He'd known she was still in her office working. He'd stopped at her door to shoo her home when he realized it had started to snow. She had looked so intense he'd decided to let her continue to work. He'd stayed late for that reason alone. She still drove that damn sports car, taking her chances the winter would stay mild. He hadn't been able to leave knowing she'd be alone in the building and possibly get snowed in so he'd come back to his office to strategize more on his portion of their case.

His hands moved, attempting to continue his unveiling. "Everyone left hours ago. You and I were the only ones left except for the cleaning crew, and they all leave by eleven."

Jordis pushed hard against his wrists. "Michael, please." She glanced at the door again, her concern about making this encounter a possible exhibition apparent. "I can't. Not here."

Knowing her history, he understood her reluctance. With eighty percent of his blood below his waist, his synapses hadn't fired quick enough to comprehend the foolishness of seducing her here at the office. Even now with his brain kicking in, the swollen part of his anatomy ruled reason and selfishly wanted to continue. "I could lock the door?"

She gave a closed-mouth smile at his hopeful tone, but shook her head.

He let out a long, slow groan. "You do realize you worked until there were piles of snow on the ground? No one is crazy enough to still be here but you."

She placed her hands on either side of his face. "Then take me home."

He dropped his forehead against hers and expelled a loud sigh of frustration.

She lifted his head, looked at him with hooded eyes, and repeated in a husky voice that made clear her intent, "Take. Me. Home. Michael."

&ed; &ed; | &ed; &ed;

Michael pulled Jordis by the hand so fast her wedge heels slid across the snowed pavement as if she wore skis. She laughed, hard. By the time they reached her apartment, she was practically hyperventilating.

He grabbed the keys from her hand and unlocked the door. He dragged her inside, relocked the door, and threw her keys on the table in the entrance. His back went against the door. "You know, I don't appreciate you laughing at me."

"I can't help it. Were you in a bit of a hurry, Mr. Remington?"

"Yes. Still am." He pulled her to him and kissed her. Lips and tongues dueled. Hands roamed frantically over cheeks and hair and shoulders. He managed to pull his mouth away from hers long enough to admit, "I promised myself the first time I made loved to you, I'd take my time and love you so thoroughly you'd scream my name over and over. But, right now, I'm so on edge I just want you hard and fast."

She dropped her coat to the floor and leaned her body against his. Sliding her hands inside his coat, she pressed two quick kisses against his lips. "Hard and fast works for me, provided—" She slid one hand down to rub the sizable bulge at the front of his pants. "You still make me scream your name over and over."

Michael flipped them so she was the one with her back against the door. "What the lady wants, the lady gets."

His hand went under her chin and pushed up, and he dropped his parted lips against hers. His tongue worked methodically inside her mouth while his other hand went simultaneously to the wall, searching for a light switch. He wanted to see her face clearly when she offered him hard and fast. "Lights?"

She reached towards the wall opposite the one he'd searched and flipped a switch that illuminated the entry-way in soft yellow light.

He glanced at her eyes. Their color had darkened way past deep green, but hadn't quite reached brown. He'd never seen that shade on her before. If it went with the hungry look on her face, he intended to inspire the color often.

Michael shrugged his coat off and let it fall next to hers. His hands found the side of her thighs and inched up her skirt. When he got it high enough to slip a hand between her legs, his right hand went in search of Nirvana. Her groan of satisfaction let him know when he'd found it.

Tiny strings and a miniscule triangle of fabric gave him ready access to what he wanted. He slipped a finger inside the barely-there underwear. The dampness he encountered forced him to concentrate on his breathing to prevent a premature end to an evening he planned to make last for several hours.

When he found his control, he asked, "Why do women bother to put on these little pieces of nothing?"

Breathing with difficulty, she replied, "Because our clothing doesn't look half as good with undergarment bulges and panty lines. Are you complaining?"

"No, ma'am." A complaint was the furthest thing from his mind. "Pull your blouse out of your skirt for me." She complied. He pressed the finger inside her thong inside her. Her head fell back against the door. "Now, unbutton it."

Her fingers unfastened the buttons as quickly as her unfocused mind would allow. Once she was done, he dropped his head to her neck to nibble his way across her collarbone. He stopped at the two bumps at the center of her neck, sucking gently in a way that made her clench around his finger. He smiled to himself. He'd found one of her erogenous zones. He filed the information away for later exploration.

Loving the picture before him, Michael slid one bra strap down as far as her open blouse would allow and used his index finger to pull the cup off a lovely breast. He put the index finger in his mouth, pulled it out and rubbed her nipple with the wet tip. He watched it bead for him and goose bumps form along her chest.

While he played with her exposed nipple and her unexposed bud of desire, her eager hands got insistent against his hardened package. His heavy breathing mingled with hers.

Jordis unfastened his belt and slid it free of his belt loops. The clank of the buckle against hardwood floor echoed around the dim room as she undid his pants.

When her hands slid into his boxer briefs, he removed his finger from its nipple play and grabbed both her wrists with the one hand. "*Bellezza*, you need to let me drive or I'm going to embarrass myself."

"You can drive all you want, *caro mio*. I just want a chance to check out the merchandise." She smiled at the surprised look of pleasure on his face.

"You've been studying Italian?"

"I looked up a few words. I got tired of not knowing what you were calling me and you didn't seem to want to tell me. 'Sweetheart' sounds so much more romantic in Italian."

He chuckled. "You know something?"

She shook her head from side to side.

"I think I may be in way over my head with you." He kissed her deeply. "You sure about that hard and fast?"

"Oh, yeah."

"Good." He added another finger to her core and immediately increased the tempo of his attention.

Her hips moved in response and sexy vocalizations hovered in her throat.

Michael grabbed his wallet from his back pocket. Not wanting to stop his manual stroking, he flipped it open with one hand and held it out to her. "Grab a packet for me, *cara*."

She smiled at his intentional use of the Italian endearment and quickly pulled an accordion of condom packets from his wallet. Not waiting for instructions, she tore a packet open with her teeth and held it out to him. "I'd help you out, but I wouldn't want you to embarrass yourself."

Laughing softly, he flipped his wallet behind him. A thud and jangle of keys indicated it had landed on the entryway table.

"Impressive."

He pushed his pants and underwear below his knees, and sheathed himself quickly. "Baby, you haven't seen impressive yet."

Toeing off one shoe and freeing a foot from the tangle of garments around his ankles, he yanked her skirt up past her hips, pulled aside her black triangle, and slid into paradise.

They both let out a deep moan. Jordis's hands gripped his shoulders and her head fell back, but he didn't tarry in the moment. He lifted one of her legs, bending her knee over the crook of his arm, and immediately started a totally different kind of stroking.

His gluteus muscles flexed repeatedly in a steady rhythm that made her roll her hips in complement. Her hands slid down his back, and she pulled him tighter against her, sending his control once again to the edge. He adjusted his breathing and wrangled his completion back into standby mode before lifting her leg higher to seat himself deeper.

A keening sound started low in her throat, letting him know he was in the right spot. "Michael!"

"I know, baby," he panted. "Stay with me a little longer."

He dropped his head into the crook of her neck, and she lifted a hand to the back of his head, holding him there. Their tempo and breathing accelerated until their bodies beat a steady knock against the door. Her erotic lilt grew louder. They clutched each other, and he thickened inside her. The increased tightness of her sheath intensified his pleasure to the point of pain. He tamped down the primitive yowl building inside him and worked it out between her thighs.

"Yes," she cried. "More."

He gave her more. Her voice rose an octave, his name getting shriller by the second.

"More?" he asked.

"*Yeeess*."

Their knocking against the door grew fiercer, a rapid aural pulse playing like a possessed metronome to their sexual tune. His pants mixed with hers. A solo groan harmonized periodically with percussive breathing, and name calling rounded out the melody. The tune played over and over, louder and louder, until she was nearly screeching his name in a subdued repetitious cry meant to keep her neighbors from hearing more of the show than they probably already had.

When her voice waivered in a tone that suggested her release was close, he gave two long, deep thrusts and commanded, "Let go, baby. Let it go."

Her spasms against his staff followed immediately, pulling his release out to meet hers. He dropped his mouth to her lips. The kiss captured the wail she could no longer suppress and kept him from emitting his own shout of ecstasy, which he suspected would sound more like the squeal of a ten-year-old girl.

He released her leg and pulled her close. His heart beat frantically, but his spirit rested easy. She didn't know it yet, but he had no intention of ever letting her go.

Whipped. His brain taunted. That's what he was, and he was thinking of a particular kind of whipped that came in a compound word and followed the offensive term for kitty.

He'd always hated that expression. He never understood it. In his other life, nowhere on the planet could a man find sex good enough to surrender his soul. He'd been enlightened at the school of Jordis, and his reincarnated psyche seeped into and displaced the jaded shell of his former self.

He kissed her again, tasting her mouth from corner to corner before he asked, "Do you know what *bellezza* means?"

She gave him a soft smile and nodded. "Beauty."

"And that you are."

He proceeded to show her how beautiful he thought she was from the front door to the living room couch to the hallway wall.

❧ ❧ | ❦ ❦

When they finally reached her bedroom, Jordis's limbs felt like jelly. She didn't think she could take any more pleasure. He'd removed her blouse, bra, skirt, panties, and shoes along the way. They'd been left behind like a trail of bread crumbs leading back from a den of iniquity. She lay before him wearing nothing. When he crawled up her body from the bottom of the bed and kissed her inner thighs, her eyes closed. With a satisfied groan, she grabbed his head and pulled him up for a kiss.

"Hey, what are you doing? I wasn't finished down there."

Her cheeks dimpled. "Darling, if you give me one more orgasm, I'm going to die of heart failure."

"How about just a small one?" He placed his thumb and index finger centimeters apart in front of her face as a visual aid.

She gave a short laugh. If he were half as good with his tongue downtown as he was with the part of his anatomy that made him male, there would be nothing small about any orgasm he gave her. "You were wrong before."

His perplexed expression made her laugh in earnest.

"I'm the one who's way out of my league with you. You're insatiable."

The corners of his mouth lifted. He placed a kiss along the top of one breast. "You're delicious. You can't fault me for being gluttonous when I'm with you." He grabbed the condom he'd thrown on the bed before she'd collapsed onto it.

Her eyes widened. "You can't be serious?"

He kissed her softly. "Don't worry. This time I'll take it nice and slow. You don't have to do anything except let me enjoy you."

Her smile turned as liquid as her limbs. When he looked at the condom packet and frowned, she asked, "Something wrong?"

"I should have taken you to my place."

"Why?"

"This is my last condom. I only had four in my wallet."

She wanted to laugh at his childish pout. The image of what his son would look like when he didn't get his way flashed through her mind. Her heart fluttered, and she went sentimentally soft. In that moment, she knew. What she'd been fighting these last few days—maybe these last few weeks—had been about something deeper than lust.

Emotion overwhelming her, she felt a rising need to have him inside her again. "Don't worry about it." She stretched for the drawer handle of the bedside table, but her arms couldn't quite reach.

He leaned slightly and slid it open for her. A box of condoms peeked up at him. He quickly looked back at her. His expression went from surprised to relieved to perplexed in a matter of seconds.

Remembering his comment about being jealous and possessive for the first time in his life, Jordis explained. "It's a new box."

He stared at her quietly.

"And the first I've needed since I gave Keith back his ring."

That made him smile. "I love a woman smart enough to be prepared."

He rolled on his last condom.

Jordis pulled a small white remote from under her pillow, clicked a button, and sighed as he slid into her to the sound of John Legend crooning *Tonight (Best You Ever Had)*. She set the song to loop repeatedly. She lost track of how many times it played as he made slow, passionate love to her. When they finally exhausted themselves, she set the music to time itself off, and they fell asleep still linked intimately, their arms and legs tangled together.

CHAPTER 16

S now fell all through the night. Jordis rolled over when she felt Michael rise from the bed at dawn. He strolled from the room naked with the same confident swagger he possessed when fully clothed. When he returned with his cell phone, she listened while he activated the firm's inclement weather notice, shutting the office for the day.

They lounged around her apartment all morning, alternating between eating, watching movies, and making love. They spent a lot of time talking in front of her blazing fireplace. In the afternoon, Michael made a store run to get sparkling wine, strawberries, S'more fixings and ingredients for a fabulous pasta dish he made her for dinner. For the first time in a long time, neither of them thought about the office or work for a full day.

After they'd stuffed themselves and worn themselves

out making love in a long hot shower, they laid in front of the fire again. Michael lounged shirtless and sockless in baggy sweatpants he had stashed in the gym bag he kept in the trunk of his car. Jordis lay in a gold negligee.

Michael fingered her damp ponytail, which had sprouted frizzy waves. "Do you ever wear your hair natural like this?"

She gave him a languid smile, still feeling the effects of his lovemaking. "Sometimes. Of course, sometimes it happens whether I want it to or not. It automatically frizzes up when it's humid or I get it wet. If I don't tame it with moisturizer or a flat iron, I end up with a frizzy bush."

"Hmm."

Jordis watched a contemplative look flicker across his face before he refocused on her. She remembered her hair had been wavy on New Year's Eve. Although she'd been wearing a wig, it had slipped during their encounter. Some of her hair had fallen out. Had he been observant enough to notice?

He'd questioned her off and on about that night earlier, but she'd deflected his comments. She'd hedged and diverted her gaze when she did so, not able to look him in the eyes as she prevaricated. He eventually let it go, but now he seemed back to putting two and two together.

It crossed her mind she should go ahead and admit the truth, but she hesitated. After his comment the other day about her never having told him no, she wondered if the added knowledge of her loose behavior on New Year's Eve would make him doubt her story about her prior senior partner. He'd told her he believed her, but part of her still expected him to reveal he had his doubts.

She ran her hand lightly against his chest. She'd originally thought it bare, but in the firelight, she saw the dusting of fine straight hairs. Their brown color so closely matched his skin tone that they were almost invisible. "I owe you an apology."

"Oh, yeah? For what?"

"You were right. I let what happened to me in LA affect my interpretation of why you appointed me to the Metra Pharmaceuticals case. You didn't deserve that."

His expression turned guarded. "It's okay. I understand."

She considered the wary expression on his face and wondered what was on his mind. She became uncomfortable. She must be right about his doubts. He just didn't want to say anything. She couldn't live with that. She needed him to speak his mind. "What are you thinking?"

"Nothing."

She pushed herself up on his chest. "Michael, you're thinking so loud, I can practically hear the words formulating in your head."

His hands tightened against her back and he stared at her. His brow creased. "I'm just wondering why you accepted a payout instead of suing for harassment."

She stiffened. "How do you know about the payout?"

He didn't answer.

"Law firms don't put that kind of information in attorney personnel files; they're too litigation adverse. The partners at my prior firm, particularly, were afraid I'd sue them if they disseminated any information that might prevent me from getting another job. So, you had to have gone the extra mile to uncover my settlement agreement." She struggled against him. "Did you find out before or after I told you what happened?"

He swallowed. "Before."

She tried to pull away from him. "You knew this whole time?"

"No." He held her tight, refusing to let her up.

"When did you find out?"

"Two days ago."

"Two days ago!" Frustrated with her inability to break his grasp, she growled, "Let go of me!" He released her, and she rolled away, propping herself against the couch. "How did you find out?"

He pushed out a deep sigh and sat up. "I had someone ask a few questions."

"You mean you had me investigated." An angry glare accompanied the clipped words.

He nodded.

"If you didn't trust me, then what has this all been about?" She moved to get up, but he grabbed her wrist.

"Jordis, I do trust you."

She gave him a doubtful look.

He repeated himself. "I *do* trust you. And that's not an easy thing for me. Don't walk away."

Something in his voice made her pause. She struggled with indecision, but ultimately settled back into a sitting position. "If you wanted to know about me, why didn't you just ask?"

"I'd been trying to get through to you for over a week, but you kept blowing me off." He reached up to touch her cheek.

She jerked her face away.

He dropped his hand, propping his wrist on a raised knee. He placed his other hand on the floor behind his hip. "Don't be mad. I thought if I could understand what happened in your past, it might give me a clue as to how to resolve the distance between us."

"Why didn't you say anything when you first found out?"

"I intended to. I sort of got distracted."

"Distracted?"

He gave her a look that made her all tingly inside. It irritated her. She was angry with him. It wasn't fair he could do that to her with just a look.

"Do you have any idea how much watching you play ball turns me on?"

Her mouth dropped open, and she blinked a few times. "I—" She didn't know what to say to that. Then, an imaginary light bulb flickered on above her head. "That's why you came looking for me in the gym the other day."

He nodded. "I know I should have said something then, but I'd been desperate to get through to you. Once you started talking to me, I was afraid you'd shut down if you knew I'd checked up on you."

She shook her head. His name slipped from her lips in an exasperated whisper. After a minute, a slow grin eased onto her face. "Desperate, huh?"

He frowned. "You don't have to look so happy about that, but yes." He shifted closer to her. "When I found you shooting hoops in the gym, all I could think about was how much I wanted—*needed*—to kiss you again. If you'd've shut down on me, I'd have never gotten the chance."

"You should have just asked me." She crossed her arms

tight against her chest, her defensive posture at odds with her amusement over his desperation.

"You're right. I'm sorry."

He must have sensed the conflict in her because he watched her intently, but didn't move closer.

She watched him back, struggling with whether to take his apology at face value. Eventually, her arms dropped and her shoulders relaxed. "Okay. I accept your apology." She angled her body towards him. "But I need to understand something. What did you mean trusting women is not easy for you?" She propped her left arm on the couch and tucked her feet beneath her.

He blew out a slow, shallow breath. "It's a long story."

She glanced towards the darkened windows. "Last I checked, it was still snowing. You going somewhere?"

෨ ෨ | ෯ ෯

"I . . ." Michael tilted his head. A little slow on the uptake, it took him a moment to process she wasn't kicking him out. "No."

He adjusted to a more comfortable position, but didn't say anything else. He'd never explained himself to a woman before. That required a degree of trust and caring he'd not yet experienced. It also required revealing how much of an idiot he'd been on several occasions. Admitting to this woman he'd been played a few times held absolutely no appeal. Exposing the cynicism he carried around as a result felt even more uncomfortable.

She sat patiently, watching him with a look that said *I'm waiting*. After dodging a bullet for his investigation *faux pas*, he didn't think blowing off her question would be a wise move. As uncomfortable as he felt, he needed to be open with her. She'd told him about the baggage from her past that made their attraction to each other even more problematic for her than the ethical conflict they still needed to resolve. What were a few ex-girlfriend dramas compared to a sex scandal and fear of career suicide?

He ran a hand down his face. "When I was a junior in high school, I started working at the firm doing various jobs—mail room, file clerk, you name it. My father cautioned me to be careful about whom I got involved with. He warned me that I would get a lot of attention, but not all of it would be genuine attraction to me. As the son of a named partner, I was a good catch and catching me any way they could would be the main goal of some women."

Her eyebrows rose. "Is that so?"

He chuckled at the sarcasm in her voice. "I was tall for my age and very athletic. Female attention always came easy to me. In fact, he'd given me a similar speech before I started high school. This was simply a reminder the situation hadn't changed although the women might be a little more persistent and a lot more sophisticated than the girls at school."

Her eyes roamed over his body. "I could see that. I never understood what a grown woman would want with a teenager, but in your case, I could see a woman with those proclivities being tempted."

"I took his advice to heart during my early years. I was extremely careful with whom I spent time and even more careful no surprises resulted from how I spent that time. If you know what I mean."

She nodded. "Surprises that took appropriately nine months to materialize?"

"Exactly." He looked up at her. "Unfortunately, when I turned nineteen, I slipped up. It was the summer after my freshman year of college. I was cocky and used to attention from older women." He shrugged nonchalantly. "Big man on campus and all with my basketball scholarship. Upper-class women propositioned me all the time. So I wasn't surprised or wary when a young associate at my dad's firm took an interest in me . . . Monica."

"How old was she?"

"Twenty-five. We had a summer fling. I was careful, except for one time. We'd been together all night. The next morning, we got hot and heavy before I realized I was out of condoms. I started to slow it down, but she pressed to continue, assuring me she was on the pill. Even as I allowed myself to be persuaded, part of me knew I was making a mistake."

He could tell she knew what was coming before he said it.

"Sure enough, right before I headed back to school, Monica told me she was pregnant. Her plan was for us to rush off and get married before we told anyone the news."

She slid her knees to her chest and wrapped her arms around them. "You didn't? Did you?"

"No." He sat up. "I was scared and embarrassed, but I went to my father and admitted I'd screwed up." His eyes lost focus for a minute, and he slid fingers through his hair. "My parents were old-fashioned. I had visions of being married and struggling to keep my basketball scholarship while I worked to support a wife and kid. I realize that sounds shallow, but remember I was only nineteen."

She dropped her chin to her knees. "What happened?"

"Lucky for me, my parents were smart enough not to let me rush into anything. They stood by me and approached the situation with calm." He winched. "Well, that is after my father gave me an upbraiding I've never forgotten. They absolutely expected me to take care of the child if the baby were mine, but they insisted I go back to school and keep in touch with the girl. My father made it clear he would cover her expenses, and once the baby was born, we'd do a paternity test simply as a means to make sure my legal rights to the child were protected since he or she would be born out of wedlock."

"So they didn't insist you marry the girl."

"No. That surprised me. I found out later they'd suspected the girl was lying. Turns out they were right. A few months after I returned to school, she unexpectedly had a miscarriage. At least, that's what she told us. We found out from another associate at the firm, who'd roomed with her, she'd let slip she'd never been pregnant. Had I married her, she would have waited until a few months after the ceremony for the miscarriage to occur."

Her expression remained neutral.

When she didn't say anything, he continued. "The experience taught me that my father wasn't being paranoid or simply dramatic about taking care with my sexual activity. I learned my lesson about protection at all times, no excuses."

The corner of her mouth tilted up. "Thus your concern last night about your last condom."

"Yeah." His head bobbed as he spoke. "I wish I could

say Monica was the last time I had a run in with a woman at the firm, but she wasn't."

Her head popped up.

He chuckled. "Wait. Wait." Both his hands flipped up. "Don't judge. Under no circumstance did I ever date another woman at my father's firm during my college years. But my second year as an associate, I dated another lawyer in my class for a few months. After I broke it off with her, she went to my father and accused me of pressuring her into a sexual relationship."

"Geesh."

He leaned back, straightening his legs and crossing them at the ankles. "It gets worse. A few years ago, I got engaged to a junior partner in the Business and Finance division. I'd learned my lesson about dating associates, but I allowed myself to be lured into a relationship with another partner. I figured since she'd already made partner, she'd have no ulterior motives. I was wrong." He went into detail about the exploits of his ex and her attempted paternity con with the help of a man she was dating on the side.

"No wonder you now avoid office romances like the plague."

He said nothing for a while. "Not *all* office romances." He moved to sit next to her, placing his arm along the couch behind her. "At least, not anymore." He held her gaze, shifted towards her, and waited.

She hesitated—a nanosecond—before she leaned to meet him. Releasing her knees, her hands found his chest, and she balanced against him.

They kissed slowly, finding truce within the unhurried press of lips and tongue.

When they parted, he leaned his forehead against hers. "I know you're nothing like those other women. Old habits die hard. I wanted to know something, and my natural instincts took over. I found a way to get the information myself." He lifted his head. "It won't happen again."

"It better not."

He flinched at her harsh tone then relaxed when he saw the softness in her eyes. He nodded. "Enough talking." He grabbed her around the waist without warning and pulled her down.

Jordis shrieked then started laughing.

He adjusted her against his chest. "How about we get back to where we were?"

Trying to get her laughter under control, Jordis stretched out on top of him. Once comfortable, she turned the conversation back to his initial question. "Why do you think I accepted the payout?"

He shrugged.

"Me against a senior partner at one of the largest firms in LA. Talk about an uphill battle, even without his partner backing him up. I was reassigned to a case of equal prominence and promised I would never have to work directly with Lowell again. I'd only recently switched firms. I had no desire to have to start over again."

He rubbed her back. "A man who was bold enough to set that kind of trap at the office has probably pulled that ambush before."

"I agree, but proving that in a court of law could have taken years. You know how the legal community is. No one would have had the guts to hire me while the case was pending. Too much potential backlash from a firm with the clout and connections of my prior employer."

She propped her chin on her hand and looked down at him. "I thought the incident would blow over. Unfortunately, I didn't get that lucky. I was branded as calculatingly promiscuous and the environment got pretty oppressive in short order. After I complained to the firm ombudsman about the hostile work environment, the firm came up with a quick settlement offer disguised as severance pay. I squeezed them for every dime I could and walked away without a second thought."

"You weren't concerned about the women who might come after you?"

She grazed two fingers over his chest, a smug look on her face. "Oh, that won't be an issue."

At his questioning look, she explained. "Apparently, Lowell's computer had a two-way web cam." She shrugged. "No one really knows how a guy who hardly ever used his computer ended up with such a sophisticated monitor." She smiled. "Anyway, the web cam facing out into the office was left on during some inconvenient times. He was caught on camera receiving fellatio favors from a few staff members, several of them noticeably reluctant."

"Fellatio favors, huh?" He chuckled, amused by her choice of words.

"Yep." She continued her mischievous smile. "Somehow, a few weeks after I left the firm, video of Lowell's sexual exploits got streamed one morning to every computer on the firm network. Shortly thereafter, Lowell decided to retire from active practice with the firm."

He laughed. "You didn't?"

She shrugged again then laughed with him. "Sometimes, it's pretty darn cool to have a brother who can do anything and find anything with a computer."

"Why you wench. And after they gave you such a nice wad of cash."

She grinned. "Actually, they sort of paid me twice."

"How so?"

"That trademark case I've been working on?"

He nodded.

"The client was originally Lowell's. In fact, it was the case we were working on when he tried to molest me. When I left, the client transferred their representation to come with me. Their engagement agreement includes a twenty percent bonus if I settle the case before trial. Which I just did." She wiggled happily against him.

"Hmm. Good job." He rolled her beneath him. "I think this calls for a celebration."

"Say that in Italian."

His right brow peaked. Her pupils dilated.

He leaned in and whispered something in Italian. The words had less to do with celebrating and more to do with what his hand was doing between her thighs. Continuing to speak in Italian, he kissed his way down her body. Breasts, stomach, hips all received his attention. When he moved lower and planted his lips for an intimate kiss, she bucked and reached for him.

"*Non questa volta, amore.*" He grabbed her hips, held her in place, and refused to be denied this time.

He ravished her thoroughly by mouth then flipped her and started over with a much harder part of his anatomy. Shortly after the third time she screamed his name, they fell asleep in front of the fire. Sometime in the night, he awoke and carried her to bed.

Jordis came awake the next morning warmer than usual. Her brain took a few moments to register the male body almost completely beneath her. She took a deep breath, enjoying the scent of him mixed with the magic of last night. She kissed his chest. He stirred but didn't wake. She smiled. She could get used to waking up like this.

Her eyes traveled down his body. The covers bunched below his waist with a long bulge in the center of their folds. She slid a hand down to unveil her morning present then stretched out on top of him. She reached a hand under the pillow he'd used last night to stash condoms, hoping to find at least one more.

He released a deep sigh and turned his head to look at her through sleepy eyes. His raspy voice greeted her. "May I help you, Ms. Morgan?"

She responded by sliding her tongue in his mouth and rubbing her pelvis against his engorged shaft.

When she released his mouth, the shadow of sleep had left his eyes. "Oh, yeah. I can help you with that."

She laughed as she sheathed him then climbed on board. She rode him slowly, enjoying the feel of him inside her and wanting to savor the moment.

Looking into her eyes, he grasped her waist and began to alter her tempo with his thrusts. Not willing to be rushed, Jordis removed his hands. She interlaced their fingers and leaned forward to stretch their arms above his head. She squeezed her pelvic muscles simultaneously.

"Jordis," he groaned.

"It's my turn to drive," she whispered against his neck.

She lifted her buttocks so his shaft rubbed against her pubic bone.

He moaned.

She repeated the move.

He moaned again. "I'm not going to last if you keep doing that," he managed through clenched teeth.

"Hmm," she responded before she slid her mouth back to his and kissed him with a sensuous fervor that corresponded seductively with the movement of her hips.

She levered back up, their clasped hands pressed atop her thighs. He watched her intently. After a while, he released one of her hands to press his thumb where their bodies joined. The exquisite pressure pushed her closer and closer to the edge. She could tell by the sounds from his throat that he, too, was near the edge. His noises fueled her excitement, pushing her to a faster and faster tempo. They held each other's gaze, coaxing one another higher with loud, wordless sounds of pleasure until the internal damn burst and shoved them simultaneously off an orgasmic cliff into a psychedelic free fall.

Sweat-soaked, Jordis collapsed against Michael's perspiration-damp chest as the sound of a door opening drew their attention.

"Was that the front door?" he asked.

Her look of horror alarmed him, and he made to move. She stopped him with a shake of her head and a palm against his chest. Only one other person had a key to her apartment.

"Jo? You here?" a deep voice called from the living

room.

"Crap." She dropped her head against his chest.

"Who's that?"

She looked up. "My brother! Quick, into the bathroom."

"You're kidding, right?" He linked his hands casually behind his head, looking as if he were settling in for the long haul.

The sound of footsteps coming down the hall made her curse. She pulled the covers up around her and disengaged from their coupling. "No! Michael, get up," she ordered in a whisper.

Michael watched her with an amused look on his face, but didn't move.

"Brandt, give me a minute," she yelled. "I'm not dressed. I'll be right out."

The footsteps stopped immediately. "Okay. I brought you something. So make it quick."

She jumped up and shut the door. The footsteps retreated.

Collapsing against the door, she made an evil face at Michael. "Really?"

"Didn't you tell me your brother lives over an hour away?"

She nodded her head.

"Then he's not here for a quick visit. He's planning to stay a while. You really don't expect me to hide out in the bathroom all day do you?"

"Of course not. I just needed a moment to regroup."

"Well, you got it. Chop chop, sweetheart. He brought you something, remember?"

She stuck her tongue out at him, and he laughed. On

her way to the bathroom, she paused. "How would you feel if you showed up at Raina's apartment and caught her *in flagrante* with some guy you'd never met before?"

The disturbed look on his face said it all.

"Well, Mr. Remington, this morning, *you're* that guy." She took warped pleasure in his change of expression and headed into the bathroom.

Jordis took the quickest shower of her life, threw on sweats, and rushed out to greet her brother. While she took her color from their light-skinned father, her brother had their mother's coloring. His medium brown skin made him a few shades darker than her, and his eyes were a light whiskey brown instead of hazel, but there was no mistaking the family resemblance. If he hadn't shorn his hair close to his scalp, it would be the same wavy mass with a tendency towards curl she had, although in a deeper brown than her chestnut locks. The shape of his eyes and the nose perched beneath them mirrored hers exactly, and the trim goatee that framed his mouth did little to hide the identical slant of his lips when he smiled.

She gave him a hug and a kiss. He immediately chastised her. Apparently, he'd been trying to reach her since Thursday night when the snow started, but she hadn't responded to any of his calls. She realized she had no clue where she'd left her mobile phone or whether it still had any battery life.

"Where's your car?" Her brother moved to pull *Lamar's* donuts from the oven warmer. "I didn't see it outside. Did you drive that thing in the blizzard that hit Thursday night?" He grabbed two plates, setting one in front of her on the kitchen island where she sat with her back to the kitchen doorway.

"No. Of course not."

"What do you mean 'of course not'? You finally get another ride?"

"Not exactly," she hedged.

"Not exactly? What does that mean?"

Michael Remington strode into the kitchen. "It means I brought her home Thursday night." He was fully dressed, hair damp from a recent shower.

Brandt's eyes widened. Jordis closed her eyes at the sound of Michael's voice. When she opened them, Brandt was staring at her.

Brandt leaned back against the counter and crossed his arms. "I see," he said to Michael. He shifted his gaze back to hers. "I guess that explains why you haven't been answering your phone."

Jordis blushed.

Michael stepped over to Brandt and introduced himself.

"Michael, it's good to finally meet you in person . . . I think." Brandt got another plate from the cupboard and set it in front of the empty chair next to Jordis. "Would you like a glazed or a chocolate donut?" Looking back at his sister, he added with a smirk, "I'm guessing chocolate."

The glazed donut Jordis had halfway to her mouth stopped in midair as she glared her disbelief at her brother. She looked quickly up at Michael when he passed behind her and fingered the waves of her ponytail. He was trying to hide his amusement, but the corners of his mouth gave him away.

He looked down into her eyes. "Works for me," he said

then strolled over to help himself to a cup of coffee from the disposable carafe of gourmet brew Brandt had brought with him.

Jordis rolled her eyes at them before refocusing on her glazed ring of carbohydrates. Surviving the morning with these two was going to be more than interesting.

CHAPTER 17

*M*ichael enjoyed watching the interplay between the siblings. Jordis was clearly chagrined at the timing of her brother's arrival, and Brandt was flabbergasted to catch his sister entertaining a man. He planned to stick around a while to see how the dynamics played out.

After breakfast, the three chatted a bit then talked about the computer forensics work Brandt was doing on their case. Eventually, Jordis decided she'd gone long enough without checking her email and went to the back room to get on the computer.

She'd been gone only a few minutes when Brandt began his man-to-man faceoff. "Well, this is a surprise."

"Is it?" Michael rose to refill his coffee mug then leaned against the counter.

"What happened? You decide to use my sister's transportation issue to extort a little weekend entertainment?"

Michael's eyes narrowed. "It's not like that."

"Isn't it?" Brandt gave him a dubious smile. "You telling me you just happened to show up this morning before I got here?"

Michael stared at him for a few seconds, holding back the smart-ass reply on the edge of his lips. He thought about Jordis's reference to how he'd feel if this situation were reversed. He'd be conducting just such an interrogation. An odd sense of irony shrouded the moment. This is what it felt like to be on the receiving end of a protective brother.

"Uh, no." He raised his mug to hide his amusement at the turnabout.

"So, what did you promise my sister to earn your extended visit?"

A muscle jumped in Michael's jaw. "Nothing. Your sister's smart enough not to let herself be used like that."

"You think so?"

"You don't?"

"Well, I'd think my sister would be smart enough not to sleep with her boss, but here you are. So, I'm wondering what's the deal. You make a habit of sleeping with your associates, Remington?"

Michael sat his coffee mug on the counter then turned back to Brandt, keeping a tight lid on his rising ire. "As a matter of fact, no. Never, in fact. This is a first."

Brandt leaned back in his chair. "What made my sister so lucky?"

Michael gave him an incredulous look. "You really have to ask me that?"

Brandt sighed. "Look, I know my sister is a beautiful woman, and I realize the effect she tends to have on men. I also realize they tend to focus so much on the outer package they fail to appreciate the inner one. You wouldn't be the first colleague who thought his position could be used to manipulate special privileges."

Michael rubbed the back of his neck. He didn't usually feel the need to explain himself, but he understood Brandt's position. "I know what happened between me and Jordis this weekend crossed a serious line. It's not something I take lightly. In all honesty, I tried with everything in me at first to avoid this situation. Nothing worked. I'm not here on a whim, Brandt. I respect your sister a great deal. I'd never do anything to hurt her. You're going to have to trust I'll do everything in my power to manage our relationship in a way that has no negative repercussions for your sister."

Brandt rose to get more coffee and a second donut. "I'm going to have to take you at your word, counselor. For now. But know this, Remington." Brandt turned to look at him. "You fail and your ass is mine."

They silently took each other's measure. They were the same height and stood a few feet apart meeting each other's gazes directly.

Finally, Michael nodded. "Understood."

Taking a bite of a caramel Long John, Brandt chewed then said out the side of his mouth, "Just one more question." He swallowed, took a sip of coffee. "Two weeks ago, you were *persona non grata*. Exactly how did you go from arrogant, domineering jerk to sleeping with my sister?"

Michael grinned. "I didn't."

Brandt raised a quizzical eyebrow.

"She still thinks I'm an arrogant, domineering jerk. She's just stopped fighting the fact that she finds that irresistible."

Gut-deep laughter shot from Brandt, eradicating the tension in the room. From that moment on, he and Brandt were at ease with each other.

Jordis rejoined them later, and the three ate leftover pasta for lunch. Late that afternoon, Michael headed out to take care of some business of his own and leave the siblings time to visit. On his way out, he asked for Jordis's car keys, promising to have her car delivered by Monday morning when she needed to leave for work.

She walked him to the door. He reached for her after she opened it, but she hesitated, looking over her shoulder at her brother. She turned back and touched her hand briefly to Michael's chest. She whispered, "I'll see you at the office on Monday."

Michael looked past her at Brandt who had parked himself across from them on the arm of the couch, making no pretense of giving them any privacy. Michael leaned in and gave her a long, slow kiss that said so much more than goodbye.

When he pulled back, he whispered, "You didn't seriously expect me to leave without a kiss did you?"

"Uhm . . ."

He tapped her nose with his index finger. Keeping his voice low, his tone turned serious. "We're going to have to talk about this, you know? About what . . ." He motioned his finger back and forth between her chest and his. ". . . means."

"I know." Resignation laced her voice.

"Okay, then." He gave her a peck on the lips. "Back to your brother."

Jordis sighed. Michael laughed as he walked away. He could tell she wasn't looking forward to what was coming now that her brother had her alone.

ᑏ ᑏ | ᑏ ᑏ

The minute Jordis shut the door, Brandt asked, "Do you know what you're doing?"

"No." She turned to face her brother.

Her honesty surprised Brandt. "Jo, this goes against everything you've ever said about the inadvisability of an office romance."

"Don't you think I know that, Brandt?"

"Then what's going on?"

"I don't know. I just needed . . ."

"You just needed what?" Brandt watched her face closely. "Don't you dare try to tell me you needed to get laid. That's not you, and I know it. There's more to it than that."

"Maybe there is. Don't worry about it."

"Come on, Jo. Talk to me."

She pushed off the door and took a seat in the living room across from him. "Really, Brandt, it was an impulse kind of thing. It's not as if this is a long-term deal."

"Does *he* know that?"

She stayed silent.

Brandt rose from his chair. "I need to get some shut-eye. I didn't sleep well the last two nights waiting for someone to call me back."

"Sorry, bro."

"It's okay. I'm just glad you're all right." He kissed the top of her head as he passed by. Before he entered the hallway, he stopped. "I did tell you you needed to get a man. Maybe I should have been more specific."

She grabbed a pillow from the couch and threw it at him.

Listening to Brandt's chuckles fade down the hallway, Jordis grabbed another pillow off the couch and clutched it to her chest. Despite her resolve only a few days ago, she'd had sex with her supervising attorney—marathon sex . . . over several days. To make matters worse, she'd done something stupid. She'd fallen for him. She'd fallen head over heels for a man she couldn't have. For a smart woman, she really wasn't acting too bright.

She'd told Brandt this wasn't a long-term deal. It wasn't because it couldn't be. She couldn't have Michael and maintain her current position at the firm. At this point in her career, another lateral move would reflect negatively on her. It would appear she didn't have what it takes to make it at a firm regardless of the extenuating circumstances that had nothing to do with her legal skills. Even if she stayed at RHM, if it took her too long to make partner, the same negative implications would apply. Her years of seniority would become a red flag.

The situation caused a major dilemma. After this weekend, she didn't want to give up spending time with Michael—in bed or out. She wanted to believe she could trust him to make this interlude work between them without risk to her reputation or career.

What if she could have her cake and eat it too? Men did it all the time. Of course, the dynamics of most office romances rarely had the male in the subordinate position. She'd known, from the start, the potential professional consequences were higher for her than him. No sense pretending that would magically change through wishful thinking. She needed to stay grounded and realistic.

With a sigh, she unfolded her legs. She needed to find her phone then she'd head for her home office. She'd uncovered some interesting medical information about the failure of the opponent's drug in what seemed like a significant number of adolescent cases. She wanted to review the details again and contact a biochemist she knew to help her understand some of the physiological implications.

Phone finally located, she settled down with her laptop and pushed all thoughts of Michael Remington from her mind. She spent the remainder of the weekend alternating between analyzing the new information she'd uncovered about the opponent's drug and hanging out with her brother.

When Brandt left Sunday evening to return home, she noticed her car hadn't yet been returned. She decided not to worry about it. Michael said he'd make sure it was returned by the time she had to go to work Monday morning, and she could count on him to get it done.

As she closed the door behind her brother, the magnitude of her blind faith in Michael hit her. She was a control freak. Normally, she'd be immediately on the phone checking on the car situation and making plans to get it done herself. What did this say about her? About him? Or more particularly, about what he'd done to short-circuit her independence-wired brain cells?

She slumped against the door. Her mind wandered through everything he'd done to her body this weekend. Her lips curved upwards with the memories.

She'd have to face him in the office tomorrow morning. Hopefully, she'd be able to do so without a tell-tale goofy grin on her face. That would certainly blow all efforts to keep their weekend encounter under wraps.

He'd said they needed to talk about this. Her gut told her nothing they'd say to each other would make a difference. Her heart whispered a completely opposite message, telling her to quit trying to control everything and take a chance. Just once, she wanted to believe in fairy tales, particularly one featuring an Italian Prince Charming.

In an uncharacteristic Scarlett O'Hara moment, she decided she'd think about it tomorrow. She owed it to herself to at least hear what he had to say. This didn't have to be forever. Maybe they could have a little bit of happy until.

∂≈ ∂≈ | ∂≈ ∂≈

Michael strolled into the kitchen of his mother's Ward Parkway home. Sofia Remington looked up. Pleasure filled her face at the sight of her only son. "Michael! You're early. I wasn't expecting you for another hour."

"Hello, gorgeous." Michael bent to kiss his mom on the cheek.

At five foot six, Sofia was the shortest member of the family. Having married a man who was over six feet tall, she'd ended up with children who were all taller than her.

"I did some shopping on the Plaza so I was close by. Didn't make sense to go all the way home then come back. So here I am." He reached for a few sliced black olives in a bowl on the counter.

His mother swatted his hand then turned back to stir the pot she had on the stove. "What were you shopping for?"

"Nothing in particular." Michael stepped to the refrigerator and took out a bottle of Coke. "It was a spur of the moment sort of thing." He leaned against the counter, twisted off the cap, and took a sip. He stood silently, watching her bustle around the kitchen.

She allowed him to stand in his silence. She glanced at him from time to time, no doubt analyzing the pensive look on his face. She always told him he was exactly like his father. He knew she sometimes found it strange to look at him and see his father's features beneath her olive coloring and coffee hair. He was a constant reminder of the greatest love of her life. The reminder often brought her sadness along with the joy.

He missed his father immensely. He suspected she missed him twice as much. Although it had been years since Austin Remington had been killed by a driver who'd lost control of his car during a snowstorm, the pain slipped in fresh for both of them at the oddest moments. Like now, he needed to talk through what bothered him with his dad. Instead, he stood in his mother's kitchen putting up a front.

"What's on your mind tonight, sweetheart?"

"Huh?" He looked up from his daze. He should have known better than to come here before he'd finished wrestling with his thoughts. The downside of being like his father was that she could read him like a book the way she always could his dad. Hiding things from her was like trying to keep scent from a bloodhound.

She smiled indulgently. "You seem to be a million miles away."

"Maybe." He started picking at the label on his Coke bottle. "Um . . . the case I've been working on took an interesting turn."

"Really?" Her eyes narrowed at his hesitation. "What's going on?"

"I think the opposition has access to our case strategy."

She raised her eyebrows. "How?"

"We've documented unauthorized access to our case database. We're not sure yet whether someone at the firm is providing them with access or they simply hacked into our network."

"Wow. That sounds pretty underhanded. I knew this was a major case, but is it really worth all this cloak and dagger?"

"Apparently so. This is a pretty big deal in the pharmaceutical world. These companies make billions of dollars a year off these drugs. Not to mention the high stakes for the lawyers involved. The article they interviewed me for last month recently ran in the American Bar Association's *ABA Journal*. The legal community is watching the case closely. Whichever firm posts a victory is going to have some major legal clout going forward."

His mother sighed and turned back to the stove.

"What is it, mother?"

"Nothing."

"That mournful sigh was not about nothing."

She looked over her shoulder at him. "I know you're pretty focused on making Remington, Hager and McCormick a nationally recognized firm, but I wish you'd focus more on your personal life. You're not getting any younger."

"Gee, thanks, mom. I didn't realize you considered me over the hill at the ripe old age of thirty-eight." He grinned at her.

She put her spoon down and turned towards him. "That's not what I meant and you know it. When are you planning to provide me with a few grandchildren?"

"Liliana has provided you with three beautiful grandchildren. And given the way her husband looks at her whenever the two of them are here, I'm sure he's going through the motions of giving you a few more."

She grabbed her tea towel off the counter and snapped him on the thigh with it. "Don't be facetious. I'm talking about *you* giving me grandchildren. Whatever happened with the woman you met New Year's Eve?"

"That may be a little complicated."

"How so?"

The Coke bottle label peeled a little more under his scratching finger. "I think she may work at the firm."

"Oh." A sizzle behind her drew Sofia's attention. She grabbed her sauce spoon and stirred the noisy pot. Dinner saved, she turned back to her son. "I can see how that might be an issue for you." Placing her sauce spoon back on the drip plate, Sofia crossed her arms. "So you've decided not to pursue the matter?"

"I've got to focus on the Metra Pharmaceutical case. It was dad's dream to build the firm into a national player.

This case is my opportunity to make sure that happens for him."

"You can't make that happen for him, Michael. He's gone. The last thing he'd want is for you to spend your life pursuing his dream instead of living your own."

"This is my dream."

"Is it? Or is it your way of trying to keep your father alive?"

He sat his soda on the counter. "Why build a practice at all if I'm not going to make it a success?"

"Success is one thing. Workaholic obsession to the exclusion of all else is another. This isn't healthy, Michael. And it's not the life your father would have wanted for you. I know you miss him, *figlio mio*. I do, too. Everyday. But you can't bring him back by slaving away in that office tower. And you can't be cowardly enough to use it as an excuse not to make a meaningful connection with another human being."

"I've tried that connection thing already. Dad got the last good woman." He walked over and kissed her on the temple.

"I think your sisters would take issue with that comment."

"Well, I'm not planning to marry one of my sisters so my comment stands."

She grabbed him around the waist. "Then you *are* planning to get married?"

He stared blankly at her.

She released him and sighed. "Your father was a family man, Michael. Work had its place, but his family—especially his children—came first. He was driven with a purpose. To build a legacy for you. He wasn't driven by ego, success for the mere sake of success. He wanted to leave something solid and secure for his only son and make sure it was expansive enough to also provide his daughters lifelong financial security. He drove himself to provide for the family he took time to eat dinner with almost every night and for the children whose ball games and dance recitals he attended. Whom are you building this for, Michael?"

He still didn't respond. He stepped away from her.

Sofia shook her head. "What's going to happen when you climb to the top of this ladder of success you're erecting and find you have no one to share it all with?"

"Oh, I think he has someone in mind to share it all with." Raina bounded into the kitchen and kissed her mother on the cheek.

"Is that right?" Sofia's voice rose in surprise. "I thought you weren't seeing anyone," she said, looking at Michael.

"I'm not."

"But he'd like to be." Raina stuck her fingers into the bowl of olives.

Sofia swatted her hand. "Do tell."

Raina grinned. "Well—"

"Raina, cut it out," Michael said between clenched teeth.

"What?" Raina batted her eyelashes at her brother. "What's the big secret about your dinner with Jordis on the Plaza?"

Sofia turned towards Raina. "Jordis? That's an unusual name."

Raina popped olive bits into her mouth. "She's an

unusual woman. Tall. Funky, in an artsy kind of way. Dresses like a runway model but's apparently smart enough to work with him." She inclined her head in Michael's direction.

Eyes wide, Sofia's glance snapped back to her son. "She works at the firm?"

"Don't worry. I'm not revisiting a past mistake." Michael crossed his arms. "Raina and I just happened to run into her when we went out to dinner one night. I'm not even the one who invited her to dinner. Raina did."

"So, there's nothing personal going on between you two?" his mother asked.

Michael glanced at his sister then hedged, "She's a brilliant lawyer. I like her style. She took over for Chase on the Metra Pharmaceuticals case so she's my new co-counsel."

Raina scoffed. "Yeah, right. Maybe *mamma*'ll buy that's all that's going on, but I was there. I saw the electricity between you two." Raina licked her index finger then pressed it together with her thumb while making a sizzling sound. "Hot. Hot. Hot."

"You know what?" His gazed pierced his sister. "You're about to get hurt."

Nonplussed, Raina meandered towards the kitchen doorway. She began to chant, "Michael and Jordis sitting in a tree K-I-S-S-I—eeek!" Raina's shriek filled the kitchen as Michael dropped his soda bottle on the counter and charged her. She fled up the stairs.

Michael gave chase, catching her right foot as she reached the top landing. "Oh, no you don't." He snatched her up and made as if to dangle her over the railing.

"*Mo-om!*" Raina yelled.

Sofia came around the bend and gasped when she looked up the steps. "Good Lord!" Her hand fluttered to her heart. "Michael! Put your sister down this instant!"

Michael jerked his arms as if he intended to drop Raina anyway then laughed when she shrieked again. As he put her down, he leaned into her ear. "I owe you. You better hope Christian doesn't stop by for you sometime when I'm around."

Raina glared at him. "Spoilsport."

He ruffled her hair. "Don't dish it out little sister if you can't take it."

Sofia headed for the kitchen. "Dinner's ready you two. Wash up and get back down here."

Michael and Raina headed for the bathroom. Raina finished and headed back downstairs before him.

When he neared the kitchen doorway, he heard his sister whisper, "This is her."

His gut clenched. Out of sight, he peeked around the open entry off the hall. His sister pressed a few buttons on her iPhone and handed it to their mom.

His mother glanced at the screen then quickly up at Raina. "Oh."

"Yeah. *Oh.* Not what you expected, huh?" Chuckling, Raina went to the refrigerator and pulled out a bottle of Snapple raspberry ice tea.

Sofia tapped on the phone and read through something. "Impressive resume. What's she like?"

Hell. They were reviewing Jordis's bio from the firm web site.

Raina leaned against the fridge and unscrewed the cap of her tea. "She's feisty, and independent, and she's not intimidated by *him*." Raina flicked her head in the direction of the staircase.

This last part caught Sofia's attention. "Well, that would be a first."

He wiped his hands down his face and leaned a shoulder against the hallway wall. His mother had never approved of his choices in short-term women.

"Exactly." Raina nodded.

"Not to mention, she's absolutely beautiful." Sofia handed Raina back her phone. "How can you be sure he's interested?" She grabbed the plated entrées and headed for the dining room.

"Oh, he's interested all right." Raina grabbed the dish of vegetables off the counter with one hand and followed her mom. "But I think this time, big brother may have finally met his match."

He frowned. *What?*

Sofia placed the dishes on the table and smiled. "So that's what's really on his mind. Hmm . . . his mystery woman shows up at the firm about the same time he goes to dinner with a gorgeous new attorney. Something tells me those grandchildren he keeps giving me a hard time about aren't as far off as he'd like to believe."

Raina burst out laughing.

The urge to sneak out the back door without a word overcame him. He quickly nixed the idea; his mother would have him hunted down and beaten. Heading for the dining room, he mentally catalogued the best criminal attorneys he knew. He'd need one later tonight because he was about to murder his baby sister.

֍ ֍ | ֍ ֍

Michael survived dinner without committing homicide, but didn't dawdle at his mom's long after. He swung by the office to take care of a few matters. When he pulled into the garage, he noted Jordis's car was gone. The service he'd called must have picked it up earlier. Glad that was taken care of, he headed for the elevators.

He stepped off on the twenty-fifth floor and went straight to his secretary's desk. As he suspected, a stack of correspondence waited for his signature. Lana had been in sometime over the weekend. The woman didn't know how to take a break. Not that he was complaining. He wouldn't be half as successful if not for Lana's tireless efficiency and dedication.

After he thumbed through the correspondence, he signed in all the appropriate places and placed the stack neatly back on Lana's desk. A sound drew his attention. Turning in the direction from which the sound had come, he listened intently. Muffled voices traveled from down the hall. He went to investigate.

The sound quieted after a minute. He paused to get his bearings. A low moaned finally sliced through the silence. Michael continued his trek, curious to know who else was at the office this late on a Sunday night. As he got closer to the sound, he recognized the decidedly sexual nature of the muffled murmurings. They led him to Eric Covington's office.

The door stood ajar. He glanced through the slit of an opening and was greeted by the sight of Alyson's naked bottom tilted up at an angle of copulatory invitation. She wore a dress, but her dress had been hiked above her waist. Loose around her left ankle hung lacy panties in a shade that matched her black stilettos. Michael noticed her fingers dallying between her thighs. She knelt between Eric's spread legs. Eric's pants and briefs were bunched at his ankles, his shirt open.

Eric moaned as Alyson's head bobbed up and down over his lap. He fisted a hand in her hair and shoved his hips hard. Alyson hummed deep in her throat, apparently enjoying his rough play.

Michael stepped away from the door. Strange bedfellows, he thought and left them to their business. They were consenting adults so what they did together was none of his business. He made a mental note, however, to get rid of that couch if Eric ever decided to leave the firm.

He went back to his office and got down to work.

About twenty minutes later, Alyson walked by. She flinched when she saw him watching her from his desk. She placed her hand against her chest and played off the edge of fear he sensed in her. "Oh, Michael, you surprised me. I didn't know you were here."

"I came in to catch up on some paperwork I missed due to the snowstorm."

Alyson propped herself against his doorjamb, trying to look sexy. Michael leaned back in his chair wondering what she had in mind.

"You work non-stop. You need to learn how to relax." She entered the office and came over to his side of the desk. She propped her butt against the edge.

He grinned at her obvious line. "Oh, I relax plenty."

Alyson mistook his humor for interest and leaned in.

"Maybe you need a little help in that regard."

He shook his head. "I think I've got it covered, Alyson. You have a good night." He picked up his pen and slid his chair back to a working position.

Alyson took the hint and stood up. "Well, if you ever change your mind . . ."

"If I ever change my mind, what?" he asked, playing obtuse.

Alyson laughed. "You know where to find me." She sashayed from his office.

No she didn't just proposition me a few minutes after her lips slid off another man's dick.

Some women had no couth.

His thoughts strayed to another woman, refined and classy, whom he'd much rather dally with at the moment. He was tempted to stop by her place when he left tonight, but it was late and he didn't want to seem too eager.

He'd told Jordis he'd see her Monday. He'd have to wait until then. Somehow, he'd make it through the night without touching her again, without holding her again.

Their last romp together replayed in his head, and his body responded as if she were in the room. No longer sure he could wait until tomorrow to see her, he glanced at the clock and felt his resolve waning.

CHAPTER 18

*J*ordis awoke Monday morning with a smile on her
face. Michael hadn't stopped back by, but he'd
called late last night. They'd talked for at least an hour.

Today, their schedule included a session to begin ce-
menting their court strategy. Working next to him after
having his arms around her all weekend would be one of
the hardest things she'd ever had to do. Hopefully, by the
time she got to the office, she'd have wrestled control over
her galloping hormones and suppressed the goofy grin
that kept creeping onto her face. She'd decided to give in
to her feelings for Michael and see where this led, but she
didn't want to telegraph to the entire office the change in
their relationship.

When she stepped outside, her joyful mood tanked. Her
car had not been returned. In its place, sat a brand new
Dodge Charger II Daytona Limited Edition in electric blue.

Stunned paralysis overtook her. What had he done!

She whipped out her mobile phone and dialed Michael's personal number. When the call went to voicemail, she couldn't contain herself. "Remington! Where's my car? Call me back ASAP!"

Battling shock and frustration, Jordis tried the door to the Daytona. It was locked. Hands on her hips, she stared at the blue V8, unable not to appreciate its racecar-inspired lines—and boy, did she love the color. But how dare he take it upon himself to replace her car?

She didn't need this this morning. She had enough on her plate with the burden of covering their inadvisable affair.

Searching around, she found an envelope taped to the column of her parking bay which contained instructions telling her where to find the keys. After retrieving them, Jordis fired up the engine and drove to the firm. She headed straight for Michael's office. On the way, she noticed everyone atwitter about something.

Halfway to her destination, she ran into Vivian. "Vivian, what's going on?"

"You haven't heard? Apparently, Michael Remington has been searching for this woman he met on New Year's Eve. Until now, he hasn't been able to find her. Well, turns out, she walked into the firm today looking for him."

"What?" Jordis croaked.

"Isn't that romantic? I think his secretary is making reservations for them to go to lunch or dinner or something . . ." Vivian's voice trailed off when she caught Jordis's pained expression. "Oh, no. Jordis? I thought you weren't—"

"It's okay, Viv. I'm fine," she lied. Her stomach roiled.

She'd told Michael she wasn't his Juliet more than once. This weekend she'd let every opportunity slip by to tell him the truth. It never occurred to her he'd keep searching until he found one. How could he believe that other woman was her? Even without her admission, if he really had strong feelings for her like those his father had experienced upon meeting his mother, he would have known despite her prevarication she was the Juliet he'd kissed New Year's Eve.

Jordis's feet continued unguided towards his office. She entered in a fog and saw a tall, tan-in-a-can model-thin woman with her arms around his neck. Upon seeing Jordis, Michael grabbed the model's arms and pulled away. Jordis's anger at his heavy-handed tactics with her car simmered up beneath a sense of betrayal over his obsession with his fabled Juliet. Considering she was Juliet, her feelings were irrational, but she failed to consider that.

"Jordis," Michael said when she entered the office.

"I need to talk to you a moment. Alone."

Michael sent the walking hanger outside to wait in the reception area.

Once they were alone, her voice dipped to a misleadingly calm tone. "Where's my car?"

His face showed surprise. Clearly, he'd expected her to go straight to a discussion of the bimbo who'd been hanging on his neck.

"Your car is safe."

"I want it back. Now. Immediately."

"No, Jordis. I want you to drive the Daytona for a week and see how you like it. It's the latest model, and it has all-wheel drive."

"Did you just tell me I can't have my own car back? Who the hell do you think you are?"

"Jordis, calm down."

"Don't tell me to calm down." Her voice crescendoed with each word.

Michael blew out a breath and ran his left hand down his face. "This isn't really about the car, Jordis. So, why don't we talk about what's really bothering you." He glanced towards the door.

"Screw her! You had no right."

"I had every right!" Now *his* voice began to rise. "What's the big deal? I bought you a car. I need you to be safe. I would have preferred to buy you an SUV so you'd have higher clearance, but I know how much you love the Charger so I thought the Daytona would be a nice compromise."

"Compromise? Compromise?" She paced away, shaking her head. "It takes two people to compromise, Michael." She turned back. "You did this without consulting me."

"Jordis, you needed another car."

She raised her hands in frustration. "You and my brother and that damn car! If you'd have both just backed off, I'd've taken care of it."

"What! Are you telling me you hadn't dealt with your car situation because we wanted you to and you were simply being contrary?"

Her lips tightened. She hadn't consciously made that decision, but she'd always hated being told what to do. She had a tendency to ignore unsolicited instructions and do the opposite.

When she didn't deny his accusation, Michael lost it. "Of all the obstinate, hardheaded—"

"Look who's talking." She stepped closer to him, dropping her voice. "What? You think because we had sex once, you own me?"

"We did more than have sex," he growled. "And we certainly did it more than once."

"Well, we won't be doing it again," she snapped. "So, you can get over treating me like some kept woman. Take that car back and give me my Bee!"

"What do you mean we won't be doing it again?" He reached for her, but she avoided his grasp. "Jordis, don't be unreasonable. I know you felt something special this weekend. We both did. Why would you want to throw that away?"

"There was nothing special about it. That's why you have your Juliet outside waiting to take my place." She shoved her hands against his chest.

He grabbed her forearms and held on. "Nobody's taking your place. Let me explain."

"There's nothing to explain. You're my supervising attorney, Michael. We knew that going in, and we knew we couldn't continue to carry on. This weekend was a one-time deal."

"It doesn't have to be." He pulled her close. "Let me appoint Eric to take over the Metra Pharmaceuticals case. You can move to the Business and Finance group and then we won't have the problem of me being responsible for supervising and evaluating your work."

"You want me to give up my position?"

"Yes. It solves our ethical problem and then we can continue to see each other."

"And since this move to Business and Finance would come after the start of the fiscal year, I'd have to wait until next year to be considered for partner?"

"Yes, but it's only a year. You know you're going to make partner."

"I do? Why? Because everybody knows I'm screwing the boss?"

He released her. "Stop it, Jordis. You don't have to be crude. And nobody knows." He glanced at his office door, which had been ajar. "Well, nobody did know."

Lana stood in the doorway with a chastising look on her face. She grabbed the door handle and pulled his office door closed.

Turning his attention back to Jordis, Michael said, "How 'bout you say it louder next time so the other twenty-four floors can hear you, too?"

Jordis dropped her face into her hands. "I'm such an idiot," she said into her palms. "I can't believe I did this to myself." She looked up. "I lose another year towards partnership. I change to a division of the firm that's not my first choice. I suffer the stigma and gossip about why I had to move to a new division. I give up the right to pick what kind of car I drive. And I do all this so we can sleep together until you get tired of me. Do I have that right?" Her voice had returned to a normal pitch.

Michael said nothing.

"Tell me, Michael, what sacrifices are you planning to make?" She crossed her arms, waiting. "Really. I'm curious. Do you have to give up anything to have this relationship with me?"

"I'm losing a great second chair. I'd much rather have you in IP Litigation than in Business and Fin—"

She put up a hand to stop him. "Poor you." She turned and walked towards the door. Before she opened it, she glanced back. "I'm flattered you thought my performance this weekend was worth a car."

Michael winched.

"Most men just send flowers. You might want to try that next time. Leave the keys to the Bee with my secretary. Once I get them back, I'll return the Daytona to you. I'll be gone for the rest of the day." She opened the door.

"Jordis, wait."

Seeing the waiting Juliet, Jordis said quietly, "Oh, and enjoy your lunch."

Upon exiting Michael's office, she caught a glimpse of Alyson a few feet away. Alyson stood at her secretary's desk with a stack of documents in front of her. Jordis doubted she was doing anything more than pretending to review the documents.

Alyson looked up and smirked. Jordis wanted to knock that self-satisfied look right off her pale face. Given the scene she'd already made in Michael's office, she wisely chose to avoid starting a live imitation of a WWE Smack-Down. Instead, she made a beeline for her office. She needed to get out of here.

జం జం | ఆ ఆ

Jordis entered her office gripping the keys to the Daytona tightly in her fist. She crossed the threshold to find

Eric Covington sitting at her desk going through one of her files.

He looked up when she entered. "Why are you going over clinical trials and medical case studies? You're working on a patent case not a malpractice suit."

"None of your damn business. I got the case assignment not you. Remember? Now get your ass out of my chair."

Eric raised one eyebrow at her tone and her language. It wasn't like her to lose her cool. He sat back in her chair. "Well, it looks like the golden girl is in a tiff this morning. Trouble in paradise already? That was certainly a whirlwind romance."

Pain in Jordis's hand alerted her she still clutched the car keys. She stepped to her desk and dropped them on a corner. Leaning across the desk, both palms flat, she over-enunciated, "Get. Your. *Ass.* Out. Of my. *Chair.*"

Eric's mouth tightened. He unfolded himself from her chair never taking his eyes from hers. "I can certainly see why Remington is fascinated with you. That fire of yours makes a man hot." He stepped from behind the desk.

She straightened. "Eric, I'm not in the mood for any of your crap this morning. Go away."

"You're not going to find a way to win this case in those medical documents. The opponent's claim is based on a legal theory not a medical one."

Jordis thought about their information leak and suspicion overtook her. "What do you know about the opponent's legal theories?"

"Enough to know you're barking up the wrong tree, and Remington obviously picked the wrong associate to back him up." He approached her. "But, of course, you know that, which is why you set me up."

Jordis's eyes narrowed. "What are you talking about?"

"Come on, Jordis. I'm done falling for that sweet innocence act. Man, Alyson was so right about you." He rubbed his hands down his face.

"I have no idea what you're talking about. Exactly how do you think I set you up?"

Eric scoffed. "I got a visit from the Chief Information Officer this morning. It would seem information regarding your case has been leaked to opposing counsel, and firm data indicates the network breach came from my computer."

She shook her head. "You're the one who's been helping the other side?"

"Hell no!"

Jordis jumped at his angry bark.

"I've been vying for that case for months. Why would I help the other side?" He stepped closer. "You, on the other hand, figured you'd get the case and get rid of me at the same time."

Jordis stepped back from the fury radiating off him. "Don't be ridiculous."

"I checked, Jordis. The computer specialist they're using for the investigation happens to have the last name Morgan. Coincidence? I don't think so." He stalked her. "Someone you know?"

Jordis nodded slowly. "My brother."

"Figures. So, you had your brother set me up, huh? It wasn't enough that you got the co-chair appointment for reasons that had nothing to do with your litigation skills."

"I know how to do my job, Eric."

"I bet you do." Eric's gaze shifted down her body.

The predatory look that overlapped his fury made Jordis wary. She moved to step around her desk.

"Not so fast." He grabbed her arm and pulled her to him.

Jordis struggled against his grasp. "Let go of me."

He leered. "That's not what you told Remington. Now is it?"

A gruff voice sounded at his back. "Take your hands *off* her."

Eric's head whirled to find Michael Remington standing behind him. He yanked his hands off Jordis and stepped aside.

Michael placed himself between Jordis and Eric. "What the hell do you think you're doing, Covington?"

An angry glare on his face, Eric shoved his hands in his pockets, but didn't speak.

"Come on. You were man enough to state your grievance when you only had Jordis to deal with. If you've got a problem involving me, grow some balls and confront me directly."

"Really? You really want me to state what's obvious to everyone around here?"

"Yeah, I really want you to state what you *think* is obvious."

"Okay." Eric pulled his hands out of his pockets. "Everyone knows the professional skills she used to get this assignment were the oldest known to man, but they certainly weren't legal in nature."

Jordis sucked in a loud breath. She tried to step around Michael. "Did you just call me a *prostitute*?"

Michael held Jordis back with one hand. Jordis spun and tried to get around him. He pivoted, grabbed her around the waist, and lifted her off her feet. "Not this time, *princessa*." He set her down behind him and ordered, "Stay put."

She bristled at his tone, but the look in his eyes warned her challenging him would be a mistake.

Once he was satisfied she wasn't going anywhere, Michael released her and asked, "Where's your annual billing summary?"

"What?" Momentarily thrown by the abrupt change in subject, she didn't move.

"Your annual billing summary. I need to see it. Right now, Jordis."

Confused, she stepped to her desk and grabbed the report from beneath a stack of papers. She handed it to Michael, curious as to what he intended to do with it.

He flipped over several pages of the report then handed it to Eric. "You might notice, Eric, that last year during the months she was here, Jordis out billed you by over one hundred hours. On top of that, her realization rate is ninety-eight percent. Since yours is ninety-two percent, that means not only did she work more hours than you, but we were able to bill a higher percentage of that time to our clients."

Glancing over the top of the report, Michael pointed to a column on the page. "And don't forget to look at last year's collections. Collections on her billed time were the highest of any associate in your class."

Eric clutched the report until it curled into a roll between his hands. "These numbers aren't everything."

"No, they're not, but this is a business after all so the numbers are extremely important." Michael leaned against Jordis's desk. He crossed his arms and ankles. "Lest you think I'm stressing quantity of work over legal aptitude, let's not forget I saw the two of you in action at the first associate meeting I attended. If memory serves me correct, Jordis won that debate."

The rolled report in Eric's hands crumpled in the middle.

"But you're right, Covington. I happen to find her a lot more attractive than I find you so I may be biased. You should know, however, Chase Hager recommended her as his replacement. I simply agreed with his assessment. You're free to question him about his rationale, but I wouldn't recommend you suggest he had any untoward sexual motives."

Eric's lips thinned. He unfurled the report and glanced over at her, probably expecting her to be gloating over his put down. She clutched her arms around her chest and worked to keep her expression devoid of any emotion. He moved to hand her the report, but she backed away. The urge to grab the report and slam her fist into his face was too great to risk getting close to him.

Michael grabbed the report instead. "In the future, Covington, if you have a complaint about how I dish out assignments, I suggest you come see me instead of bullying another associate. Or, you're always welcome to take your complaints to Hager or McCormick. Neither of them would tolerate me doing anything to jeopardize the reputation of this firm."

He slapped the report against Eric's chest. "Just make

sure you take the latest billable hours report with you, and make damn sure your stats out shine whomever you're complaining about. Otherwise, both Chase and Roy will laugh you out of their offices."

Michael stood up. "You're a smart guy, Covington. And you might actually make an outstanding attorney one day if you ever drop that cloak of entitlement you wear around yourself like a security blanket. Quit assuming you're the best man for the job and start putting in the effort to prove it."

With a parting glance at Jordis, Eric turned to leave.

"Oh, and Eric?" Michael shifted his stance.

Eric stopped mid-turn.

"One more thing." Stepping close to him, Michael dropped his voice to a dangerous growl. "We're at the office so I had to control myself today. But the next time you put your hands on Jordis for any reason, it won't matter where we are. Know that I won't bother giving you a warning. I'm just going to proceed to *kick your ass*. Are we clear?"

Eric gave a terse single nod and left.

Michael turned towards her. "Jordis—"

"I hate to say 'I told you so,'" she interrupted, "but neither of us should be surprised by Eric's attitude."

"He's entitled to his opinion, but his behavior was out of line."

"Well, I doubt he'll be the last to demonstrate negative sentiments about our liaison. And now that he thinks I set him up, I'm sure it won't be the last time I hear from Eric."

"Set him up?"

"Apparently, IT traced the computer network leak to

his computer. He thinks I had Brandt set him up."

Michael shook his head and sighed. "I'll deal with Eric later on that. Right now, we need to talk about what happened in my office."

"No, we don't."

"Give me a chance to explain."

"I'm not in the mood for explanations at the moment. I've had it up to here—" She raised her flattened hand horizontally above her head. "—with overbearing, domineering, arrogant male jerks." She threw several files, a notepad, and a reference book into her tote. "Right now, all I want is to get out of here."

She passed him to leave. He reached for her, but she shook off his grasp. "Don't. Let me go, Michael. I need some space."

❧ ❧ | ❧ ❧

Jordis blew out of her office.

Chase Hager stepped aside to avoid being run over and snagged her by the arm. "Whoa, where's the fire?"

She jerked her arm away. "The next man who grabs me is going to get decked!"

He threw up his hands and grinned at her. "O-*kay*. Sorry. What did I do?"

Jordis closed her eyes and dropped her head with a shake. "Nothing, Chase." She looked back at him. "I'm sorry. This has nothing to do with you. I just need—" She glanced up and peered over Chase's shoulder.

Chase twisted to see what she was looking at and saw Michael standing in the doorway to her office.

"I need to get out of here for a while. Excuse me."

Chase watched Jordis board the elevator then looked at him.

"Don't ask." Michael waved off his buddy and stalked away. He went to shut the door to his office only to find Chase's hand blocking the move.

Chase slid through the crack in the door. "You really didn't think you were going to get off that easy, did you?"

Michael turned from him.

Chase shut the door. "What did you do this time?"

Michael whirled back around. "Why do you assume *I* did something?"

"Because I know you. So spill. What gives?"

He told Chase the story.

"You bought Jordis a car?"

"Yes."

"A car?"

"You said that already," he gritted between clenched teeth.

"Right. I'm just trying to make sure I'm clear on this." Chase adjusted his pant legs and sat. "You got rid of her car without her permission and replaced it with what you think is a safer model."

"I didn't get rid of her car. It's safe and sound in my garage."

Chase grinned. "So, you're holding her car hostage until she spends a week driving the car you picked out for her . . . the car you picked out without consulting her."

When Chase put it like that, Michael sounded like the overbearing jerk Jordis had accused him of being.

"Okay, maybe I should have consulted her first. But,

damn, I handed her outright the keys to a brand new car in a model she loves. Most women would've been excited by that or at least appreciative."

Chase laughed. "You mean those twits, attracted by your money and power, who bat their eyelashes at you and coo 'how high' when you say jump?"

Michael scowled at him.

"You're right. Those women would have been very appreciative. How have those relationships been working for you?"

"Cut the crap, Dr. Phil. What's your point?"

"My point is this. Jordis isn't like any of those other women. She's the complete opposite. I dare say her sass, her independence, and the fact that she doesn't take your crap lying down is a big part of the attraction for you."

Chase stood up. "I get why you bought her the car, Michael. Better than you do. It's not about the weather. Until Jordis, you've only been fiercely protective of four women: your two sisters, your mother, and my Grace. You need to ask yourself what those four women have in common. Then, you need to find Jordis and fix this."

Michael let Chase's words sink in. Yes, he needed to fix the situation with Jordis, but she'd asked for space. He'd give it to her.

He turned to his desk after Chase left. He had other things to handle immediately, starting with Eric Covington and the IT issue.

He sat down at his computer and woke up the sleeping machine. He scanned through his emails until he found his carbon copy of the one from Brandt to the CIO about Brandt's most recent investigation report. The email included an attachment detailing forensic information that traced network logins, system downloads and the piggy-backing of access routers. He didn't understand all the computer lingo, but Brandt had included a spreadsheet of key times and dates. Michael printed out the spreadsheet and went over the information looking for any recurring patterns.

Half an hour later, he finally got a clue. He double checked his calendar and corresponded dates on the spreadsheet with days of the week. Shaking his head, he rose from his chair and went in search of Eric.

CHAPTER 19

*E*ric Covington glanced up as Michael Remington walked into his office. Tossing down his pen, he looked squarely at the partner. "Should I be clearing out my desk?"

"That depends on you. At this point, I don't suggest you push your luck."

Eric frowned.

Michael sat in the guest chair opposite Eric's desk. "I understand you take issue with the computer forensics report we received on the network breach investigation." Michael tugged at his pant leg and crossed his left foot over his right knee. "Why don't you tell me about it."

"I'm sure Jordis filled you in."

"I'm asking you. Now's your chance to give me your side of the story."

Eric didn't say anything. He'd acted rash this morning.

He'd let his temper get the best of him. He wasn't foolish enough to walk into another trap. He'd take the Fifth on this one.

When Eric didn't respond, Michael said, "You know, Eric. In our profession, arrogance often comes with the territory. I've found, however, that a man who makes the mistake of being arrogantly sexist leaves himself open to having his balls put in a sling by some woman he underestimates."

"Believe me, I won't be underestimating Jordis again."

Michael's fingers flexed against his knee. "Your obsession with Jordis is making you stupid."

Heat warmed Eric's face.

"If you're going to hang with a woman who likes to spend Sundays on her knees, you might want to try one who prefers doing so in a house of God rather than while servicing you." Michael leaned forward and tossed a spreadsheet onto his desk. "Especially, since it seems your woman of choice has an interest in more than how long it takes to get you off."

Eric's brow creased, and he picked up the spreadsheet. "What are you talking about? I haven't—" The don't-bullshit-me look on Michael's face made him hesitate. How could the partner possibly know about his fraternization activities? "Alyson?"

Michael settled back in the chair. "Sundays seem to be a popular day for transmission of case data. The last one occurred last night. Know anyone who had access to your office, and thus your computer, last night?"

"That bitch!"

"Yeah. Looks like you were set up all right. And you

gave the perpetrator free reign to do so in exchange for . . . whatever. I guess the next time you accuse someone of being swayed by the 'oldest profession known to man,' you'd do well to look in the mirror first."

Michael unfolded himself from the guest chair. "I'm going to give you a chance to get back on my good side. Everything we have on Alyson so far is purely circumstantial. The IT investigation team will be contacting you for assistance catching Alyson in the act. I suggest you cooperate. You do and I'll give you first crack at any case on Alyson's docket you want and the opportunity to first chair the next major IP case appropriate for a senior associate."

Eric waited for the other shoe to drop.

"Do we have a deal?" Michael asked.

"That's it? I help nail Alyson, and I get a clean slate?"

"Clean slate?" Michael scoffed. "Let's just say I'll forgive your prior transgressions, but I don't intend to forget them. My warning still stands."

Eric had no doubt as to what warning Michael was talking about. Jordis. He'd play with fire with that hellion one too many times already. As long as he got a caseload that gave him the opportunity to prove himself to Remington, he didn't care what Jordis did.

He stood. Cautiously, he offered Michael his hand. "Deal."

ॐ ॐ | ॐ ॐ

Two days later, Michael stood at his office window staring at the tangerine glow rising with the dawn. Sleep and he no longer had an amicable relationship so he found himself at the office earlier than usual.

The IT group had progressed with Eric on arranging their sting for Alyson, but Michael hadn't seen Jordis since Monday morning. She'd made herself scarce. The look on her face when she'd walked away still haunted him.

She'd taken his gift as a vulgar expression of thanks for the lay. He didn't understand how she could possibly think he saw her simply as a notch on his bedpost. Granted, he'd made the mistake of referring to her in anger as a piece of tail before, but he'd thought they'd gotten past that.

He'd never bought a woman elaborate gifts before, not so much as a tennis bracelet. Last weekend, he'd gone out and bought her two. He'd been looking for something to express the seriousness of his feelings, and he'd come across a trinket that had made him think of her. He'd bought it on impulse. He hadn't gotten a chance to give her that second present—the one he still hadn't quite come to terms with buying. She'd been too preoccupied with the car.

Dammit. He should have handled that better. He'd known her independent spirit would make her turn down the car so he'd taken the easy way out, hoping she'd fall in love with the Charger Daytona on sight and he wouldn't have to convince her to accept it.

He'd thought the Daytona a good compromise. It had the sporty power she loved with all-wheel drive to give her maneuverability in challenging terrain. That she'd thought it payment for her sexual performance galled him. He'd simply wanted to see her safe.

His father had died as a result of a car accident during a winter snow. Another driver with a vehicle not properly equipped for inclement weather had lost control of his car. The other driver had died at the scene. His father had managed to hang on for a few days in the hospital before succumbing to his internal injuries.

He needed his father's guidance right now. He felt lost. He'd been happy until Jordis had crashed into his life. Okay, maybe not happy, but he'd been content.

His hand found the silver chain he'd pocketed with his loose change out of habit this morning. He hadn't thought about it much in the days since he'd met Jordis. Fingering the chain, he said out loud, "Talk to me, dad."

He thought about his parents' fairy-tale beginning. At the age of ten, he'd once asked his father after hearing his parents' love story for the zillionth time, "It was a miracle you found her, huh, dad?"

"No, son," his father had responded, "the miracle wasn't that I found her. The miracle was that I recognized her and accepted it."

Michael went numb. *Was it really that simple?*

Yeah. He shook his head at his own folly. It was that simple.

Chase had been right . . . again. Purchasing the car hadn't been simply about the weather. The thought of Jordis driving a car that wouldn't handle snow well had made him nervous. He'd been afraid of losing her. What was that old saying? Women fall in love with the man they want to live with; men fall for the woman they can't live without.

His fingers tensed around the chain he'd been fondling.

He pulled out the silver bracelet. Five charms linked at equidistant segments stared back at him. For the first time, he looked closely at each charm. His heart thudded and then he smiled. Glancing up at the heavens, he gave a silent prayer of thanks. Despite Jordis's denials and the address discrepancy, he'd had a way since day one to identify his mystery woman, a way as unique and individual as the infamous glass slipper.

He'd known that night on the balcony she was his true Juliet. When she'd shown up at his firm, his body knew who she was and his heart had recognized her even if his conscious mind hadn't yet understood. He'd found her and he'd recognized her not once but twice. The problem was he hadn't accepted it. He'd been fighting it. He was still fighting it, trying to have her without losing his heart when this whole time she'd already stolen it.

She'd become the fifth in a set of unique women who had one particular thing in common: he loved them.

Michael laughed softly. He'd joked he'd not find his perfect mate at a masked ball. He'd scoffed at love at first sight. And here he'd fallen victim to both.

Maybe you're not really a dinosaur, but my Prince Charming. That's what she'd said to him as they'd lounged in front of her fireplace last weekend.

Yes, he was, and he needed to go claim his fairy princess.

Michael turned and strode from his office at a furious pace. He headed straight for Jordis's office. It was empty. She'd left her desk clear of files and the room tidily organized. It looked as if no one even worked in it.

He stopped at her secretary's desk, but the secretary

wasn't in yet. It was an insanely early hour for most anyone else to be in. He returned to his own office and paced impatiently while time ticked by.

When he finally heard his assistant Lana at her desk, he stepped to the office door and barked, "Lana, have you seen Jordis this morning?"

Lana gave him a look that could have melted steel. That was the downside to having a secretary who'd known him since he was in diapers. He often felt like he was dealing with a parent. "Since I just arrived, that would be a *no.* And, good morning to you, too, Michael."

Michael blew out a loud breath. "Sorry."

Lana put her purse in her bottom drawer and sat down. She noticed a stack of files on her desk. She picked up the note on top and read it before handing it to Michael. "It looks like she dropped these files off last night. The note says for me to make sure you look at the memo she left on top."

He quickly flipped through the documents. She'd prepared a draft motion for sanctions in case they could link adverse counsel to the breach of the firm's computer network and a memo detailing medical information she thought could be used to pressure the other side into settlement.

When had she had time to do all this?

He sat the documents down on Lana's desk and ran his fingers through his hair with a deep sigh.

"Something wrong, boss?"

Lana rarely called him "boss." Hearing her do so now made him think of the one woman who called him that out of facetiousness. Where was she? "I need to find Jordis

Morgan. Would you mind checking around for me?"

"Have you asked Vivian? She and Jordis are pretty close."

"Good idea." He headed for Vivian's office and burst in without knocking. "Vivian, do you know where Jordis is?"

Vivian looked up from her file, surprised to see him. "No. She—"

"Never mind. That's all I needed to know." As he was about to leave, he looked down and noticed the file Vivian had sitting in front of her—the Gardner pro bono file. Jordis was pretty passionate about getting that young mother what she needed to provide for her son. Seeing Vivian with the file made him uneasy. "Did Jordis turn the Gardner matter over to you?"

"Yes. She wanted to make sure Cynthia had someone who would fight hard to get her what she needed."

"Why isn't Jordis the one fighting to make sure Miss Gardner gets what she needs?" His unease grew. It finally dawned on him why Jordis's office had looked so neat.

He spun and headed back to her office. When he walked in, the evidence of abandonment jumped out at him. Not only had she cleared her desk, she'd taken all her personal items and bared her walls. Her diplomas, awards and pictures had been removed. His heart sank. She wasn't away from the office. She'd left permanently.

He grabbed the cell phone off his belt. He dialed Jordis's number, but got voicemail. He left a quick voice message then immediately typed two text messages. He turned as he hit the *Send* button for the second time, nearly plowing into Vivian. He steadied her with one hand so she wouldn't fall over. "Vivian, are you trying to kill us both?

What were you doing behind me?"

"Michael, we need to talk."

"I'm sort of in the middle of something right now. Maybe we could do this later?" He glanced at his phone. No responses to his texts had come in. He tossed the phone onto Jordis's abandoned desk with a huff and stalked to the north windows.

"If you're looking for Jordis, you're not going to find her."

Michael's heart palpitated. He turned around. "What do you mean?"

"Take a look around." She motioned to the empty office then closed the door to give them some privacy. She looked into his eyes and watched`his face closely as if she were looking for something in particular. "She left grumbling about idiot men who can't keep their Juliets straight."

"I *can* keep my Juliets straight, dammit." He paced across the room. "She'd have known that if she'd given me a chance to explain."

He couldn't believe his luck. He'd spent weeks trying to track down a particular Juliet. The one he wanted turned up under his nose at his own firm, and the other walked into his office Monday morning thinking he'd been searching for her. She'd been as grab-handy as she'd been New Year's Eve. Of course, Jordis would walk in right when she'd made a pass at him. Her timing sucked.

He turned back to Vivian. "How can she be upset with me for that when she repeatedly insisted she never attended that costume party?"

"What did you expect her to say, Michael? She's trying to avoid an affair with her boss only to find out said boss is looking for this mysterious woman he made out with on New Year's Eve—who happens to be her—so he can hook up."

His face tightened. Her rendition of the story made the whole thing sound tawdry.

Vivian stepped further into the room. "Look, I only recently found out about the whole New Year's Eve slash Juliet encounter so I really can't judge. What I can tell you is after that steamy kiss between you two in the elevator, she was never the same."

"Jordis told you about that?" His eyes flicked to hers.

"No. I saw you. I was chatting with the guard at the front desk late that night when the security camera flashed to the view in the elevator."

So much for confiscating the security video, he thought. "You drive a silver Lexus SUV."

He phrased the sentence as a statement, but Vivian answered anyway. "Yes. I didn't think it was any big deal, but when I razzed Jordis about it, she was extremely embarrassed she'd been seen."

Vivian sighed and sat down. "She confided in me about what happened at her prior firm, and I realized what was going on between you two was tearing her apart. She was attracted to you, but she didn't want to be. She stressed about what would happen to her reputation if she gave in to her feelings for you. She wondered whether you were genuinely attracted to her or if this was just some sexual challenge for you that would put her back in the same situation she'd gone through before."

He sat down in the seat opposite Vivian's. The knowledge of Jordis's emotional turmoil weighed heavy on him.

"Where is she?"

"She doesn't want you to know."

"Today would not be a good day to toy with me, Vivian," he warned. He saw the shudder that ran through her, but she squared her shoulders and maintained her ground. Despite himself, Michael admired her fortitude.

"She didn't tell me where she was going. She suspected you'd grill me about her whereabouts." She surprised him by grinning. "Looks like she was right about that."

"Great." He reached over and picked up his cell phone. He still hadn't received a response from Jordis or Brandt. "I need to find her."

"Why?" She was watching him closely again.

He wondered what she expected him to say.

"You know, Michael, she's really not interested in being known again as that associate who banged her boss."

He frowned at her language. "I wish you wouldn't talk about it that way. You make it sound cheap."

Vivian stared at him, her pointed glare sending him a not so subtle message.

His voice quieted. "Is that the way she felt?"

"Pretty much." She leaned forward in her chair. "Was she wrong?"

"What do you mean?"

She looked at him with an expression that suggested she thought he was an idiot. "Are men really that clueless?" She shook her head. "Given your behavior recently, I figure you're in love with her."

He'd only accepted it himself a few minutes ago. Somehow, it didn't seem right that Vivian be the first person he told. He didn't say anything.

She nodded. "That's what I thought." She rose from her chair. "Because I happen to think she's in love with you, too, I'm going to share something with you that you have to promise to forget you heard from me." She waited for him to acknowledge her condition. "Jordis didn't just leave the firm, Michael. She's leaving the city."

He stood rapidly. "What!"

"I don't know if it's permanent or simply time away to clear her head, but I saw her get into an Executive Limousine about forty-five minutes ago."

Executive Limousine gave service to the Kansas City International Airport. Michael left the office at a dead run. He almost tore the office door off its hinges in his haste to open it. He glanced at his watch as he rounded the corner where Lana sat. "Lana, I need you to keep trying to get ahold of Brandt Morgan for me. When you get him on the line, transfer him to my cell phone. Also, call Doug Corbin, General Counsel of Metra Pharmaceuticals. We have a meeting tomorrow, but I need to send Covington in my place."

Lana frowned at him. "Corbin's not going to be happy. He pitched a fit last time you tried to send someone else to meet with him."

"He'll have to get over it. I'm on my way to the airport, and I can't be in two places at once."

"The airport! I haven't made any plane reservations for you."

"No, you haven't and neither have I." Her confused look would have been humorous if the situation weren't so dire. "I'm not planning to go anywhere. At least, I don't think I am."

He looked at his watch again. Counting Jordis's head start and guessing her goal was to be at the airport at least an hour before her flight, he'd be cutting it extremely close even leaving right away.

He looked at Lana. "I gotta go."

Finally, she smiled at him. "Let me guess. Jordis?"

"Yes."

"You planning to stop her?"

"Yes."

"It's about damn time."

Michael startled at her comment and her use of profanity. He'd never heard Lana swear before. "Does everyone know how I feel about that woman?"

Lana laughed. "Yeah, everyone except apparently you. Now, get out of here before you miss her plane."

CHAPTER 20

*M*ichael rushed into the garage and pulled up short. He swore. He hadn't driven a car today. He had his F350 monster of a truck because he had an appointment after work to get his motorcycle serviced and prepped for the spring riding season. Cutting through rush hour traffic in that would be a nightmare.

He paused, staring at the motorcycle strapped into the truck bed. Or, maybe not. Without his leather jacket, he'd have a cold ride, but the motorcycle gave him the best chance to get to the airport in time.

He hopped into the back of the truck and freed the cycle. He put it on the road in less than five minutes. As he hit the on-ramp for the highway, the Bluetooth in his helmet buzzed. It was Lana. "Michael, I have Mr. Corbin on the line."

"Put him through, Lana."

"Michael, what's this I hear about you sending another lawyer in your place tomorrow? I thought I'd made myself clear the last time. I expect you at the helm of this case, and I expect you to give me personal service not pawn me off on some lower level associate."

"Eric Covington is not a lower level associate. He's a senior associate and soon to be junior partner."

"I don't care if he's a senior partner. I hired you, and I expect to see you."

"Mr. Corbin, I have a matter I have to address that may take a few days. I'll be available by telephone should you need me, but I need you to work with Covington in the meantime."

"It's you or no one, Remington. I'm sure I can get another firm to take this matter on. It's a pretty high profile case, and the payout from a win will garner legal fees that could set a lawyer up for generations."

Michael took in a deep breath. The threat to take this case elsewhere should have made him edgy. It had the last time Corbin issued the ultimatum, but this case didn't seem all that important anymore. Winning this case would mean nothing if the woman he loved disappeared from his life forever. Everything of value in his life, he wanted—needed—to share with her, and here he was dealing with a corporate brat who thought he could blackmail him into cooperation.

"Do you understand what I'm saying, Remington?"

"Yes, sir."

"Good. I'll see you tomorrow."

"No." Michael weaved around an SUV into the passing lane. "You won't."

"Excuse me?"

"You've made it clear you can easily find other counsel. I'm glad to hear that because if you're not willing to work with Covington in the short-term, then you'll want to take care of that as soon as possible."

"What the—"

"When you've selected replacement counsel, let my secretary know where to send your files. I'm unavailable as of now."

"*Remington—*"

Michael disconnected the line without letting the man finish. He'd have a lot of explaining to do to his equity partners, but he'd worry about that some other time.

A few minutes later Lana buzzed in again. "Michael, I've got Brandt Morgan on the line."

"Go." He heard the line click over. "Brandt, where's your sister going?"

"I have no idea what you're talking about."

"She's on the way to the airport. Where's she headed?"

"She didn't say anything to me about traveling. And if you don't know where she's going, I'm guessing this isn't a business trip. So what happened?" There was silence on the line. "Remington, what did you do to my sister?"

Michael huffed out a breath, cutting sharply back into the middle lane. "Nothing. There's just a little misunderstanding I need to clear up."

"What kind of misunderstanding?"

"One that has your sister running away from me . . . again. I can't let her get out of the city. She's smart enough to find a way to disappear for a long time." Or permanently, but he didn't want to think about that possibility.

"My sister doesn't run. She faces her challenges even when it's sometimes not wise."

She could face all challenges but him? What did that say about how she really felt about him? "Well, she's leaving town in a hurry."

"What aren't you telling me, Remington?"

Michael sped in silence for a minute, thinking about how to answer that question. "Your sister and I sort of met New Year's Eve."

"New Year's Eve?" Brandt's voice modulated from perturbed to curious.

"Yes." Michael checked the speedometer and gave the bike more throttle. "Did she happen to mention a guy she met at a party dressed like a gladiator?"

Brandt burst out laughing. "Jordis didn't, but our cousin Narisa did. *You're* her gladiator?"

"Yeah."

"I bet that threw her."

"Yes and so did finding me in my office with another woman who claimed to be the Juliet I'd met that night."

"Ah."

"A*h*, indeed. Look, Brandt, your sister once told me there's nothing you can't do or find with a computer."

"True."

"So find me what flight she's on."

"Are you asking me to break into airline flight records and retrieve personal traveler information?"

Michael grinned at Brandt's unctuous tone. "May I remind you I'm on a mobile phone?"

"Doesn't matter. I'm on an electronic phone that scrambles not only my signal but also the signal of anyone on the line with me. No one could eavesdrop on this conversation even if they wanted to. Something I patented and licensed to Uncle Sam for a trial run by various alphabet agencies."

Michael would have to ask him the specifics on that some other time. "Well, then, yes. That's exactly what I'm asking you to do."

"Why should I help you?"

Michael continued to weave in and out of traffic at breakneck speed. If he wanted Brandt's help, he suspected he'd have to tell the man the truth. "Because I'm in love with your sister."

This time the silence was on Brandt's end.

"Morgan, you still there?"

The silence continued for several seconds then finally Brandt asked, "You ever happen to tell her that, counselor?"

"No. And if I don't get to the airport and figure out what flight she's on, I'll never get the chance."

"It's amazing how dumb some smart people can be."

Michael was getting really tired of people taking pot shots at his intellect today.

"I'll call you back, Remington."

Only ten minutes away from the airport, Michael accelerated. His heart raced with the fear he'd be too late. When he saw the exit for KCI, he darted across two lanes of traffic, narrowly missing another speeding motorist. He exited to the steady blare of a car horn.

He pulled into the first terminal, and his phone beeped. "Remington."

It was Brandt. He gave Michael the airline and flight number he needed.

Michael whipped to the curb adjacent to the boarding entrance for the appropriate airline. He reached for his wallet when a skycap approached to tell him he'd have to move his bike. Michael shoved his helmet and a hundred dollar bill into the man's hands and promised him another if his bike hadn't been towed on his return. He sprinted through the airport doors and pissed off people in line to check in when he cut to the front and demanded a ticket for Jordis's flight.

"Sir, you'll have to step to the back of the line."

Michael looked behind him and apologized. Looking back at the ticket agent, he said, "This is an emergency."

"It always is. Step to the back of the line, please, sir."

He dropped his eyes to her name badge. "Look, Nikki, I really need your help."

She raised a hand, pointed a finger over his shoulder and swirled it in a circle. "So do all those people behind you, and they managed to get here in plenty of time to handle their business *and* board their flight on time."

Several people behind him grumbled their agreement with her statement. Michael swore under his breath. Today was not the day he needed a rule stickler behind the counter. He fumbled for his wallet and removed his platinum card. He slid it across the counter, trying to contain the anxiousness that made him want to shout at her. "It's not my flight, but I really *really* need to be on it."

She rolled her eyes. "Let me guess. The love of your life is on that plane. Yada yada. Blah blah blah."

"As a matter of fact . . ."

Her eyebrows rose.

Michael checked his watch. He only had fifteen minutes

until Jordis's flight was scheduled to depart. His heart dropped. If this were another era, he'd take a chance and race to the gate without a ticket. Doing so under current Homeland Security regulations would likely get him jailed, if not shot.

With a sweaty palm, he pushed his card further across the counter. "Nikki, *please*."

ॐ ॐ | ॐ ॐ

The plane doors of Flight 203 whooshed to an airtight close. In her first-class window seat, Jordis curled up and covered herself with a fleece blanket she'd brought from home. She'd been sullen for three straight days. At times like these, she wished she were a crier. She needed a good cry to release all the tension and angst built up from losing a job, a potential partnership, and a man in the span of about a week.

She'd struggled with her moods for two days. She'd berated herself for ignoring the warnings in her head that said stay away from Remington and for believing a man who controlled the world in which he lived and worked would be capable of not wanting to control her. The woulda-shoulda-couldas had left her emotionally drained until she'd realized the truth. Her feelings had transitioned from mere lust long before she'd given in to her physical craving for the man.

Once she understood that, she gave herself a pass for the foolish hope that the worst-case scenario wouldn't happen this time, and her course became clear. She couldn't continue to work at RHM and pretend nothing had happened. No partnership in the world warranted that kind of self-torture. So, she'd cleared out her office. She needed to get as far away as possible from the man who inspired her to emotions she didn't know how to handle right now, but she hadn't expected walking away to hurt so much.

It hadn't hurt this bad when she'd broken up with Keith, and she'd been with him a lot longer than Michael. No matter. She would take a two-week vacation then pick somewhere to hang out her own shingle. No more playing the game with the good ole boys. No more waiting for someone else to deem her worthy of the partner title. The time had come to take her future into her own hands. At some point, the work would heal her heart, and she'd never have to see Michael Remington again.

"Is this seat taken?"

Jordis's head jerked up. The sonorous voice made her heart thump. So much for never having to see him again. "Michael, what are you doing here?"

He sat down next to her. "Stopping you from running away and ruining both our lives."

She sat up and put her feet on the floor. She eased away from him. "How did you figure out where I was?"

Michael shrugged. "Sometimes, it's pretty cool to know a guy who can do anything or find anything with a computer."

Her grip tightened on her blanket. "That traitor! I'm going to kill him." The angry flush on her face deepened as she asked, "Shouldn't you be with Juliet?"

Michael gave her an indulgent smile. "I am with Juliet. Why she continues to lie to me about it, I don't understand.

Maybe she'll explain it to me one day."

"Michael, I—"

He leaned over and placed two fingers over her mouth to shush her. "I know you're my Juliet, Jordis. On some level, I think I've known since I saw you standing across the conference room that first day. I couldn't figure out why you seemed familiar or why I was so drawn to you, but something inside me knew you were the one."

He sat back in his seat. "From the moment I kissed you in the elevator, visions of you kept swirling together with the woman I'd kissed on New Year's Eve. By the time I figured out why, you'd already driven away.

"That day with you in the locker room?" He waited until she gave a silent acknowledgement. "I knew you were my mystery woman, but I didn't know how to broach the subject because it was clear you didn't want me to know."

Denial pushed strong against acceptance of his words. "For a man who seems to think I'm his long lost . . . whoever, you certainly have a funny way of showing it."

He rubbed the back of his neck. "You mean the other woman."

She nodded.

His shoulders rose and fell, but he didn't make a sound. "She was the first Juliet I met that night."

"The one you were looking for when you kissed me?"

"Yes."

"I see."

He turned more fully towards her. "No, you don't. I'd only met her that night. She'd propositioned me earlier in the evening, and I'd turned her down. By the end of the night, I was frustrated and bored and, yeah, a little horny.

I went looking for her merely for a one-night hookup."

Jordis's eyebrows rose.

"Okay. I'm not proud of that, but if I hadn't, I wouldn't have found you. And kissing you that night changed my life."

Jordis shifted into the far corner of her seat and crossed her arms. "Michael, don't do this to me. I saw you with her. I know you weren't sure—"

"I think I'm doing this wrong," he interrupted. Lifting the seat arm between them, he pulled her into his arms and kissed her, hard. He kissed her until her resistance melted. Then, he lifted his head enough to breathe into her lips, "I love you."

She blinked rapidly. "W-What?" Surely, she hadn't heard him right.

He pulled back to more clearly see her expression. "I love you very much, Jordis, but I've fallen down on my duties as Prince Charming. So, do me a favor? Quit arguing with me so I can do this right."

Too stunned to speak, she bobbed her head.

He reached into his pocket. "What kind of Prince Charming would I be if I didn't bring along a talisman to prove I have the right fairy princess?"

He leaned over and attached the silver charm bracelet to her left wrist. Her mouth dropped open.

"I've been wondering why you always fool with your wrist when you're distracted. I thought maybe you'd lost your watch or something. I realize now you've been missing this." He pointed to the bracelet.

He fingered each charm, as he explained, "The number twenty-three for the college basketball champion, a giant redwood tree for the Stanford graduate, the Eiffel Tower for the student who spent a year in Paris, the scales of justice for the lady lawyer, and a glass slipper for the little girl inside who loved the Cinderella carriage. You dropped it during your taxi escape on New Year's Eve."

The woman who never cried felt dampness roll down her cheeks. Michael wiped her silent tears away with his thumbs.

"Stay with me, Jordis. You don't have to switch divisions, but you won't be working on the Metra Pharmaceuticals case anymore. Actually, neither will I."

"How's that?"

"I fired the client this morning."

"You did *what!*" She jerked her face from his hands. "Why?"

"Because I had to choose between losing the client or losing you, and there was no contest." He reached into his other pocket. "You once asked me what I was giving up to be with you. I can answer that now. I'm prepared to sacrifice or give up whatever it takes. I just need to know one thing."

"What's that?" she whispered.

"Do you love me?"

The tears flowed stronger, but she didn't respond.

"Jordis?"

Finally, she nodded her head, her hands gripped tightly together in her lap.

Michael's tense shoulders relaxed. "Good, because a car wasn't all I picked out this weekend."

He pulled out a small box from *Tivol* jewelers and opened it. "As you can see by the bauble I selected, I've never had any doubt as to who my true Juliet is."

She peeked in the box and started laughing. Inside sat the most beautiful princess cut diamond solitaire she'd ever seen. It was mounted in a twisted white and yellow gold setting, which meant she could wear her silver bracelet without clashing or wear gold if she so chose. The most unique and the most touching aspect of the ring, however, was the three-carat stone was chocolate. He'd bought her a chocolate diamond!

"I have to admit when I bought it, I thought I'd be putting it on your right hand as a way to express to you how serious I am about our relationship." He pulled the ring out of the box and set the box aside. "Now . . ." He looked up. "I find myself hoping you'll want to wear it on your left."

Her eyes found his slowly. She dared not interpret what his words implied.

"Jordis Morgan, I know you're the woman for me. I want you to marry me. I love you, and I want to spend the rest of my life proving that to you. I realize this may be a bit sudden. You may need time to think about it, and that's fine as long as you wear my ring in the meantime. I'll be content with you wearing it on your right hand until you're ready to move it to your left."

He looked down at her clasped hands. He didn't reach for them. He simply waited for her to decide which hand she wanted to give him.

She sat unmoving, trying to absorb her shift from severe depression to near euphoria in less than fifteen minutes. This man did dangerous things to her body and her psyche. She didn't think she should trust herself to make a major, life-altering decision under the current circumstances. The practical side of her fought to intellectualize this turn of events, wanting to be cautious and avoid the mistake she'd made the last time she'd accepted a man's ring. Her heart struggled to ignore the clearest sign of his feelings for her, and it wasn't the ring he held waiting for one of her hands to move.

She lifted a hand towards him.

Michael let out a long, slow breath. "You'll marry me?"

The joy inside her commingled with amusement. She nodded and waggled the fingers of her left hand.

He smiled. "For the record, counselor, I'll need you to answer that question out loud."

"Yes, Michael. I'll marry you." She grabbed him and kissed him deeply. "I love you."

What wasn't there to love about a man who, to be with her, threw away a multimillion-dollar case he'd waited for his entire career?

Something she had no intention of letting stand.

She didn't know whether Michael had read her memo on settlement strategy, but as soon as they landed, she had a phone call to make. Their involvement in the case was far from over.

ও ও | ও ও

Michael slid the ring onto Jordis's left hand and kissed her again.

Pulling back, he realized he'd lied when he'd said he'd be content with her wearing his ring on her right hand. There was only one hand he'd wanted to put that ring on, and he was more than relieved she'd seen fit to give it to him.

A bell dinged indicating everyone needed to fasten their seatbelts for takeoff. He fastened his safety belt, glad he'd managed to shoot off a quick text message to Chase about his bike. It didn't look like they were getting off this plane until it reached its destination.

Jordis looked up at him, mischief dancing in her eyes. "You know, this doesn't get you off the hook about my car."

He sighed deeply. "Yeah, right." He rubbed an index finger along the band of her engagement ring. "About that."

"Yes?"

"I didn't handle that so well. Can I get a do-over?"

"What did you have in mind?"

"How about we really compromise this time?"

"I'm listening."

"I give you back your Bee, but you allow me to buy you the SUV of my choice to drive when conditions warrant."

She laughed, noticing he'd said when *conditions* warrant and not simply when the weather warranted, which left room for broad interpretations. "An SUV of your choice?"

"Yes." His tone was adamant. He glanced at her. "It's a gift. I know I have to work on not stepping on that fierce independent streak of yours. But you have to work on accepting my desire to take care of you. Not because you're incapable of taking care of yourself, but because it makes me happy to do certain things for you." He ran his fingers gently along her cheek. "And perhaps, learning to do that for each other is going to truly be the greatest compromise of all between us."

Jordis nodded. "I think you may be right." She leaned into him and said in a soft voice, "Okay, Mr. Remington. We'll do it your way. This time."

"Good." He laced his fingers through hers then sat back to enjoy the flight. After the plane lifted off, he rolled his head against the seatback to look at her. His brow furrowed. "I'm curious about something."

"What's that?"

"When I was searching for my New Year's Eve mystery woman, I remembered the markings on the taxi you left in that morning. When my investigator traced the address you were taken to, it wasn't the same as your current address. That threw me for a bit."

"I didn't go right home. I had the driver take me to my cousin Narisa's house. I was shaken by our encounter and didn't want to be alone. Plus, I needed to give Narisa a tongue-lashing."

"Why?"

"For standing me up that night. She convinced me to go to that party then left me hanging. If I'd known she'd be a no-show, I'd never have gone."

He nodded his understanding. "Boy, am I glad you did."

Jordis arched up and brushed her lips against his. "Me, too." She pulled her legs up into the seat and placed her head on his shoulder.

Michael looked out the window. While he watched clouds engulf the plane, it occurred to him he had no idea where he was going. He'd been so focused on the departure gate number, he hadn't paid attention to the flight destination on his ticket. He looked down at the woman curled against his side and decided it didn't really matter. Wherever she was going was exactly where he needed to be.

QUARTERBACK CASANOVA

(A *Kansas City Griffins* Novel)

by Lisa Rayne

Professional quarterback TALON "DASH" JANSSEN just had his big break threatened by the league scandal of the year. The last thing he needs is a relentless reporter digging through his life, especially one he used to date. She used him once to get a story. It wouldn't happen twice, even if seeing her again *does* set his body on fire.

To save her job, sports reporter NAOMI PELLIER needs an exclusive on the truth behind the rumors surrounding football's favorite bad boy. But facing Dash revives feelings she thought long buried. This time, saving her career might mean losing her heart.

AVAILABLE WINTER 2016

TURN THE PAGE TO READ A PREVIEW

Preview:
QUARTERBACK CASANOVA

QUARTERBACK TALON "DASH" JANSSEN wanted to hit someone. White-hot heat boiled through his veins and fired his blood way past angry to downright pissed. Beneath a sun-drenched September sky, he tamped down the itch to strike out and forced himself to put one foot in front of the other.

A black microphone flew towards him, halting mere centimeters from his face. He jerked to a stop. A plague of reporters—who swarmed like locusts outside the downtown headquarters of the *Kansas City Report* newspaper—pressed close. Instead of crops, the hungry throng devoured his peace of mind and nibbled at the edges of his professional future.

"Janssen, who's the guy in the picture?" A balding newspaperman with an eager face shuffled forward.

A television broadcaster cut him off. "Janssen, how

long have you two been an item?"

Dash reversed direction, turning away from the interrogators. More questions bombarded him from the other side. The commotion caused by the relentless bunch, and their jockeying cameramen and shutter-happy photographers, grated against his eardrums and created bedlam on the otherwise calm city block.

No comment, Dash told himself. *Just say no comment and keep moving.*

His agent and publicist had briefed him thoroughly. He wasn't to react or respond to the press, and he certainly couldn't hit one. He'd made that mistake once, and it hadn't gone over so well. If he ended up with another fine from the Kansas City Griffins organization or the NFL Commissioner, he'd be screwed.

Another black mic swooped towards him, nearly hitting him in the mouth. Pain radiated through the molars he clenched to refrain from swearing out loud. He believed in the First Amendment, but when journalists practically mauled you while shoving one microphone after another in your face, you should have the right to defend yourself.

"Janssen, how have your teammates reacted to finding out you're gay?"

He didn't think his teammates gave a crap whom he slept with, but that was beside the point. His sleeping habits—or, more accurately, what he did in bed while not sleeping—shouldn't warrant this farce. It wasn't anybody's business.

"Janssen, why did you choose to hide your sexual orientation?"

Dash's fists clenched at his sides. "I'm not gay," he said

in clipped tones. He hated that his pro athlete status turned this gossip into breaking news. He'd worked hard to keep a low profile after his last faux pas. Now, all his efforts to stay out of the headlines amounted to naught. Just his luck, the press couldn't be content to twist the facts of real events any more. They had to start manufacturing their own.

"So, you're saying you're bisexual?"

Crap. Not the direction he intended to take this media circus. "No. That's not what I'm saying." He pushed through the buzzing paparazzi, whose fingers clicked furiously.

So much for no comment. His agent and publicist were going to kill him. He couldn't afford to be at the center of another gossip-rag-worthy story. The Griffins owner hated scandal and negative publicity of any nature. The press had already branded Dash as a hot head and featured him in several *R*-rated headlines over the last season and a half. He didn't need this sexual brouhaha highlighting behavior that would place him opposite the owner's conservative values—again. The guy already didn't like him. He'd been warned: one more misstep and they'd bench him for so many games his season would in essence be over.

He couldn't have that. With the starting quarterback temporarily out due to injury, he finally had the opportunity to show what he could do as more than a backup and position himself to take the first string spot permanently. He had no intention of letting this fiasco derail his chances.

He tilted his wrist to glance at his watch. *Ten minutes.* He had exactly ten minutes to get inside for the meeting his agent had scheduled. How he'd manage that and keep his cool he couldn't fathom, but somehow he had to get through this mob so his personal representatives could handle business. Someone needed to start doing damage control, like yesterday. In his opinion, his people should have immediately sent out a press release and skipped this diplomatic powwow.

Screw diplomacy. He wanted the rag shut down and the job of the cretin who had phonied up that picture of him kissing another man.

Tension settled into his muscles. After hours of practice, he craved a soak in his hot tub, a full body massage, and a woman wouldn't be bad. He'd showered away the sweat he'd worked up earlier on the field, but the heat from his frustration had his perspiration back on the rise. His jeans and athletic t-shirt clung to his damp skin, doing little to improve his disposition.

Dealing with this media nightmare, while trying to mind his *P*s and *Q*s, felt like torture. He'd welcome needles under the fingernails before he'd willingly walk this gauntlet again. Luckily, the *Report*'s front entrance stood only twelve short feet ahead. Once he got inside those revolving glass doors, he'd be free. The vultures couldn't follow him inside the building.

"Dash, come on. Give us something here," someone begged.

Dash shook his head and kept walking.

"Dash, surely you have to know your fans are curious about that photo?" a honeyed voice asked. "Especially with starting quarterback Shave Stephens out and you leading the team for the next few weeks."

Naomi. He knew that smooth as molasses Southern

cadence without having to see her face. He slowly turned to his left. Time suspended as his eyes tracked the crowd then locked on the sports journalist with whom he'd had an affair almost three years ago. She, out of anyone here, should know he was all heterosexual male. He shot her a look that telegraphed that thought, but she only smirked. He should have known. Hell hath no fury after all.

"Are you here because you're planning to sue the *Kansas City Report* for the article it ran yesterday?" Naomi finessed her way to the front of the crowd and stopped about a foot away from him.

He swallowed the lump in his throat. She looked good. She always looked good. From the moment he'd first seen her at a league party, he'd been attracted to her like steel to a high-powered magnet. That night she'd worn only a simple black cocktail dress and clear stilettos, but she'd taken his breath away. The dress's skinny straps had shown off her tempting shoulders and neckline. She'd tamed her mass of long, curly dark hair into some fancy up-do and worn no bling except a pair of diamond studs in her ears. The warm glow of her light brown skin and her luscious curves had been all the adornment she'd needed.

His gaze moved up and settled on her face. She still took his breath away.

Today, she'd styled her thick mane into a high ponytail and let her wild curls cascade down the back of her head. The large drop earrings she wore nearly brushed her shoulders. Their five uneven strands of tiny dangling beads matched the color of the coral blouse she'd paired with tailored black slacks.

His eyes roamed over her lower half. She had a great

pair of legs. Her designer pants currently shielded them from view, but he remembered what those long, shapely legs had looked like. More significant, he remembered what they had felt like wrapped around him in the heat of passion.

For a moment, longing assaulted him, stealthy longing so deep it reached beneath the years of resentment he harbored and tightened his chest in the vicinity of his heart. The unexpected bout of sentimentality caused unease to trickle along his nerve endings. Naomi's jewel green eyes narrowed, hinting she suspected he'd taken a stroll down Memory Lane.

Dash mentally shook himself. He covered his emotional slip with a cold stare. "Ms. Pellier, you know the drill. Any official questions regarding legal matters should be forwarded to my lawyer."

She frowned, not happy with his response or his proper form of address. Tough. Once upon a time, he'd given her special access to his life. Then she'd betrayed him and acted such a nuisance after their breakup he'd cut her off completely.

He'd never intended for their relationship to go the long haul, but her underhanded act had accelerated their inevitable breakup. The premature end to their interlude had blindsided him. He'd thoroughly enjoyed Naomi. He'd gelled with her in ways he'd never experienced with any other woman, and they'd proved extremely compatible sexually—in bed, in the kitchen, and anywhere else he could get her primed and willing. For her to take part in this misdirected homosexual outing struck him as not only absurd, but also disloyal.

Leave it to her to betray him yet again.

"So, are you saying your lawyer is meeting you here now?" a masculine voice asked from behind him.

Dash ignored the follow-up question, nodded a dismissal at Naomi, and strong-armed his way towards *Report* headquarters. His brash movement knocked Naomi off balance. His hand shot out, landing on her hip. Pulling her to him, he placed his other hand on the opposite hip to steady her. The familiar scent of her sweet perfume wafted up, eliciting an olfactory Pavlovian response in his nether region.

Twin emerald pools with the power to undo a man focused on his face. The look in those large eyes had gone from haughty to questioning. The pulse at her neck beat erratically, and Noami's lips parted to release light breaths, syncopated in time with her gently heaving bosom. Dash's mind drifted once again to the erotic before he caught himself.

Leaning into her, he whispered for her ears alone, "You know better than this, Naomi." His fingers tensed against the rayon blend of her slacks. "The erratic beating of your heart and the throbbing of my . . ." His voice trailed off. He crushed her hips closer to let her feel the hardness Mother Nature wouldn't let him control. ". . . ought to be a clue."

With a glare, he moved her aside and entered the building. His long-time agent, Pete Daniels, paced a dull path onto the shiny black tile in front of the elevator bay.

Pete looked up. "It's about time," he fussed and steered Dash into a waiting elevator.

Right before the elevator doors closed, Dash glanced out the glass front of the building and caught Naomi's vexed stare. She challenged him with a tilt of her head, letting him know he hadn't shaken her bravado. His lips pressed into a thin line, and he slid his hands into his pants pockets as he wondered what her next move would be.

~ *END PREVIEW* ~

FIND OUT WHAT'S NEXT FROM

LISA RAYNE

visit

www.lisarayne.com

ABOUT THE AUTHOR

 LISA RAYNE graduated from Princeton University with a bachelor's degree in Comparative Literature, went on to obtain a law degree from Stanford, and pass the bar exam in two states. Her passion for the creative arts led her to practice intellectual property, entertainment and media law for many years before she decided to produce her own creative works instead of simply representing others who did.

An avid reader, the only thing she likes more than curling up with a good book is writing one. She won a Top 10 Finalist berth in the Harlequin global *So You Think You Can Write* contest with her first manuscript. As a former practicing attorney, naturally, she loves to write about lawyers, but the athlete in her ensures she also infuses her love of sports into her stories.

She currently lives in the Midwest with her two daughters.